THE STRANGER IN MY SOUL

Saige-Annette Jarrett

Dedication

For KJB: My pride and joy. Remember, there is always honor in being a first fruit.

For BG: There are some friendships that move beyond personal struggles and heartbreaks. They transcend life and death. Always in my heart.

Acknowledgment

To all the BEAUTIFULS who have supported and
encouraged this endeavor.

Table Of Contents

About the Author

Saige-Annette Jarrett is a Southern Belle with a passion for various genres of music, reading, writing, and education. She spends her free time enjoying family and friends.

THIS PAGE INTENTIONALLY LEFT BLANK

Foreword

When she was six years old, she did it! Madison jumped off the back of Mr. Jack's truck covered from head to toe. With dust on her eyelashes, black fingernails, a dirty face, and matching eyelashes, she was proud of herself. To anyone outside her small town, she looked like she'd spent the day in a volcano.

From the truck, she marched right up to the front porch, poured dirt out of her shoes, took her head rag off, and received the biggest hug ever from her mother. Using her garden hoe, an egg sandwich for breakfast, and penny-candy in her front shirt pocket, she accomplished something. Madison had "made a day!"

Yes, there were others bigger and older than her, but not nearly as proud because she succeeded in her first attempt. In the South, going to the cotton fields in the summertime, chopping weeds, morning glories, Bermuda grass, and cockleburs away from cotton stalks was known as "making a day."

She had no idea spending 10-17 hours from Monday to Friday waking up early to catch the truck, drinking out of pop cans to prevent virgin lips from being inducted into the Redman/ Bull of the Woods Chewing Tobacco Hall of Fame was an artform.

Listening to the embellished tales of the previous night's activities and hoping the transistor radio batteries would last until lunchtime highlighted her will. She loved all types of music and needed those lyrics to keep her moving. The experience was forging a spirit she would carry for the rest of her life.

Madison continued to smile as she ran the foot tub of chilly water to heat on the stove. Her smile didn't fade as she filled the bathtub with the mixture. She quickly scrubbed her body clean before the dirt "foam" settled against her skin. She was glowing long before she applied the imitation Vaseline. As the ritual of swatting mosquitoes under the illumination of the television light commenced, she maintained her smile.

Yes, looking back on it, that $6 per day eventually became $17. Over the next ten years, that money contributed to buying school clothes and funding extracurricular activities. As an adult, life and hard work take on different meanings when you've "made a day."

It took a special person to survive those blistering summers. She was unaware of the test awaiting her. God was girding her soul with armor because the devil was coming. He was coming for Madison Elise St. John in a powerful way and all the angels on high would have to work overtime to protect her!

Day One

Maybe it was because she was another year older. Perhaps it was because she was now a mother herself. Madison didn't know what triggered the dream again. She spent twenty-one years with her mother before she passed away. Why was the only vivid memory she could recall of that weekend? Why was it tormenting her dreams at night again?

What was it she was supposed to remember? What was she missing? Whatever it was, it always came to her in the same way...

She was a junior in college when her mother called and asked her to help pick pecans. Madison agreed to come home for the weekend. They spent the entire two days underneath trees down in a field. They'd taken turns throwing sticks and boards into trees and running clear of pecan showers. Afterwards, they put the pecans into buckets and sold them to markets by the pound for Christmas cash.

Those two days were spent talking about life, people, dreams, clothes, cars, dishes, money, the lack of it, and Christmas. School and studies were also discussed. She realized her love for all genres of music was inherited from her mother. The songs they listened to were always indicative of their moods. For the first time Madison realized her mother was a woman.

Sometimes children forget their mothers are people too. Mothers had lives before they had kids. They had a name, and it wasn't "Mom." Her mother's childhood memories came flooding back and she explained when "she used to be tall." Madison still laughed because her mother was only 5'4 inches. However, in her mother's mind, she was a 6'6 Amazon in her heyday!

"All of those are good memories. Why do I wake up with my heart racing and my chest about to explode every time I dream about that weekend?" Why did it occur sometimes and not others? When it came,

1

why did she always wake up remembering things she knew her mom never said?

The dream always ended the same way. Her mother would respond to some profound questions Madison desperately needed answered yet, she would fade midway sentence. Madison could never recall the exact questions, but she understood it was a vital part of an important conversation. Because of this, she had not experienced a good night's sleep in weeks, and it was beginning to show.

Was her conscience haunting her for a sin she couldn't recall? She freely admitted she was not the ideal daughter. To her mother's disdain, there was a rebellious streak within her that made all her wayward ancestors proud. Her mother had difficulty sustaining expressions of happiness and satisfaction. Later, she would learn her mother had symptoms of undiagnosed depression.

Frustration or deep-rooted sadness were the typical resident emotions in her household. Love was an understanding, not an announcement. She knew her mother was proud of her, but it never came from a direct statement. It was always overheard in a phone conversation or one-on-one remarks with others on the front porch. Laughter dropped by on occasion, but it was sparing and always unexpected.

Consequently, Madison found her consolation in her paternal vices, alcohol and sex. Her absentee father passed down his sins, and she handled the torch proudly. In stark contrast, her mother was a churchgoing, God-fearing woman.

The teenage years were a power struggle between decency and predisposition. The principalities of her father's world outweighed the morality of her mother's by a landslide. There was never a struggle between her and her mother; that was an understanding. Mother won, always. Maybe her mother understood, "if it's in you it will come out somehow or some way" and was trying to run interference for her daughter.

Madison faithfully attended the Sunday prayer sessions held

every 1st and 3rd at her home church. They visited neighboring ones on the subsequent 2nd and 4th. Those were the days when the struggle wasn't so violent. She assumed it was because the angels gathered with the Hosts of Heaven and salvaged her. Oh, but miss one! Those had to be the days her angels were granted reprieve because the deviants raging within her came out for an unsupervised stroll.

Through it all, Madison maintained excellent grades, held a hypocritical position as Sunday school secretary, and church choir member. Surely, God would grant forgiveness. At least she was counting on it. Otherwise, she was in big trouble!

Lately, she felt the effects of poor judgment and restlessness. Not only was she tired physically but emotionally, mentally, and spiritually as well. Madison asked Pedro to pick Grayson up earlier than originally agreed for their six-day excursion. She pledged loyalty to her daughter's pet fish and vowed not to stay at home feeling down. She closed the door after waving goodbye to them.

Grayson noticed her mother's growing restlessness and fatigue a few days earlier. Madison started crying over accidentally burning some toast for a grilled cheese sandwich. Being the loving protective child she was, Grayson gave her mother a big hug and explained she knew how to make peanut butter and jelly sandwiches for lunch if that was okay.

Through her tears, Madison thanked God for the blessing of her child. She also knew her emotional state was not up to standard. She fought to hide it from Grayson as best she could. Pedro heard something in her voice on the phone when she called. He loved spending time with Gray so picking her up early was an easy decision for him. Plus, his mom Marisol was in town.

She loved her daughter, but Madison's lack of energy was no match for the typical six-year-old handful one would expect. She would welcome Grayson home. However, Madison needed to regroup and reconnect with someone she had not spent time with in a long while. Herself.

Next week, the new job search will start. This week, however, her soul needed pampering with bubbles and music. She had an uneasiness she could not shake. It was getting stronger, and she needed to understand why.

Madison went to the stereo and put Najee and Damien Escobar compact discs on shuffle. Then went into the bathroom and turned the tube jets on full blast. As she pulled her ponytail loose and slid out of her jeans, undies, and sweatshirt, she listened. All she heard were the patter of horns, saxophones, and smooth jazz in the background. She was alone.

She realized it had been a long time since she'd been alone in the house for any length of time. Normally, she and Grayson would be cooking together or watching television. Today, however, it was her, the music, and her thoughts.

At 37 years old, she was attractive, standing at 5'10", a flawless size 14. She was well educated with a C.P.A., an M.B.A., and a B.S. in business administration management. "Huh, the degree for people who had no clue about their life goals but had to declare a major," she thought. That epiphany hadn't taken place until much later.

Pedro was inspirational in helping her obtain the other two accolades. She told him she made a promise to herself and Helen to get the C.P.A. because Helen recognized her gift for financial management. She just always wanted an M.B.A. He wanted her to attain whatever she desired and supported her through it all.

By all means and standards, she'd done well for herself and Grayson. They were debt-free, Grayson had all the whimsical toys for her age group, and she had married well. The water was hot, and the cable was on. She quit her job eight months prior as the Chief Financial Officer (CFO) for an accounting firm. The job turned her life upside down for ten months in exchange for the six-figure salary. The whole exchange ended with a platinum "there's cake in the breakroom so kiss my ass exit!"

She shivered as those memories felt like icicles trickling down her spine. She recalled the endless phone calls at all hours, the lack of respect for her private life, the implications of fraud, the bribery attempts, and numerous other criminal activities she discovered about her counterparts. Because she refused to engage in "black-on-black" conflicts and offer up a fall guy, she had been labeled the angry Black woman who was "difficult."

She could still recall the day she was introduced to the woman who would become her replacement. She used the term loosely. Karen Boston was the perfect patsy for them. She thought she knew everything and was too stupid to realize she was being used strictly for the color of her skin.

Without her, a discrimination lawsuit was headed straight toward that company. Pedro convinced her to walk away from the idea. Not because she would lose but because he did not want her to deal with the nuisance. Madison was a firm believer in karma. She handed Karen a ticking time bomb.

Madison decided clients should be aware of the corruption within the organization. So, she sent an anonymous letter to the Better Business Bureau and copied the contents for the defrauded firms in duplicate envelopes. The packets included receipts, bills, check stubs, deliberate markups and errors, memos endorsing the actions, and the bonus checks received by Karen and other managers. She thanked Dominic for his detective work to gather the latter two items.

Meanwhile, Karen inherited the lovely task of explaining the fraud to the BBB and the companies that had been swindled. She was also tasked with saving the company's reputation. She failed miserably. Amazing how twice the talent is only required when your skin has the slightest hint of melanin.

Just yesterday, Madison marveled at the media's ability to stitch together corporate secrets using the Freedom of Information Act (FOIA). She put on fresh lipstick and blew kisses when the pictures of key-figure heads flashed across the screen. Blake Drysdale's ass was still fine as hell! If only he had used his powers for good.

Madison was saddened to hear Karen suddenly packed up and went back to New York. Her stint as replacement had been so short-lived. Bitch. She thought of a saying her mother had, "every dog has his day, and if you are a really good dog, you have two!"

That foolishness was a whole lifetime ago. Today was the beginning of her recovery. Grayson would be back on Sunday, and she would be ready to resume her role as mother. However, the next few days would be spent being a woman.

Madison shrugged as she eased into the tub. As if on cue, Najee and Damien began a slow, seductive serenade to soothe the spirit of the exhausted. Strange is the journey that takes us from being born to being us.

The gospel group Lee Williams and The Spiritual QCs crossed her mind. How she loved their songs "Come See About Me" and "I Can't Give Up." God only knew the purpose behind the journey. All she knew was up Calgon was calling her name and it felt rude not to answer.

Somewhere in the distance the phone was ringing. She didn't even glance in its direction. Madison waited a long time to experience the melody of water caressing her skin this way. No one except Jesus himself could come between her and it. And even HE needed to tell her the gates were closing on her opportunity to get in to disrupt this moment. Messages were meant for tomorrow.

The warm smell of peaches and jasmine saturated the air. Their scents were intoxicating as she found the perfect position. She wallowed in the silkiness of the bubbles against her skin. "Aah" was the only sound that escaped her spirit.

She must have fallen asleep because a "clink" from the forgotten bottle of wine caught her attention. It obviously found its own form of relaxation in the ice bucket. Slowly, she opened her eyes and observed the cork's look of "do not disturb." As she shifted in the tub, she noticed the water was lukewarm and the bubbles had dissipated. Her lemon-puckered skin was a sign to either reheat or get out.

The Stranger in My Soul

The candles cast a dusky glow over the bathroom like an intimate whisper. The flames licked the wallpaper in hisses and spits. "Time to get out, St. John," she groaned.

As she stepped out of the tub and reached for her bathrobe, she caught a glimpse of herself in the mirror. She glanced at the reflection with a hint of shyness before stepping back. Taking one step, then another, she stood in front of the mirror confronted the attributes she had been given. The interplay between reality and perception can twist the mind in curious ways. In this moment, Madison did something she never did, scrutinize her body.

Most women wanted to know every inch of their bodies, whether good, bad, or indifferent. She stared at herself blankly. It was flesh supported by bone structure. Almost unwillingly, she was drawn to the person inside her face. Her eyes were controlling the show and they stared back at her inquisitively.

"We're still here," they taunted. Eventually, she will have to confront what's behind us. For most of her life, Madison knew her eyes belonged to someone. She just didn't know who. She usually avoided them as they probed and searched for clues and answers to questions for which she had no idea.

Her eyes had a life of their own. Madison couldn't handle them looking at her any longer. They were like strangers waiting for their formal introduction to the world. What would their reflection reveal? How could she open those curtains if she didn't know who was inside?

The familiar churn of bile started to rise uncontrollably and crept up her esophagus. She hurriedly moved to position herself over the toilet. The acid erupted from her throat like a volcano that refused to be silenced. When she thought it was over, another wave held her captive for several more moments. Per normal, the stench was awful. This was always her reaction when her eyes made her acknowledge them.

With flushed cheeks and reddened eyes, Madison brushed her teeth savagely and let her mouthwash add to the scalding in her throat.

She decided hunger was calling and went off in search of dinner items at the grocery store.

Although she was physically gone, the spirit within her eyes remained in the mirror. "She'll be back. She will always be a prisoner until she comes to terms with the message we're conveying. We are the windows of her soul. It's been dark for far too long. Daylight always comes."

Madison decided on an elaborate dinner. She was craving seafood so, she selected some lobster tails, shrimp, clams, and stuffed mushrooms. Fettuccini with alfredo sauce and fresh Parmesan sounded appealing so they were added to the basket. She was headed towards a formal introduction to a head of romaine for her Caesar salad when she heard her name. "Madison!"

"Hey there." She turned and saw a smiling Dominic Charles. "What's been going on with you?"

"Not much, the same old stuff on different days. Did Pedro pick up Grayson?"

"Yes. I have a full six days to myself, and I am starting with an adult dinner and a nice bottle of wine." She forgot she mentioned her hiatus from motherhood to him a few weeks ago.

"Well, it was good to see you. I ran in to pick up a few Dinty Moore beef stews and some beer." "Goodness Dominic, you haven't changed a bit, have you? I'll tell you what, you choose a beverage and some garlic bread, and I'll be gracious enough to allow you to intrude on my evening for a while."

"All right, I'll even bring dessert. I saw a chocolate mousse over there with your name written all over it."

"Don't even start with me Dominic Charles, just bring the accompaniments. I'll meet you at my place in about fifteen minutes."

Madison hurried through the self-check lane and headed home. She felt relieved to see Dominic for some strange reason. She missed his friendship. She was trying desperately to reconnect with the comforting things in her life.

She and Dominic became the friends they were destined to be. Yet, she remembered a time when that was questionable. She put the groceries in her trunk and drove away. Yes, their friendship had been difficult to maintain she thought, as she waited for the stoplight to change.

Eighteen months earlier, she and Dominic worked side by side at the accounting firm. He was the Chief Accountant. Many people questioned his abilities and his drinking, but Madison believed in his talent. She understood the pressure. She began exercising. Dominic turned to alcohol.

He possessed an aptitude that needed to be highlighted even if the first epiphany needed to be his own. Madison refused to give up on him. She was happy standing by her decision. However, there was a time when she and everyone else questioned her sanity.

At first, it wasn't noticeable. She thought he was going a little too heavy on the aftershave. He mentioned he was trying out some new ones. Rumor at the office was he was a little "sweet on her." She dismissed it as the typical "Black people can't work together without sex syndrome." Little did they know she and Bob, the white partner from the law firm downstairs, were actually "getting through the night" together.

She made a mental note to check on Bob. He wanted to be a little more serious than she. The ink was barely dry from her and Pedro's divorce. Bob was awaiting the judge's signature on his.

He did not want to wait for her to ease back into the waters of dating. Bob knew she was a great catch and wanted to cement the relationship immediately. Madison's hesitation was firm. They were each other's "firsts" after emotional breakups. No one should make life altering decisions immediately after one of those. After several entanglements over a three-month span, she realized they would never work.

The secret meetings in quiet out-of-the-way places had not bothered her because "you can't get used when you're using." The office would have misconstrued it as an interracial mishap. She gave zero-damn, but some women become overly aggressive when a "good catch" is taken off the market by an "other."

Anyway, she and Dominic discussed his choice of colognes on many occasions prior to the altercation. She assumed he was trying to impress the many single women in the office. Personnel mentioned the faint smell of bourbon on a few too many consecutive Fridays and she had to address it.

Madison tried to give Dominic the benefit of the doubt. She jokingly referred to his "weekend starting earlier" than was appreciated. She hoped he would tone down the nipping during office hours. He didn't. Things intensified. The powers that be had been lying in wait for their opportunity to pounce on him. They took it when she went to Toronto for training on a new software package. All hell broke loose upon her return.

She was summoned to the Vice President of Operations office for a small chat on the matter of Dominic Charles. Her fingers were crossed hoping her suspicion was not the topic of discussion. Luck was not on her side.

Blake Drysdale, a man in his late thirties and exuding handsomeness from every angle was renowned for his debonair smile and uncompromising demeanor. Talent had not gotten him the salary or position. He compensated for that minor oversight with cunning and charm.

The moment Madison stepped into his den of iniquity the fireworks began. Blake always gave the impression he was "waiting for you," even if you were prompt. She hated it.

The judges evenly split their previous rounds. He was willing to cut any throats necessary to get his point across. If Madison's financial expertise had not been invaluable, she would've been the first line item crossed off the profit-and-loss statement. Their disdain was palpable because it held a sexual tension that screamed, "if I caught your ass in another time and place, it would be on!"

Quite early in their relationship she realized his only allegiance was to himself and Satan. Consequently, every move, verbal, nonverbal, implied, or factual required a calculated counter move. Their meetings were a chess match. Every time. The stage was set, and the sparring began.

He immediately went into detail about his observation. He came into the office the previous Friday and Dominic avoided him at every turn. It never occurred to Blake that Dominic was unimpressed by his charm, so he went into Dominic's office and waited for him. Upon entering, he recalled being hit with a strong scent of bourbon.

He knew his relationship with Dominic was tense, so he decided to mention his observation to Madison. He wanted to give Dominic the benefit of doubt on the off chance it was a foul aftershave or an ointment. He wanted no harder feelings to surface. It was no secret he and Dominic were not subscribers to each other's fan club.

Madison sat as Blake explained his tolerance for Dominic was a professional courtesy to her. She made it clear Dominic's head would not be delivered on a platinum platter with a cold chianti. However, she would address the situation and clear up any further "misunderstandings."

Blake smiled and told her he was sure her measures would be in the company's best interest. He also commented that everyone should have a warrior as a manager. She flashed Blake her best son-of-a-bitch smile and went in search of Dominic. He had substituted her ass for his without one ounce of lubricant!

Dominic was in his office talking to a client on the phone when she found him. He was smiling and being quite pleasant and efficient. Yes, that is what he got paid for but damn him! There was nothing more annoying than having to wait to chew on someone's ass.

Madison shut the door and began pacing back and forth. Dominic glanced up and instantly recognized the fury in her eyes. He quickly made some excuses and got off the phone. She tore into him!

She told him about the allegations against him and the request for his head at brunch. She screamed what a jerk he was for placing her in this position and how hurt she felt that he did not confide in her earlier. Hell, they had discussed everything from the mating habits of crickets to the best pain reliever for her period.

She demoted him immediately to Accounting Business Assistant and told him his office hours were changing to 12-8p. She was out of breath. She stared at him in anger and frustration. He heard every word but was more affected by the look of hurt and disappointment. They worked hard to pull off the numbers for the firm.

He knew they would be scrutinized down to the last drop of urine because they were the first all-Black group of managers in the firm's history. Why hadn't he trusted her enough to protect him before it came to this? She could have arranged emergency leave or something.

Everyone has a long-lost, unaccounted-for cousin who is suddenly ill. Why fight this hard in the trenches with her only to self-destruct? Most importantly, why couldn't she fire him? She also ignored Blake's implications that his salary should be reduced. Fuck him! He would not get the satisfaction of waving Dominic's balls in the "we took down another one parade."

Madison was so deeply lost in her own thoughts that she did not see Dominic move in front of her. She noticed nothing until his fingertips brushed the tears from her cheeks. He lifted her chin and looked her squarely in the eyes.

"I'm sorry. I let you down both personally and professionally. You have done everything imaginable to help me and I failed you. The pressures are different as captain than as a passenger.

When you went to Toronto, I felt like the little boy in the "big chair." Honestly, I had no clue my feet would not touch the ground. The added pressure of Pamela's whining at home made me start drinking again to relax. One drink became two. Suddenly the weekend stopped meaning Saturday and Sunday. Any day with 12:00 started being an opportunity.

I told myself it was a one-time occurrence. You were polite enough to refer to it as aftershave. I thought I could get it under control by myself. I never wanted you to look at me the way you are now. I chose a familiar outlet when all the meetings, deadlines, and expectations got intense.

I will never hurt you like that again. You believed in me. It will not be something you have to be ashamed of." They forged a pact in blood that day. They both knew the end was coming.

Blake and company were not going to stop until Dominic was served as the main entrée with au jus and tip. Madison would be collateral damage if she continued to protect him. She learned a valuable lesson from that experience. When the powers that be want retribution, saddle up and be prepared to ride at dawn. Take nothing that cannot be used as a weapon.

They had sufficient grounds to terminate Dominic. Madison simply refused to do it. Watch "shit get real" quickly, when you come for me and mine was the attitude she took. In a war zone, allyships instantaneously transform from professional to personal.

Dominic's performance was stellar after their discussion. They didn't care. He was a marked man. She was prepared to die on whatever hill they marked as his burial site. She would protect him. Why? Because she was sick and tired of oppression taking the scenic route when it came to some but was swift to cry for justice when it came to others. Also, because deep down, she recognized a few of the demons haunting him by name.

The light turned green and jolted Madison back to the present as she sped towards her house. The shrimp would steam rather quickly. Oh, snap! He was allergic to shrimp. Well, she would put it in the freezer.

She pulled into the garage, and he was right behind her.

"Grab some of this stuff, please." He laughed and took everything from her before it tumbled to the grass.

"This is why I love you, your impeccable timing. I do not know why I am sharing my bounty with you!"

"Because you love me."

"You better be happy about it too, Charles!"

He rolled his eyes upward and smiled. He recalled a time when she was remarkably close to meaning that in a vastly different way.

Dominic worked feverishly on the lobster tails as Madison chomped away on the fettuccini.

"This is absolutely fabulous!" "More wine?"

"Sure, while you're up, would you grab some more garlic bread too?" "Okay."

She missed him. He had an uncanny ability to make her smile. He nearly broke her heart once. However, he was still good people.

She used the word "nearly" because she was not emotionally available at the time, and neither was he. Their involvement began after their professional relationship ended. Madison closed her eyes as she let her mind drift backwards to a time when they often dined together.

She and Dominic were incredibly open about their lives and lovers. He exposed himself to various female love interests during his twelve-year marriage to Pamela. Yet, through all of them, he had never been tempted to leave her, except once.

Pamela seemed to accept his infidelities as part of his personality. It always puzzled Madison how a woman could lose herself so completely to a man. She did not drill him about Pamela because it hadn't bothered her that he was married. If she had considered their involvement more than pain relief after her divorce then, maybe she would have.

Dominic filled a void when she was not sure she wanted to love anyone other than her daughter. She prided herself on the fact that they had not gotten involved while he was her direct report. Madison had been around men her whole life. She let him believe she did not notice his growing affections. It was easier. The repercussions at that time would have provided a layer of ammunition to the enemy that they couldn't afford.

It began innocently. He dropped by as he did sometimes when Grayson was spending the weekend with Pedro. They were having dinner on a night similar to this one. They had drinks and watched a movie. A discussion about one of the scenes was underway. Dominic gently placed his hand in her hair to prevent her from shaking her head in a negative direction.

The touch excited something inside them both. Slowly, he began to massage her scalp. Madison moaned because it felt so good. Unconsciously, she made an "O" formation with her mouth. He ran his fingers along her lower lip. Instinctively, she slithered her tongue out to trace the pattern of his finger.

They stared at each other for a moment. Both were sober enough to realize if they crossed this bridge it would burst into flames on impact. Yet, they were intoxicated enough to ignore the warning signs. He did not want to lose her friendship. He also knew he had desired her for months. Desire won. Dominic was unprepared for what Pandora's box held in store!

In the office he witnessed the hard-laced, meticulous CFO they all respected. He smelled her perfume and watched her hair change from sexy to hot and back again. It was painfully arousing. She was his boss. An affair never crossed her mind. It consumed his thoughts.

He went home aching for her after he offered to massage the tension from her shoulders. In reality he just wanted any excuse to touch her. Their work relationship was over. All those longings culminated with a single touch of her tongue on his fingertips. The line to purgatory was crossed.

He knew she would never have given in to the vulnerabilities between them without the catalysts of wine and a broken heart. It was not another infidelity for him. He was in love before he ever touched her. Her heart would never belong to anyone but Pedro. Dominic didn't care.

In her mind, Dominic was a loyal friend. That night she realized he was a man. She needed to be close to someone who gave a damn about her.

Loneliness can make bedfellows of any two people whether the timing is right or wrong. Dominic listened without prejudice or opinion as her marriage fell apart. He understood her hurt even though she initiated Pedro's departure.

Suddenly she heard Dominic shouting something to her from the kitchen. Her eyes popped open and refocused. Damn, she thought, did I really need all of that to move forward? He appeared with the end of a bottle of wine and the beginning of another.

"I wasn't sure which you would prefer, so I brought out both." "It doesn't matter."

Her mind was trying hard to return to the present moment. She shifted in the chair and rearranged her blouse. The memory of his touch made her nipples erect. Recapturing those moments was not on her list of things this evening.

He inquired about Grayson, and she was thankful to have something else to focus on besides the memory of his lips on her body. The mention of her daughter brought her forcefully and solidly back to the present moment.

She talked about Grayson's latest desire to take ballet. She deduced in a six-year-old way that ballet would help her grow taller because of all the time spent on her toes. Unsuccessfully, Madison attempted to explain genetics to her daughter.

Madison told Grayson she would be tall because she was the product of a 6'3 father and a 5'10' mother. She left out the probability that she would be full-figured as well. Grayson was not convinced her 4'5 stature would improve with age.

Dominic was laughing so hard he was crying. "Well, she is stubborn like her mother."

"Very funny!"

He kept trying to stop laughing but the exasperation on her face as she relived the plight of explaining biology to her child was hilarious. Madison surrendered and playfully hurled a crab leg at him. He ducked, and the crab leg hit the wall with a resounding "thump." They both burst into laughter.

"Help me remember why I tolerate you in my kingdom as we do these dishes. If you wash, I'll dry. Everything is still in the same place it used to be."

Everything but us, he thought. Damn, he missed her.

As they stood with the water running, Dominic's mind made a time travel of its own. During the few months he had been allowed to love her, how many nights had he stood right here? She always washed, and he always dried. How many times had he longed to be here with her since then? The simplicity of dishwashing became pleasurable with her.

She was chattering about something as she ran her hands over the pot handle that previously contained the crab legs. He never found himself envious of a pot until now. His mind recalled the way she caressed him when they were lovers.

Why doesn't being a fool whisper to you in time to fix it? Instead, it always screams loudly after the fact in ridiculous moments like doing dishes. Standing here, it felt like all his foolish decisions and behaviors were on display like the scrolling ticker at the bottom of a CNN broadcast.

She was a woman. Pamela was simply female. She intimidated him. The strength and determination required to recover her life with Grayson without Pedro scared him shitless. On his best day, he knew he was not the man Pedro Santiago was.

Madison never told him, but truth is not always kind. It is, however, always true. He knew he was a rebound experience but, he loved her in a way he never loved a woman then or still. She came to him without reservation the first night they made love. Amidst the intensity of their passion, he realized sustaining her love on that level created exhilaration and fear within him.

Pedro was an idiot! Who leaves a woman like her? He also understood being the man she needed was a challenge. Madison was the kind of woman a man never wanted to disappoint. Dominic suspected Pedro let her divorce him because he felt he failed that test miserably too.

On the other hand, Pamela lived off his very existence. She did not breathe without checking with him first. It drove him insane. The weight of being someone's everything is as difficult as not understanding how to be what they need. Disappointment is inevitable when one person is responsible for all the decision-making. Just once, he wished before they ended their 12-year marriage, she had known how to take the wheel.

Madison was not a bystander in her own life unless she chose to be. A woman like her thrives on acts of service and quality time, not whose check is bigger. Pamela needed constant affirmation she was enough. He had simply burnt out. Sadly, his demons prevented him from being the partner Madison needed.

Madi was a one-woman show. She scared the hell out of him because she represented possibility. She appeared to always be in control. The day she cried on his shoulder about her marriage shocked him. He listened as the wall crumbled. He got a glimpse of the woman deep inside the female capable of defeating Goliaths.

When his alcohol addiction almost cost him his job, she taught him coping strategies. She never disclosed her own demons, but he could tell there were some. Otherwise, why would she be so proficient with the strategies she taught him? Her favorite saying "begin at the beginning" when something or someone is bogging you down.

The more he understood her, the more he recognized she would never genuinely love him as a partner. Pedro would always be the beneficiary of her heart. She was too stubborn to admit it. Had she ever decided on a relationship with him and then needed out, Dominic did not know if he could have let her go.

She and Pedro were on hiatus. You could tell because he was still too concerned about her under the guise of checking on the mother of his child. Time made him realize his mistake by letting her divorce him. It was visible to everyone except Madi. Eventually, she would see it too.

Dominic knew she wanted to save him because in some way it meant saving some part of herself. He wanted to triumph over the bottle to show her he could love her the way she needed. It should be as easy as people think to simply stop. It is not.

So, he took the road most familiar. Out. Walking away was never difficult for him until Madison. Pamela was safe because she would never be strong enough to leave him.

As he stood in Madison's kitchen, he gazed at her. Who was this woman rinsing a skillet and confiding her secrets to him? Why hadn't he fought harder to be the one she yearned to return home to? Now, after months of rehab and actually attending the Alcoholics Anonymous meetings, he could be the safety and security she and Grayson needed.

Dominic glanced at her hair. It was cut above her shoulders again. He remembered when it used to fall over her breasts as they made love. The feel of it drove him to distraction.

He could still hear Glenn Jones' "Let It Rain" and Euge Groove featuring Jeffery Osbourne's "What I Could Do (With a Woman Like You)" playing in the background. By the time Estelle started singing "Set Me on Fire," they were always deep in the throes of passion. He burned a CD with the songs in the exact order for his personal collection!

She was chattering about something. He guessed he supplied the correct "uh-huh" responses at the right time. She seemed unaware he was not listening. He was loving her.

His mind fell victim to the first time he ever touched her auburn mane. It felt so silky as it slithered through his fingers. The memories of stroking her bottom lip with his fingers while she nibbled on them transported him back in time.

No longer was he standing in this kitchen at the sink. They were lying on the living room floor. The chemistry between them was the closest thing to insanity he had ever known. The experience became an insatiable ache, not a desire.

He shifted and recalled the taste of peaches and white zinfandel on her lips that evening long ago. He purchased the exact same vintage tonight. Maybe, just maybe, tonight it could help rekindle their romance. Hell, he loved her enough to wait until she caught up!

Back then, the combination caused her to lose inhibitions and touch him. His tongue licked her lips as he kissed her. She let a moan escape her and stroked his erection.

Passion was an understatement for what he felt. In the beginning, new lovers can be a bit clumsy figuring out the pleasure zones of their partners. Madi fit into his arms like they were designed specifically for her.

He was honest about the impact of the wine on the outcome. If she had not been drinking and lonely, the permission he was granted would have never been. However, all his passion stemmed from her. The wine was in the wrong place at the wrong time. It got used that night and he had no regrets!

His tongue invaded her mouth. He assaulted her lips like trespassers. He probed; she opened. He asked; she answered. His mouth begged her for access to the rest of her.

He needed to see her acceptance not simply hear it. Once she acknowledged it was him and granted permission, he lost control. Those big, beautiful cognac eyes held a passion he still remembered.

Dominic created a masterpiece on the side of her neck with his lips. He ran his hands underneath her tee shirt and freed the strained breasts and nipples held captive. In appreciation, she pushed her nipples between his lips like a breastfeeding baby who was running behind schedule.

She cried out his name in pleasure. He prayed she would not ask him to stop. He was never forcefully convinced anyone in his life to make love but, she was as strong a candidate as a naked hooker on a corner of newly released parolees.

Madison arched her back in excitement. Dominic suckled her nipples until they passed the "blow" test. They stood at attention. She shivered violently.

She ran her fingers over his bald head and licked his earlobe. A bolt of lightning shot through his heart. The way he kissed her stomach made her jump with pleasure. He crawled back up to be sure what he wanted to do next was acceptable. The kiss she planted on his lips was so slow it was painful.

Madison moved on top to grant him better access to her body. His erection greeted her there. "I need to feel you around me." "I guess we better get started then."

He parted her legs in anticipation as she held herself open for him. Damn! His head lodged between her thighs. His lips began their salute to greatness. She moaned and slid across the floor. He applied the pressure of his tongue until she lowered her hips.

She felt like guajillo peppers to his penis when he finally entered her. Her movements kept time with the ticking of his organ until she overflowed. Damn he should've brought biscuits!

She was a truth serum to him. Afterwards, they lay under a blanket on her sofa. He told her he was in love with her. She smiled and told him love was a good thing between two people who just committed the acts they had. He tickled her and reveled in the sounds of her laughter.

Madison seemed comfortable with her nudity. She did not cover herself when he sat up to admire the expansion of her breasts or the mole inside her thigh. In his mind, this is what real women looked like underneath the designer suits and diamond studs.

Madison was considered full-figured by the fashion magazines. But, to any man who ever made love to a real woman, she was a trophy. Her legs and ass muscles were strong enough to rock you back in a moment of passion.

When your lips slid over her breasts, the sternum never interfered. Caressing her hips was never interrupted by the sharpness of protruding bone. Men will not admit that shit is uncomfortable and keeps you switching positions throughout the night.

He became erect. She moved and gave him access. There was no hurrying this time. She took control of their journey. A smile crossed her lips as she heard his intake of breath. The starting point she chose left him speechless. Madison did not pretend oral reciprocation was offensive. Some women act like it is their first time. They know damn well they've blown every man and half the wildlife in the state!

Dominic tangled his fingers in her hair and screamed her name. She knew he was out of control. Madison did not stop him as he sprayed his seed all over her breasts and neck. He collapsed with exhaustion. By dawn, there was no doubt whose needs mattered most. He could join her, or she would go alone. Satisfying herself with his body was her only thought.

"Dominic? Dominic Charles, are you listening to me?" Madison asked impatiently. The tone snapped him back to the present moment.

"Yeah, of course I am." "Then which do you think?"

"I think the blue one looks best."

"You didn't hear a word, did you? If you did, you would know the answer would be Kem or Joe as a better balladeer, not blue!"

"Madi, my mind drifted off for a moment. I was listening. I didn't realize I got momentarily sidetracked." Hell, she could have been talking about hamsters on a wheel.

He set the dishtowel aside and began a slow painful stride down the hall to the bathroom. He could not let her see his erection. The need in his eyes afforded him no dignity. Hopefully, the chilly water would camouflage his desire.

What carried him so far away, Madison wondered? Whatever it

was, it held him completely captivated. "Oh." She blushed. Dominic envisioned himself in the same place she had been. They were in the same surroundings doing the exact same things. The difference was her guest bedroom sheets were not ablaze!

Always the guest bedroom. Another man in Pedro's bed was not an option. She should've known then she wanted him back. Her bed knew.

Dominic was standing in the bathroom with the water running. He found the obvious painful and visibly true. She still made him forget his place in time. He splashed water on his face to clear his mind. It did not matter. The water only intensified his thoughts.

Was tonight the right time to confess his error in judgment by choosing Pamela? Would she trust his words? Did she even care after all this time?

Somehow, he had to find a way back inside her heart. He was okay never being the love of her life because she was the love of his. That was enough for him. He would never be Pedro. Second was the highest ranking any man would ever achieve with her. It did not matter to the men who loved her.

Dominic Charles, you haven't even asked her if she is seeing anyone? The thought of another man touching her made him wince with pain. It hurt sometimes to look at Grayson because he knew she was someone else's.

He and Pamela never had children. He did not want the responsibility of raising twins. One would grow up. The other would just get older. Raising an adult woman was already difficult. He would rather own a dog than have another adult cling to him the way she did.

Madison was sitting on the floor when he finally emerged from the bathroom. She was thumbing through her vast collection of CDs. The disc she selected was Busy Body.

"Hey, you. The National Guard said they'd be here in fifteen minutes to perform an evacuation attempt." "Ha, ha, ha, very funny," he replied and joined her on the floor.

"This was when Luther Vandross used to sing." The stuff he reverted to later in his career was so haphazard because it was out of his range in my opinion. Artists should remember when experimenting with contemporary music us older fans. We still want to hear some original sound blended into their new albums.

Some songs on these albums make you wonder who you purchased. "I'm not sure what became of his first album. It had a song called "This Is for Real" and used to get me right in the heart. Whenever he interviewed, he only talked about "Never Too Much." Some of us remember the older one." It had a little bit of the group Change in the background."

"Madison, you are probably the only person I know who can recall music and isn't a critic or in a band."

"Does church choir back in the day count? Seriously, the lyrics were a powerful testament to heartbreak."

Dominic stared at her in complete and utter amazement as she sang the bridge. The lyrics were precisely what was on his mind. How had karma done this to him? Madison's voice was not bad either.

"Well damn, Mad. And he did not re-release it!" "Nope."

The lyrics to "Make Me a Believer" began to flow over them in a whisper. "See, this is when music took you over and didn't assault you with directness. You were in the mood to get some or give some up before you knew what hit you. Subtly is still the best way to romance a woman who knows what that means.

I feel sorry for some of these young girls because all they have ever been exposed to is vulgarity, insults, and grinding. Romance seems outdated. They have never known what it represents. Put on some Whispers, O'Jays, Isley Brothers, or Frankie Beverly and Maze and croon away a nun's virginity."

"Really?"

"Yes. The only women who like to be berated and degraded by blunt lyrics have never been "courted." These days, it is supposed to be complimentary to receive two calls before the request to "hit it." Daylight better not catch the man at the wrong woman's house."

"Speaking of being at someone's home, are you splitting evenings with anyone?" "Is that South Carolina subtleness for asking if I am dating? No, Dominic, I am rediscovering me. Until I know how that plays out, it would be cruel to pull someone into the vortex of "Madison undefined.""

"Cruel is knowing you choose to sleep alone. A man can accept another lover. Knowing you prefer no one, is a different brand of cruelty."

"Men do not understand when a woman says she needs time to gather herself it is a compliment. Especially, if the woman is actually doing it. What it means is I respect you enough not to put you in a situation I know I cannot handle right now. Instead, most men assume there is someone else and get insulted. It is actually a favor when you discover a woman is truly choosing to be alone for a while to get her head together.

In terms of us, I am flattered. You want to travel down that freeway intentionally swerving to miss all the barriers, construction workers, and potholes we hit. You do remember our road was destroyed by a catastrophic event called us, right?"

"Madi, we both know I was stupid. Letting you go was a colossal mistake. I realize it every time I think of what could be happening between us now."

"I know I can be intense, Dominic. You made the only move you knew how. Out. It gave me a chance to take a step backwards and realize I was not ready for us either. I didn't know what I wanted. You didn't know if you could give it. I always respected your decision.

It was no one's fault we did not make it. We survived the carnage. We were two self-destructive people on a collision course with no brakes. You at least had the sense to veer off the road. Thank you. Now, we have a few fantastic memories that didn't destroy the relationship we were meant to have. Friends."

"If you weren't describing us, I would say you put that very eloquently. Do you know how much I still love you? You are a very tough act to follow."

"Thank you. I think everyone should have a standard."

She threw a pillow at him and laughed to lighten the mood. He tackled her and beat her on the head with it. He tickled her until she screamed.

"I will pee on you, I swear it, if you don't stop!" "You wouldn't dare!"

"Not only would I but, I would send you the bill for my carpet. I cannot have my place smelling like Bigmama's slop jar, can I?"

"You really do know how to kill a mood, don't you?" He smiled and released her.

"Yep. Seriously though, sometimes the best friends don't make the best lovers."

"You have already dismissed the idea, haven't you?"

"I've learned left and right limits. Temporarily crossing margins can be more detrimental than tasting the fiery benefits on the other side."

Madison got up and looked out into the back courtyard. She let the magnitude of her actions strike. At this point in her life pacification was not an option. Involving herself with Dominic again would be equivalent to a liquor store owner attending Alcoholics Anonymous meetings.

He was similar to a high school romance. Someone to remember fondly. You could relax and enjoy the 15th class reunion because someone else was waiting at home. The "friendly stamp," as they called it in college. Now, it affectionately described her feelings toward him.

The term meant you felt secure he would not disclose your intimate secrets. He was safe with the knowledge you slept with silk panties on your head to protect your curls. He was the friend who helped you remove paper sack rollers after a bad hair idea for prom.

It was not a term used for the subject of your nocturnal emissions. Was it even possible to have a healthy relationship with someone when it began through dysfunction? Madison turned slowly and looked at him for a moment before she spoke. She wanted all the awkwardness to diminish.

"I remember when I had to explain to Grayson why you weren't coming by anymore. She was upset you did not even say goodbye. I tried to reassure her you were busy and had not forgotten her. Healing for children takes longer. It is especially difficult when you don't have a decent explanation yourself.

You only get one opportunity to break my child's heart, Dominic Charles, deliberately or not. I will tell her you came by. She will be thrilled. Maybe you can take her out for a movie or a day of Skee-Ball at the arcade like you used to do. No pressure. I know she loved it. I won't mention it in case you get busy again. It will be a surprise for her."

"Is this my cue to leave?"

"This is our cue to take the left at Albuquerque on this remember-when road of awkwardness. The last time you and I were together, I listened to Teddy Swims' "Set the Bed on Fire" for weeks."

"If I tell you I'm never giving up on doing us right, would it matter?"

"It will always flatter me. Especially when my ass is the size of Texas, the Mississippi is rolling through my midsection, and my teeth have wandered off for a bite to eat without me." She smiled at him.

"You and your visuals St. John-Santiago." He smiled and let her escape into her way of letting him down easily.

"Will you at least sleep on it?"

"Will you accept an "I'll get back to you?"

He kissed her, held his heart like Fred Sanford, and left.

What the hell? she thought as she showered and crawled into bed.

Madison fell into a deep slumber only to toss and turn. The dream came again. She was standing under the same pecan tree from years past staring at her mother waiting for a response.

"Mama? Mama?"

She sat upright in bed as her mother's image faded. She was reaching out to her. Her movement caused her to open her eyes.

Madison lay still trying to focus on something other than her dream. Her eyes wandered to the lines in the wallpaper. They were gold and bronze with alternating stripes intertwined by paisley Bordeaux. The colors were rich and warm compliments to the pattern she loved. The colors made her feel a relaxation and coziness she felt nowhere else.

She and Grayson snuggled under these covers during thunderstorms numerous times. Grayson always jumped in to wake her, so it seemed strange for it to happen naturally when she was at Pedro's. It was amazing the way a child could transform your life. They are blessings that anyone afforded the opportunity to give or be loved by one should relish. It did not matter whether the chance came through biology or otherwise.

At one point, Madison was unsure she could have a child of her own. The thought did not distress her the way it did some women. She always felt one could enjoy other people's children and respect their places in your life just the same. Shopping sprees with Roz and her children were equally as expensive for her throughout the years prior to Grayson Marisol's arrival.

In the meantime, she opted to have a career. She had not postponed fulfillment for events that may not occur. She reflected on the early years of her marriage to Pedro. Making love was the only thing she felt she did well other than manage the restaurant. Consequently, she tried to pencil in quickies or marathon sessions.

His career kept him busy too. Mistakenly, she thought he was not upset about the amount of time if she maintained consistency in her appearance. His primary love language valued time and then appearance.

He knew she would never allow herself to become a "her." A "her" is woman who lets the most basic feminine upkeep decline with no regard.

She prioritized acts of service then quality time. "Well, that's where you got out of sync St. John." An image of JoAnne popped into her mind's eye as a strong visual representation of a "her." She had not thought about that woman in years.

As Madison's career began to flourish quality time became a juggling act between them. The sex was conducted via phone when not interrupted by a conference call. Time together became a good intention.

The morning they conceived Grayson was comical in hindsight. Pedro called her office and said there was an emergency. Her husband had been driven home. It was urgent that she get there immediately. Terrified, she dashed out of her meeting in tears. The client wished her god speed and agreed to reschedule with Dominic.

She broke into a full sprint across the parking lot. The stoplight tested her patience, so she ran it. By the time she got home, she was shaking so badly she dropped her keys at the door. Pedro opened it in a grey silk bathrobe and a smile.

"Well, this isn't quite the reaction I'd anticipated," he teased. He noticed the tears streaming down her face.

"What's wrong? Are you hurt? Why didn't you let them take you to the hospital?" "Hospital? Oh, baby, I am sorry I scared you. I am fine. Really, I'm okay. I wanted us to spend some time together. I knew if it wasn't an emergency we would both try and fit it in." She stared at him in utter disbelief. He suddenly felt like such an asshole.

"Pedro, how could you! You know how I feel about phone calls described as an emergency!" Madison slammed her fist into his chest as hard as she could. He winced.

She was so pissed she could hardly see straight. She stormed into the living room, took off her pump, and threw it at his head.

"Don't you ever fucking do to me again! Do you hear me? I damn near killed three pedestrians by running a stoplight to get here. I can see me in court on murder charges. "My defense Your Honor is my husband had an erection. They had to die!"

He walked over and wrapped her in his arms. "I'm sorry. I missed loving my wife. This was a stupid way to get your attention but, I need you as much as your clients."

"If you didn't look so goddamn good I'd walk right out of here barefoot and…"

He began a slew of kisses down her hairline that made her forget she was angry. She forgot she was supposed to be anywhere else doing anything except this man.

Just like that, they were two young lovers making love for the second time. The first time is always a bit awkward. The second time you really lean into it. If Grayson Marisol hadn't been conceived, it was because sheer exhaustion shut down every body part they owned.

She could still feel her ovaries take a deep breath. She recalled the seductive music, bubbles, baby oil, honey, and the chocolate mixture he poured on a plastic tablecloth in the backyard. They pretended to be on a water park slip and slide. The Maestro would have appreciated their attempt to duplicate his lyrics in "Love Serenade"!

She remembered the neighbor's dogs letting out a series of tormented howls because her heat matched theirs. Pedro jokingly said, "See, that bitch will have me if you won't. She knows a good thing when she smells it."

The wind started to blow softly while they slept. They awoke to leaves stuck to body parts typically unexposed to nature. A soft spring rain began, and they let it wash them free of debris. They created a different kind of stickiness. Nine months later, Grayson Marisol Santiago was introduced to the world.

Madison turned over in bed still glowing nearly seven years later. "Aah, pain has a way of upsizing," she whispered. What a shame their relationship took a detour and headed full speed towards its own collision course. Pedro Miguel Santiago will always be in my heart, she thought.

Four years, five months, two hours, and thirty-five minutes from the day Grayson was born it whirled through. After surveying the damage, it was determined their marriage was the casualty. They forgot how to be lovers and friends while learning to be parents and juggle careers.

Pedro was deeply rooted in his bid for Assistant District Attorney. She was running Satyre's and trying to finish her MBA. Her goal was to create an international Satyre's.

The restaurants' residual incomes would build generational wealth for Grayson if she were successful. She had every intention of relinquishing control to Ashley and becoming a silent owner. By structuring it that way, she could reduce the stress on her marriage and place priority on the quality time they needed as a couple. Unbeknownst to Madison, Father Time and The Good Intention Fairy had a falling out years ago.

She and Pedro alternated schedules so Grayson would always have a parental presence regardless of their chaotic careers. Generally, they met via telephone. More often than not they succumbed to exhaustion after handing Grayson off to the parent of the hour. By the time they did crawl into bed together, one of them was already asleep.

The toll was more severe for Pedro than for her. The smell of liquor increased as the stock in the cabinet substantially decreased. Madison was more experienced in the area of functioning with alcohol and maintaining performance than Pedro.

One night anger and frustration burst through the door and ripped off all bandages. Grayson was fast asleep. Madison was in her office crunching numbers. She was tired and trying to prepare for a forecast meeting with the London investors the next morning.

They were only in town one more day and interested in opening a Satyre's. They asked her to draw up some preliminary plans to take home and discuss with their venture capital group.

The smell of bourbon appeared before Pedro. He was slightly intoxicated and wanted to make love. "Dammit, Pedro, stop it! Can't you see I am trying to get this done?"

The next fifteen minutes halted everything. Madison was about to be the victim of a head on collision. Straight with no chaser!

"Where's Gray?"

"It's two o'clock in the morning, and she is four years old. Where do you think she is?" He came around the desk and tried to kiss her. She pushed him away.

"Where is my Madi? The one I married. The one who could not keep her hands off me. You are so cold and unfeeling I almost hate coming home anymore. Sometimes, if it were not for Gray, I'd think about it a lot harder.'

"What! What do you mean, where am I? I am the person home every night being the bedtime story parent. The one making excuses to our daughter about why it's just the two of us at the dinner table again. I am the person who goes to bed wondering if you forgot where you live!

I used to get a return phone call during the day. Now, if I do not see your dry-cleaning hell, I don't know if you came home or not! Yet, you are pissed because I'm not wearing the latest Victoria's Secret outfit in case you do remember us! You are not the only one who wishes some nights you didn't bother to come home!" She had not meant to say it aloud.

"Damn you, Madison! Damn you for making it sound like I am the only person who has abandoned our marriage. You used to care if I'm satisfied as a man or not! When was the last time we made love? Do you even remember? Or is that irrelevant in your current state of asexuality? Well, it has been two shitty months! Two months too damn long!"

"Why, Pedro? Do you think it gets me off to crawl up next to a bottle of bourbon when you are here? I mean damn babe can you at least share one of the two glasses you pour? Can you tell me the last time you treated me like someone you deserved to make love to?"

"Oh, now you have an issue with alcohol. I clearly recall your days at the firm before Gray was born. You went to the liquor store more than the grocery store Madison. Marry them, and they get rights! Date them, and you get all the ass you want! Now, I must deserve to be loved by my wife!" He mocked her in a falsetto voice.

"Stop it! You came in here tonight with fighting on your mind. I am not in the mood for it!"

"You are not in the mood for anything, are you, Madison? I should have stayed with Tamara tonight like she asked!"

As soon as he said it, he wanted to hit autocorrect. Pedro knew he had driven into a head-on collision with no survivors. Their sparring match was over. GAP insurance nor apologies would fix this crash.

"What the fuck did you say?" Pedro was frustrated but he also knew what she was trying to accomplish. She did not deserve this.

Tamara was not a reason to end his marriage. There was no such reason. He ran his hands through his hair and prepared for her reaction. The pain he saw in her eyes was more than he could stand. He ran across the room and tried to pull her into his arms. If he could get her to listen, maybe, just maybe, his world did not have to end tonight.

She swung so wildly he confused her with Laila Ali. A left hook connected with his jaw when he attempted to restrain her. He pounced on her to knock her off balance. She cursed him and the day they met. She threatened to kill him and tell God he died. Still, he restrained her.

Finally, she wept. It was the most gut-wrenching sound. He had only heard her cry like that one other time. She struggled. He would not let her go. He could not let her go. This might be the last time he ever touched her.

Madison's mind raced as she sobbed. How many nights with Tamara had there been? How had they got to this point? Her blind stupidity was harder to accept than his betrayal. She contributed through her silence. Her gut told her something was wrong. She thought she had time to fix it.

How many times had she made excuses when she knew differently? One thing she should have learned from women in her life were signs of betrayal. Hell, she had been the side whore before. She knew the tricks and the rules. "You always know. How long it continues depends on when you woman up to the knot inside your gut," one woman said.

She saw his remorse when she finally looked at him. Madison did not know what was next. Why hadn't this tirade occurred before he betrayed them? Her entire marriage rested on his answer.

Madison got up, went to her desk, and sat down. There were no words to ease her mind. She couldn't process anything else right now. Pedro moved toward her but halted as the sound of little footsteps came down the stairs.

"Mommy, what's going on? Daddy, are you hurt? Mommy, why is Daddy crying?"

"Because Daddy is moving out tonight, sweetheart." "I don't want Daddy to move, Mommy!"

"Daddy has some things he needs to handle. He can't stay here to do it." She picked Grayson up and carried her back upstairs to bed. Suddenly, Pedro realized he was no longer a part of her family. Being ostracized by her was worse than never being forgiven.

Madison recalled lying in Grayson's bed listening to him hurriedly pack. The next morning, she walked into their room. Painfully, she realized he had taken the essential things in his life. She was not one of them.

Those next few weeks were frenzied. To this day, she was not sure exactly what happened during that time. She knew she obsessed over every minor detail in Grayson's life and played make-believe about the status of her marriage. Until, one night she turned over in bed and there it was. It waited patiently like Communion Sunday. Silence.

The wee hours of the morning do not lie. They confront you for the coward you are. If you are alone or lonely, they make damn sure you know it. Madison realized they had pulled up a pillow and waited for their turn to chat.

She stretched across to Pedro's side of the bed. It was cold and he was not dead. The tears she refused to shed came down in torrential sheets. She bought into "til death do us part and forsaking all others," and she had been cheated. This time, she experienced payback from the side of the wife not the side whore.

Finally, she understood the view was different when paperwork was involved. She owed a few apologies to nameless names. Not simply an "I am sorry," but actual heartfelt admissions of wrongdoing. It was her turn to feel the wrath from another "good dog's day."

Pedro completely turned to another. His words echoed," I should have stayed like she wanted me to." When the side piece is comfortable enough to ask for the whole night and you consider it, their status has elevated from passive to active participant. It was apparent the one-night stand had staying power.

Tears rolled down her cheek for the lost commitment of the man she loved. She also cried for her part in the whole thing. She opened the door. Tamara curtsied in and danced away with her role as significant other. Madison could not even call her a worthless whore because Tamara Stone was an excellent attorney.

She was so good professionally she applied those skills to listen her way into Pedro's bed. Now, she was inside Madison's head with images of Pedro thrusting his common sense between her thighs.

Tamara put in the quality time and heard the signals of loneliness. She patiently waited for an injury to get her chance as starter. She was rewarded for showing up to practice every day. She did not squander her opportunity.

The one-time Madison prayed for the recurring dream to haunt her. She got the cold hard truth. It pretended like they had been together a lifetime. Why is it uncertainty and diversion can never be found when you want them to stop by and visit?

So, Madison got out of bed and met with the one old friend she knew very well, a bottle of vodka. She always kept it around when the need for mindless oblivion occurred. Once again, her bet on love had proven unwise. Next time, all her chips would be on alcohol. It had always proven itself consistently faithful in the destruction of her life and others.

The next morning, after she met with the investors, she came home to find Pedro waiting for her. He called the restaurant and Ashley told him she had gone home ill. He decided to purge his soul and provide her with the details. Pictures. Exactly what she needed to complete the torture.

Tamara Stone. They worked together on the McRayland case about six months ago. It was a bitch to win. They spent tremendous hours together, alone. Those were the times when the tie was slung across a chair and shoes were kicked off. The smell of stale Chinese food lingered in the air. You really get to know someone, whether you want to or not.

One evening they started to discuss their personal lives. Tamara began by stating she saw more of him than her boyfriend. She had been engaged for two years. Their schedules had not matched up to find the perfect wedding date. She thought they were both pleasantly avoiding the subject.

She discussed their friendship and how he supported her during her finals in college and bar exams. Dennis was a physician, which compounded their lack of availability. However, they did try to make the most of their quality time. At thirty, there was plenty of time for her career and perhaps private practice. She had desires to one day slow down and have a couple of kids. She asked Pedro to divulge his life and times with Madison.

Pedro told her he had been married for eight years. Madison stared deeply into his eyes as he moved through the recitation. Her eyes posed the question, "and you didn't hear the sirens?" He noticed but continued while his nerves were still intact.

Breaking the heart of someone you love is tortuous to watch. Especially when it's all your fault and they didn't deserve it. Pedro looked away from her.

He told Tamara they did not spend a lot of time together anymore. Their work schedules were not compatible. Increasingly, he found himself lonely.

"You never told me," Madison whispered, barely audible.

He did not know exactly when it happened. Sometime during one of his nightly "I'll be late coming home" calls, she had not answered. It hit him particularly hard when he saw couples making out the way they used to. He never meant to share those feelings with anyone.

He thought maybe it was a phase and it would pass. It did not. Tamara was a good listener. Madison used to be. He did not see their conversation as a betrayal or an invitation.

Anyway, the evening it happened began as any other. There was no indication it would end the way it did. They danced and celebrated the victory of the trying case. One too many rounds of drinks was served. He drove her home and she offered him some coffee to sober up. Pedro shifted uncomfortably. He put some distance between him and Madison as if the proximity made the pain less intense.

He had reached for the cabinet to get the mugs and some dishes shattered as they hit the floor. Both burst into drunken laughter and ended up on the floor with tears and coffee all over them. He brushed some coffee grounds from her hair, and she kissed his palm. He tried to pull away, but she would not let him. She crawled across the floor and kissed his cheek then his lips.

He thought of Madison and stood quickly. He got his things and left. When he got to his car, he dialed home. Madison painfully reminded him it was late, and she was asleep. After driving around trying to calm his nerves and his passion, he drove to the park to think.

Being needed is one of the most powerful aphrodisiacs in the world. Nothing positive ever forms when need is combined with loneliness. He did not want to be alone. So, he and his rejection went back to Tamara's. She was not who he wanted. She was who wanted him.

He rang the doorbell and saw her pleasure at his change of heart. Standing there in the lateness of the night with a towel on and a bar of soap in her hand, she accepted him. Animal instinct took it from there. He pushed her against the wall, closed the front door with his foot, and destroyed his marriage against the doorframe.

It was not about love. They did not make dismissible after-orgasm daylight promises. It was loneliness, simple and complex. He pretended she was someone else. She needed to be needed.

Ironically, the song "Nobody's Lonely Tonight" by Chris Stapleton was playing somewhere in the background. How appropriately the lyrics described their feelings: "You be her, and I'll be him..."

Pedro was ashamed as soon as it was over. He meant his wedding vows. All he could recall was how much they had been through to be together. Now, he had betrayed Madison in a way he could not take back. And so, it had begun.

Hotel rooms or her house when her fiancé was away. It always began and ended the same. Afterwards, he would pour a drink and stare out the window. Tamara would sit quietly in her corner of rejection. He lingered for an hour because he owed her more than the "I left the money on the dresser treatment," but there was nothing to say.

He wasn't sure what she expected from him. He didn't care. She would never be more than a drive-by. He took all the necessary precautions to ensure there were no "accidents" left as evidence. He accepted his role in the affair.

It ended because she was a constant reminder that he had lost his wife. He simply couldn't pretend Tamara ever filled the void that started it all. The longing in his heart for Madison.

He would come home freshly showered to her soundly sleeping. His eyes did not have that luxury on the nights he betrayed her. Instead, he always found the bottle she kept hidden and replaced it the next day. He would empty it watching the sun rise on his shame.

Madison recalled standing there two years ago and watching the emotions flash across Pedro's face. She understood loneliness in her own life. She had done some stupid things based solely on that fact. The mind can twist events to rationalize actions. Loneliness is the demise of more relationships than loss of love.

Loneliness chooses you not the other way around. It is not a proud emotion. Yet, it is a living, breathing thing that shows up without warning or invitation and makes itself at home. Pedro's day of reckoning forced Madison to concede that "love alone does not a good relationship make."

Relationships thrive when respective parties feel their individual needs are being met. She had been remiss in her provisions to Pedro. She owned her failure. She wanted him to understand what drove him to cross the line instead of talking to her. Yell, scream, or curse, but get her attention.

He expected her to accept the affair meant nothing. Six months. That's how long it lasted. Nothing. Was that the standard line all men used when they cheated? Now she had her own card in the rolodex next to Victoria's.

Madison believed anything that continued for thirty days became a habit. Generally, a habit is created to fill some kind of void. She wanted him to identify the void before they could continue.

He said his affair was strictly about the sex he was not getting at home. In truth, the reason he was not getting it was because neither of them was home! He did ask her to take a break from the restaurant until Marisol was old enough for school. She agreed to reduce her hours, but she wanted to use her education. He accused her of not valuing their home life or relationship enough.

In their twelve-year history, Madison had learned that Pedro listened well in life-or-death situations. It made him an outstanding attorney. He was not always as deliberate in his personal life. If he felt stress of any caliber, he became a bull in a china shop. Alpha male. Their first reaction is to take charge, not listen. Patience is not their virtue.

She tried to explain lack of love was not the source of their problems. He wanted to be her savior. Madison did not need to be rescued; she needed to be supported. She wanted to be a working wife and mother. She stood by his career choice. Why couldn't he stand behind the one Helen left her?

Madison shook her head because these memories were interrupting her child-free week. She had focused on the madness too long already. Pedro's own words from their first dinner here answered the question he would not. He had stopped enjoying their marriage. Their divorce was finalized nearly two years ago.

She retained the house and her car. He paid off all her student loans. He wanted to pay her child support and alimony; she refused both. Lack of money was not the issue either. The desire to contribute to their life in every way was. She wanted to help keep their finances stabilized. He did not want or need her focus to be divided. It was a source of pride for both for different reasons.

Pedro felt a man should be able to do whatever is necessary to provide for his family. Moreover, he was independently wealthy thanks to the similar beliefs of his parents. Madison grew up poor. Although education had eased her poverty mindset, she understood life throws shit at the wrong times. Preparation was never a bad virtue. They were both right.

They shared joint custody of Grayson. Weekend and holiday schedules were created. They agreed to attend all relevant events together. Their divorce was a parting of assets. Their souls would never be separated. He was the true love of her life.

Madison was the reason he would never marry again Pedro told Joshua. One day maybe, she would forgive him, and he could put his family back together. In his mind, the only difference between their current state and their wedding day was where they spent their nights. The few women he entertained since their divorce were merely filling space until he could go home. The ringing of the phone brought Madison back to the present.

"What are you doing with all these days alone? Are you still in bed? I am on my way over and we'll have lunch. I think you can treat me!"

"Well, Rozalyn Crenshaw, I see the ballots have been cast, and I like you that much whether I actually do or not!"

They drove into the city and ate at this sweet soul food restaurant with great jazz and blues. Roz was craving deep-fried chicken and potatoes smothered in gravy. Madison loved their crawfish cakes and hot water cornbread with collard green stuffing. After these sessions, the gym memberships they held were really useful. Once a month, they came to reconnect with their Southern roots.

"So, what have you been doing since Ms. Marisol isn't home? Any long nights of wild sex ending with exhaustion and margaritas? Has your knight in shining armor with the single brother come along?"

Madison almost spit cornbread across the table at how close Roz had been to her evening. She loved this woman who shared her life in a way no other could for the past 30 years.

"I've not completely done any of those things however, thoughts have crossed my mind. I did have an imitation knight come to my rescue last evening. We shared a couple of bottles of wine and some great seafood."

"Well, you do know I never touch anything stronger than Coca-Cola. Alcohol is for people who try to be incoherent about their surroundings. I have three kids who take care of that for me. Now, about our knight with the brother I can have."

Madison told her about the evening with Dominic and her thoughts on Pedro. "Men should all be medicated and comatose until sex

41

is required. She took another bite of her chicken. "I don't understand either of them, she continued. They both had you, not to put your puss on display, but they did.

Now, each has decided to be an adult, and you are the best thing since call waiting /caller ID. I always thought Pedro was a little nuts, but you love him. So, I stood at the altar while you gave away your sanity. If he had not looked so fucking good in that tuxedo…"

"Dominic, on the other hand, with his egg-head ass, always had issues he couldn't manage alone, and you were the perfect Florence Nightingale. You know they have a syndrome named for her." Madison rolled her eyes. "Well, they do!"

"Anyway, why should you be a victim again because he wanted to keep the needy freak? If one must backtrack, my money is on Pedro. At least in a pinch, you can look at him and ease some troubles. I told you to let me evaluate the waters first, but no! You had to remember we were friends and all. Did I ever tell you I still feel deprived?"

Roz paused, "Okay, now, I am listening to your version of these events. Pass me the coleslaw. I might as well be full before you sell me this line of bullshit!" Madison roared with laughter.

"I do not sell you a line of crap. I try to see things from the perspective of other people. Give me back my coleslaw! I cannot believe I am paying for this kind of abuse!"

The women's jovial exchange was not a surprise to the staff at Gloria's House of Sinful Soul Food. They were used to these two sistas coming in monthly. They were happy two women, who obviously made it out, came back to support the mom-and-pop joints. They also tipped very well, usually $70-100 dollars.

The staff fought over taking their orders. A calendar was posted in the back for the week of their anticipated monthly visits. Hell, their tip was a water or cable bill for somebody.

However, the ladies attracted the attention of someone else. An older gentleman sitting across the room was mesmerized. He was in his early fifties and intrigued by their playful bickering. His hair was salt-and-pepper gray, and he stood about 6' tall.

Barring the scar creasing his brow and continued to his left eye, he was quite attractive. One could tell, even with it, he did not hurt for companionship on long summer nights. He had the most piercing eyes!

"My goodness, she is more beautiful than I remember. She has become quite the woman." They were still friends after all these years.

For years he had looked for her. She was the hardest one to find. It was more than worth the effort. He had stabbed an inmate in the throat with a sharpened rock after seeing a picture of her in the society section of the paper. The guy deserved it for spilling coffee on the page number.

He had an acquaintance track her through her social security number. She had been quite busy professionally. Silently, he applauded himself for the drive he instilled within her to never let anything hold her back.

His plane arrived this morning. His hotel was on the south side of the city. With his luggage discarded in a heap on the floor in his room, he headed straight for her address. He was parked nearby when her friend came over. He sat there for hours debating on whether to ring the doorbell.

After assessing the neighborhood online and its $350-$500,000 homes, he rented a Jaguar and parked at an angle from her house. The house had character. It was the faintest gray brick with black marble etched around the windows. The circular drive was inviting with its rose bushes and cypress tree adornments.

The address, 13951 Cherokee Lane, commanded respect from the beholder. This is where she lived for eight years with someone pretending to love her. She gathered her senses and divorced him two years ago.

Pedro Santiago would never be the man he was or love her the way he did. There is a difference between loving someone from the heart and having someone possess your soul. Her daughter, Grayson Marisol, was six years old. He looked forward to meeting her. They were about to become a family and prove love transcends time.

He followed the ladies to lunch. Nice to see they were still in touch with their Southern upbringing and spent their monies with common folks. These types of meals required appetite and fingers, not four forks on the table. She had proven to be the angel he remembered from long ago. Yes, Madison Elise St. John was a somebody.

Roz and Madison left the restaurant and went for a small stroll. Roz wanted to window shop.

"Rozalyn Crenshaw, you know damn well you are not going to buy anything.

You never buy anything, and you always talk me into this!"

"Oh, stop whining. Miracles happen daily, you know. I only do this to you because I know you hate it so much. Anyway, you have four more days to go home and do nothing while the rest of us work. This is my revenge for all the little people in the world!"

"Fine, where to next?" Madison shivered and rubbed her arms with her hands. "It's seventy-two degrees out here; where did that come from?"

"I don't know. It felt like someone ran feathers down my spine. Let's walk faster and maybe I will generate some warmth. If not, at least you can buy me another soda and this trip won't be in vain."

The tall stranger stopped and pretended to stare into a window, so he did not draw attention to himself. He inhaled her perfume in the air. "Jasmine," he thought. He paused in his pursuit; he knew where she would end up.

Right now, his attention turned to the primary adversary on his list. He hurt Madison; therefore, he deserved agony on his torturous road to hell. There were others awaiting his arrival.

"Mr. Santiago, you have a package. The driver says you have to sign for it personally."

44

"Okay, send him in." "Pedro Santiago?" "Yes." "May I see some identification, please?" "Excuse me?"

"I have strict orders for this package, sir. If l don't follow them, I could lose my job."

"Well, never let it be said I contributed to the unemployment rate by withholding a pictured identification." Pedro pulled out his driver's license and showed it to the courier. "Did you need DNA as well?"

"Just doing my job, sir."

"And quite thoroughly. If l ever need anything delivered, I'll make sure to request you. Hey, wait a minute; there is no shipper's address on this package. Where did it come from?"

"They pay, I deliver, sir."

Pedro opened the envelope and pulled out its contents. He reached over and called Joshua. "Can you come down here? There is something I need you to see. Thanks."

"Karla, can you get an address and phone number for the courier service? I need to know who thinks this much of me."

Madison and Roz finished window shopping. They arrived at Madison's house just as a delivery van pull into her driveway.

"Well, well, what have we here?' The driver got out and announced his delivery was for Madison.

"I am Madison." The man went around to the back of the van and brought back a beautiful bouquet of twenty-eight pink roses with seven carnations disbursed.

"Those are thoughtful."

"Everyone in the world knows I despise pink. I would not think it was asking too much for the men in my life to pay a little attention."

"Well, let's hurry the ungratefulness along, so we can see who are they from? Roz snatched the card from the arrangement. "What the hell kind of card is this?"

"Well, if I could see it, perhaps I would be able to tell you. Tip the man, Crenshaw!" Madison made her way inside with the flowers. Roz followed her with the card and handed it to her. The inscription read "28/7."

"Does it mean anything to you?"

"Maybe it is a sweet way of saying they think of me twenty-eight hours a day, seven days a week. Hell, I don't know."

"Well, duty calls dear so, I'll stop by and bug you tomorrow. Tell Dominic he gets a zero for originality."

"And how do you know they are from Dominic?"

"Because Santiago would have sprung for the string of harps playing a serenade in the background." Madison flashed her " finger" and stuck out her tongue.

"Careful, with my latest drought, I might take you up on it!" Roz closed the front door and left.

Madison placed the roses in water and sat them on the fireplace. "There," she thought. They are displayed for Dominic but out of the way, so I do not have to look at them. "Yuck!" She would call Dominic later and say thank you. She decided a nap was a promising idea. Her pillow was fluffed and calling her whole name.

"No, no, stop!" she cried out as she wept in her sleep. She sat up with tears rolling down her cheeks. She sat there immobilized. She could not recall the dreams, but they left her shaken. "That'll teach me to eat crawfish in the middle of the day," she scolded herself.

It was early evening. The sun was setting and casting a beautiful shadow on her walls. She climbed out of bed and called Grayson.

"Hi, Mom! Dad and I are about to go to the movies. Can I call you back later? We're taking Ms. Jennifer and Melissa."

"Oh, okay, sweetheart."

"Would you remember to feed my fish for me, Mom?" "I love you."

" I love you too," Grayson whispered as if her father and Jennifer did not know.

She hung up the phone. So, Pedro had a date.

Madison went into Grayson's room and inhaled deeply. She always felt the love emanating from the walls in there. Cartoon caricatures adorned the walls and doll clothes were always on the bed. She loved to read so plenty of literature was about.

She drifted over to the goldfish and watched them shoot bubbles for a time. She laughed as she imagined their cries of S.O.S She had forgotten them yesterday.

After changing the water, she sprinkled food in the tank. She felt another odd sensation of frigid air shoot through her body. She touched her forehead. She must be getting ill. This was the second time today she felt strange and chilled.

Madison ran her hand under the blinds to make sure Grayson had not raised one of her windows. No, they were closed. The feeling of cold was more intense this time. "Next time, Judge Rozalyn Crenshaw gets the crawfish if this is what it does to me." She turned off Grayson's light and decided to read a book of her own.

"This Present Darkness" by Peretti was always a favorite." It was a good refresher for her state of mind. Maybe it would provide a clue to the uneasy feeling she couldn't shake. The sofa cushions were very accommodating as she settled among them. The sensation hit again. This time, it felt tangible. She looked around the room, got up and took a sweep of the house and the locks.

She passed the pink roses and stopped as they glared at her.

"Must you stare at me? I did not get this feeling until you entered my home. I will be glad when you have been viewed and then the trash is where you're going. Learn some etiquette if you are going to be here. If you must stare, do it quietly!" She picked up the phone to call Dominic to get this over with. Of course, he was not home. Too much to ask. She left him a message.

Madison's uneasiness had been provoked only she was not aware of its source. He stood outside her windows and moved from room to room with her as she roamed throughout her home. Her grace and beauty were breathtaking. He watched her sleeping and felt his body respond to the parting of her lips and the sound of her moans.

It visibly aroused him when her tousled hair and exposed breasts showed through an opening of her robe. How generous of her to share. She moved him. Watching. He was careful not to make too much of a disturbance to her flowerbeds and draw attention to himself. He longed to rap on her windowpane and say, "I'm here, darling, you're safe now."

He walked away with images of making love to her with TEEKS' "Change" softly repeating in the background. "Our souls are entwined more than you know, my love. You and I will always be a part of each other." He had done so many things for her. And yes, he could change.

The thought of kissing her consumed him since he saw those luscious full lips and tantalizing smile at the restaurant. "Be patient, our reunion is close." She will welcome me back into her life with open arms.

With the speed of a mountain lion, he quickly moved along the outside edge of her lawn and drove away. The lady next door was lowering her blinds and saw him. She made a mental note to mention it to Madison tomorrow.

Day Two

Madison was deeply engaged in her book when the phone rang and startled her. "Hello."

"Hello Madi. How are you?"

"Quiet, how are you? More importantly, how was the movie and Melissa's mom?"

"Oh, Madison, you can be very direct, can't you? Jennifer and I are only friends. The movie was fine. It was very squeal-laced and giggly."

"Where's Grayson?"

"She's spending the night with Melissa. Jennifer is having a birthday party for her tomorrow. Since Gray is the best friend and all, she had to be there the night before, or she would "die!" He mimicked a six-year-old girl exceptionally well. "The way you call her Gray and I call her Grayson keeps people confused when I say we only have one child, you know."

"When have we ever given a damn about what people thought? Speaking of which, the reason I called is the office is having this masquerade ball on Saturday. I was wondering if you would like to go?"

"Hear me out. I know this is strange, but it is a thank you for the city's finest. Before you say no, it starts at 8:00 o'clock with a 6:30 appetizer set. We wouldn't have to attend that part if you don't want to. And before you ask, my mother is going to be in town to watch Gray." There, he said it. At least she let him finish before she rejected the idea of being alone with him for more than twenty minutes.

"What are you going as?"

"I hadn't really given it much thought."

"How do you feel about Pepe Le Pew?" She was toying with his emotions, and he knew it. Pepe Le Pew was her absolute favorite cartoon character. He was also befitting for all her feelings about Pedro.

"I guess I don't have any aversion to being that particular skunk."
"Good, I'll be Penelope, and you can pick me up at 5:30."

"You'll go?"

"Did you not really want me to? Pedro people typically don't extend invitations to be rejected."

"No. I mean, of course, I want you too. I wanted you to all those other times before, but you wouldn't."

"It's been a long time since I've been to a masquerade ball. However, this is not a date. We are two people helping each other pass the time on a Saturday evening, okay."

"Okay, Madi, take care."

He got off the phone before she talked herself out of going. "Hot damn!" He had a non-date with his wife. There were going to be some restless days until Saturday.

Madison sat down on the sofa again. She could not get comfortable, so she laid back and put her feet up. It had been a long time since she was made aware of her free-agent status. She could see anyone she chose. Dominic tonight, Pedro tomorrow night, and any new man she met at the grocery store the next night. She smiled.

Dating was what they called it these days. She was entitled to a little fun and leisure. When was the last time she subjected herself to dating? One name came to mind and one name only, Brock. The road to hell is paved with good intentions they say. THEY got that right!

Everyone should be privileged enough to be with someone who enjoys every essence of them. All should frivolously indulge in loving to the point of obsession at least once, not dangerously but passionately so.

Madison smiled at the passion that convinced her she was certifiably insane. When the Brock "thing" ended, the experience allowed her to freely open herself to love. She still shared Pedro's name. He did not ask for it back in the divorce, and she didn't offer.

Sometimes fortune smiles on the brave with a passion to accompany them for a lifetime. Other times, simple gratitude for an invitation to a party left unattended is better than the memories. Madison and Brock classified as "other times." The invitation she accepted was adorned with the most beautiful wrapping of heartbreak she had ever received at the time.

His name was Brock Andrews. Brock Julius Andrew to be exact. It was a long, scorching summer twelve years ago. Brock was the reason she and Pedro found each other and came crashing onto the scene of marital partnership. Thoughts of him took her to polar opposites of the emotion spectrum. The only things that travel faster than the speed of light are lust and stupidity.

He was the produce vendor for Satyre's while she was studying for her C.P.A. exams. She managed the restaurant for six months but never noticed him until that day. It was the beginning of a slow and excruciating lesson on love and betrayal.

She recalled it vividly as though it was this morning. Yesterday was too far away where thoughts of Brock were concerned. Thinking of him now made her feel as though she were overdue for a confession. He was the Catholic. A good old-fashioned baptismal for backsliding should have been her request.

Madison overslept the day they officially met and was trying not to be too late for the 5a.m. delivery. She threw on some "coordinated" clothing exposed to the right lighting and passed moderately for business casual. Off she had sped with a ponytail and a swipe of lipstick. She arrived at the restaurant at approximately 5:20. He was waiting.

With a brief acknowledgment, she greeted him and dashed inside to unlock the back door. He began placing the items in the cooler. He meticulously aligned each item and rotated stock. Brock stood back as he examined his work. He did this with all his accounts. He tried to make sure the items were aligned by season and use. This kept them as fresh as possible.

One morning he decided to rearrange the romaine lettuce next to the tomatoes instead of peaches. It would be easier for the person stocking the salad bar. After he was satisfied, he found Madison to explain his reason for rearranging her cooler. She would not mind. Madison St. John was a young, easy-spirited woman. He guessed her to be about 20 years his junior; making her about twenty-five.

She took over the reins at Satyre's about six months prior. The grapevine offered she was working on her CPA and needed something flexible. She got the job because she went to college and befriended the owner, Helen's daughter Victoria. Helen Cromwell established Satyre's in 1980. She instantly fell in love with Madison and became her surrogate mother of sorts.

Victoria and she used to come home from school and take Helen on those wild, adventurous day trips. It all was to get her "out and about" since her husband Richard passed away. The three of them would have these outrageous makeovers or pull all-nighters with movies and popcorn. When they went back to school, Helen could not wait until the next break to bring her girls home again.

The grapevine also offered Madison lost her parents early, so she was open to the opportunity to have a family again. The connection between the three women grew into a beautiful trio of mutual respect and love. When one of them took an unexpected departure, the remaining two were never quite the same. The whole sordid mess had been an unwelcome exercise in strength and provided a fiercely protective bond of love. Travesty would be the only word to describe it.

Helen knew her clientele' exceptionally well. She still served her customers as if she were part of the wait staff. She was exceptionally good at judging the way people would perceive an added item on the menu. Perception, along with Madison's unique gift for management, made the restaurant a stellar success.

She and Madison were quite the pair. Brock came in sometimes and overheard them engaged in conversations ranging from politics to constellations to men and back. Helen respected Madison for her drive. She got what she wanted and did not settle for what she did not. She often proclaimed herself the" new generation" of women because the 1990's definitely represented a new set of differences and challenges than the 1970's posed.

On the other hand, Madison seemed to exchange pain for passion and found a way to make it work for her. She lowered her guard for Helen, something people sensed was not easy for her to do. She was polite to all but in-depth with few. In his conversations with her, he always respected the wall placed around her and tried not to offend by asking for the privilege to enter.

Observers were tolerated by not encouraged to participate. She had a way of looking at people with her eyes that could chill to the bare bone. They told a story of a woman who had seen more than she was supposed to at too early of an age. Helen once commented on her ability to look into your soul in an instant. She did, however, keep whatever it was she saw to herself. Helen adopted a "she will tell me when she is ready attitude." She had her own demons to slay.

She told Brock she often thought of Victoria and their relationship. Brock's heart often ached for his friend. Victoria would have to explain everything to her mother whenever they spoke again.

It all began five months earlier. Helen was awakened from a

deep sleep by a drastic chill. It was the kind of chill only mothers feel. She had spoken to Victoria a few hours ago. Victoria made a doctor's appointment because she missed her period.

She was hopeful the news would be what Stephen wanted as much as she did. She loved Stephen and wanted to have his children as soon as possible. Stephen Carpenter had proposed, and their wedding date was set for August.

Victoria decided to detour on her way home to look at the latest in infant wear. The doctor heard two heartbeats. Twins! What a beautiful wedding gift for Stephen! She walked out of the store, got into her car, and began to pull away when a familiar stride caught her attention. Two people were laughing and cajoling as they exited a hotel across the street. She knew that stride.

Stephen was holding the blonde woman's hand, and he gave her a kiss as they approached the corner. The light turned green. Victoria froze. Cars behind her started honking their horns. The commotion made the couple turn and focus on the culprit.

Stephen's eyes locked with Victoria's. He looked like a man caught with no excuse available to explain his infidelity. Sometimes, there are no words. He dropped the woman's hand and made a dash into traffic toward Victoria's car.

Victoria stared at him with the look of a woman who knew. Clarity can be earth-shattering when it removes all doubt. She finally knew the reasons for the last-minute cancellations. He said it was because of extremely critical patients who required him to extend his nights at the hospital.

Doctors have easier alibis than others who cheat. No one wants to be the reason someone loses their life. Therefore, random, and sudden absences are part of the relationship DNA between medical spouses and partners. She sat there and stared at him with all those answers crystal clear in her eyes.

It was over, instantly. As Stephen reached her car door, her limbs came to life, and she pressed the accelerator. The force was so significant it threw him backwards. Damn, she thought, why didn't he fall in front of the car!

Victoria ended up at Helen's house. Amazingly, no matter how distraught, children always know their way home. Equally amazing, parents always know when to be there. Victoria stumbled from the car. She was screaming something incoherent. Helen ran from the house and cradled her daughter in her arms in the driveway where she lay.

They sat there for what seemed like hours, Helen recalled for Brock. Helen had been around long enough to know a woman only released an agonizing scream like that about a child or a lover.

Victoria had no children.

At first, all she understood was it was over between Victoria and Stephen. No explanation would take the pain away.

When she finally calmed down, Victoria recanted the whole story for her. The missed period, doctor's visit, pregnancy, and Stephen's infidelity. All within two short hours.

"I do not ever want to see him again! I know he will try to come by my house after he discards his bitch. I will not give him the satisfaction of the lie he has spun together.

I am going home to gather some stuff. Mom, I need to stay here until I figure it out. I do not want him to have the opportunity to catch me alone in a weak moment."

"I'll go with you," Helen said.

"No, Mom, I'll only be long enough to put everything together. It will only take a few minutes. I will be back within the hour. I am so happy you are always here for me. I love you so much, Mom."

"She was much calmer than when she arrived. Not wanting to upset her any further for the welfare of those babies, I let her go alone.

Okay, baby girl. I am only a phone call away if that bastard shows up. Do not try to argue with him. You have more important things to focus on. We will get through this. I promise. I love you, Vicki, and we will figure this thing out."

Helen sat in her recliner and waited.

She must have dozed off because she awoke with a start. The phone was ringing quite annoyingly. Victoria was not back yet. Helen got in her car and drove over to her daughter's house. The crowd of people surrounding it drew her immediate attention. Neither her sight nor her soul ever recovered.

Police tape tried to hold her away. Helen was wrestled to the ground by an officer who tried to find out her identity. Paramedics and the stretcher made their way outside. Black plastic is what you use to take out leftover food, not the remains of one's only child.

The scream that tore from Helen's lips held a familiar ring. She felt as though she was standing outside herself. It could not have come from her. It was the same agonized cry of desperation she witnessed from Victoria earlier, but for the other reason.

When she awoke, she was at the hospital with Madison and Brock by her side. The neighbor knew Madison was like a second daughter to Helen and called her. She found the number on Victoria's refrigerator. The note listed contacts in case of emergency for me or Mom. Madison used the same detective skills to locate Brock, who was listed as a secondary contact for Helen.

Helen recalled the whole story as she remembered it for them. "She's dead, isn't she?" It was not a question. "Yes," Madison answered softly.

"Do you know how?" Brock shivered as he tried to find a less graphic way to answer her. There was none. Madison recalled how difficult it was for him to say the worst words he had ever spoken to another.

"The police said they received a 9-1-1 call from her neighbor who heard something that sounded like a gunshot. They dispatched a vehicle immediately. When they arrived, her neighbor was attempting CPR. The paramedics took over, but it was too late. She was gone. There was a single gunshot wound to her abdomen. Victoria died instantly; she did not suffer Helen."

Brock would never tell her Victoria languished in pain. Horrific images should never accompany a parent's loss of a child. She took her own life and the precious twins she carried inside her. Within Helen's heart, her daughter was murdered.

Helen had only two requests for the service: 1) small and intimate, and 2) Stephen Carpenter could not attend; the rest of the service details she would entrust to Brock and Madison. They succeeded with the first.

Victoria was laid to rest in a cherry wood chamber with copper lining. She was draped in cream and burgundy rose petals. Her dress had an eggshell tone which accentuated her beautiful olive skin. She looked like a reincarnated Sleeping Beauty. Helen was pleased when she viewed her daughter's remains.

The services were concluded, and the viewing went well. All the invited guests were standing in preparation to exit when Stephen burst in.

"No! "Let me see her one last time!" He screamed as the attendant was about to close the chamber. As he approached the coffin, Helen recovered from her shock. "How dare you! How dare you show your face here!"

Brock and Madison tried to restrain her, but she broke free and lunged at him from around the pew.

"You animal, you never gave a damn about my child or the babies she carried! If you had, we would not be here today! Where is your bitch? The one that helped you create this havoc and destroy my child's life? They may have reported it as a suicide, but your hands are permanently stained with the blood of three lives.

Go ahead, touch her! Touch her! They say if a murderer touches his victim, they will point them out even in death! May you greet the devil on the lowest rung of hell!"

Stephen looked at Madison and Brock in sheer horror. Pregnant. Twins. He hadn't known. Victoria never spoke to him after she found out. Silently, they escorted Helen from the chapel and took her home to confront the necessary task of living.

Brock and Madison agreed to close the restaurant "until further notice." He called vendors and told them to withhold any orders until he contacted them. Each extended their deepest sympathies to Helen. He also gave the staff two months paid leave and took an extended one himself.

Madison went home, packed some things, and forwarded her phone to Helen's. She closed Victoria's house and packed up photos and mementos for Helen to distribute later. A cleaning service came and removed the blood from the carpet in the bedroom and the walls.

For the next few weeks, Madison settled into caring for Helen. One evening, Brock and she were sitting in the den when Helen came downstairs. "Hey, you two, why don't you go out and get some air?"

"Where would you like to go?"

"I have no intention of tagging along. You have been fussing over me like a wet hen for weeks. I am sick of seeing the two of you. You are officially fired from policing me for a few hours anyway. If you are worried about my being alone, Reverend Calvin is coming over and bringing a few people from church. I'll be fine."

"We'll wait."

They chose a restaurant not too far from Helen's house. They felt like parents sending their child out on a first date. Awkwardly sitting in silence, it occurred to them they had never been alone outside of Satyre's or Helen's.

Finally, they chatted about the service and Helen's state of mind. The conversation turned to people at the service and some of the outlandish dishes brought to Helen's. Smiles were forming more easily when someone interrupted.

"Excuse me. I know I'm probably not welcome here, but I need to talk." Brock and Madison looked at each other uncomfortably as Stephen waited for permission to join them. Madison slid over.

"Okay." Brock found his voice.

Stephen ordered a drink to accompany the nervousness in his hands. He slammed it down and relieved the server of the bottle. He took a deep breath, and the whole sordid affair untangled from his lips as if he were on trial. Madison and Brock resented their roles as jurors.

He told them he genuinely loved Victoria. He explained she wanted to get married, and he had not, not yet. But he did not want to lose her, so he proposed. Deafening excitement radiated from her.

Meanwhile, he had a patient in remission. However, her ovarian cancer came back vigorously and metastasized to her other organs. He spent a great deal of time with her family explaining the options and trying to make her as comfortable as possible. Her sister took her relapse especially hard.

They went for a drink one night and purged themselves of their ills. She was in town to be by her sister's side and was rotating shifts with her parents. She did not want to go back to the hospital, plastered with alcohol, so they went to a hotel not far from the hospital, and she got a room. He stayed. They eased each other's frustrations. He intended to tell Victoria he wanted to postpone the wedding date and take some time to review his feelings.

He inhaled deeply as the tears began to flow. The next day, they checked out after breakfast, and he was saying goodbye when they heard the horns blaring. He saw Victoria. His voice began to falter. He never meant for her to find out. He knew the awful mistake was exposed when he saw the look on her face.

Stephen continued after he expelled some of the pain lodged within him. He knew she would be angry so he thought he would give her a moment to cool down. He called her numerous times. Ready to face her wrath, he went to Helen's to see her. The neighbor told him Helen was at Vikki's funeral and shared the details.

They had been right. He had not known of the babies until Helen spewed her venom upon him at the service. Dear God, it had been an awful place to be for all of them. A mother grieved for her child, another would never become a mother, and friends stood by helplessly through the entire tragedy. Even now, it felt equivalent to the description of "whole crush pressure" described by submarine personnel watching a disaster occur.

"I know it is cliché, but it truly meant nothing to either of us. We were two overwhelmed people with a bottle."

"So, let me get this straight: My friend is dead because of NOTHING! You and Miss, I AM SO AFRAID let's fuck, devastated Victoria's entire world for NOTHING? Well, I hope you feel better because I sure in the fuck do not!

I found some comfort in the idea that maybe, just maybe, you had fallen for someone else. And maybe you were searching for the right words to tell Victoria because she could be dramatic when she really wanted something. But NOTHING!" Madison was shouting. Brock touched her shoulder to quiet her because people in the restaurant were starting to stare.

"They can go to hell too!" She shouted. The waiter came over and asked if everything was all right.

"No, my friend is dead because her cheating-ass fiancé slept with someone else while she was pregnant with his twins, and he says the fuck meant NOTHING!" The people in the restaurant all turned their gaze pointedly at Stephen.

A patron came over and told the waiter, "Put their bill on my tab. His too, as he glanced at Stephen. He has enough to atone for if this is all true.

"Thank you," Brock said.

"No thanks necessary. More people need friends like the two of you to tell an asshole off on their behalf. I am only sorry this one cost your friend her life." The patron walked away.

A few weeks later, Brock sat thinking about his dinner with Madison. They were both in need of a change of scenery. It turned into a TikTok video when Stephen showed up. He wanted to know the woman behind the cognac eyes and wry sense of humor he had watched for months.

"How about we have a real dinner, uninterrupted this time? Brock wanted to see if the attraction he felt for Madison was mutual.

"Brock Andrews, are you asking me on a date?"

"And making a damn poor attempt if you need clarification."

She laughed, "The restaurant is in Ashley's capable hands this evening, so sure, why not." She reopened the restaurant two months after the tragedy. Partly because Helen asked her to and partly because she needed to circulate some fresher air.

Grief had a chokehold on all of them. It needed to be released. Madison ventured into her office to review the day's receipts when he sauntered in.

"You do realize you walked off in the middle of a conversation, right?"

"I thought it was finished. You asked me out. I said yes."

"People typically decide on a place and time. Wow, Madison, you really are bad at this, aren't you?"

"Well, Mr. Andrews, let's make this simple. Given our history of sabotage by well-wishers when we have attempted to eat out, how about my apartment at 7:00 p.m.?"

"Oh, you're cooking?"

"Hell no! But I will let you choose and grab a bottle of wine."

"And you are doing what exactly," he teased.

"Opening the door, setting the table, and chilling the glasses. You know, the heavy lifting." He rolled his eyes, and she cracked up. "She was beautiful. It was a nonintrusive, naturally innate beauty. The kind women have when they are not focused on it. It took your breath and thoughts away without warning. The kind men left home for."

"Somehow, I am getting the short end of this dinner, but okay, lady. I will see you at seven o'clock. By the way, what is your address?"

"Oh, I guess we have only seen each other here and at Helen's."

"You really are terrible at this!" Now, it was her time to roll her eyes at him.

She scribbled her address on a piece of paper and handed it to him.

She dashed home and gave everything the 20-minute to clean ritual. It had been a while since she had been home. She was used to picking up her mail at the apartment office and rushing off to Helen's. It was not too hard to dust a place unoccupied for months.

When she decided it was as good as it was going to look, she ran a comb through her hair. Brock rang the bell.

He arrived with multiple bottles of wine and cartons of Chinese food. "There is really only one kind of takeout in a pinch," he joked. "So… you already have excuses before you even get inside the door? Whew! Some things about men are classic!"

One of everything soon lined her coffee table, and they settled into a nice round of mindless and meaningless chatter. For hours, they ate and simulated old dance steps from days gone by. The level of comfort was amazing to them both. There was no drama to undertake or reality to whisk in.

She reached for her shoulders and gave them a mild massage. The weight of the past few weeks seemed to hit her all at once. He poured her another sympathetic glass of wine and refilled his own. He reached out and replaced her hands with his own.

Without a word, he stood behind her and pulled her backwards into the sofa for a better angle of her back. His touch was warm and thoroughly therapeutic. "This is dangerous," they both thought.

She smelled of jasmine, and honeysuckle radiated in the air. Her hair was soft as it slid over her shoulders and caressed his hands. Hypnotically, he gathered it and placed a small kiss on her shoulder. It was as natural as one foot in front of the other. To her surprise, a small moan escaped her lips.

How long had it been since her last massage? How long had it been since relaxation was not a struggle? How long since a man's touch wasn't a clumsy attempt to stroke her hand when she returned his change?

They spoke no words as he nibbled her neck and ear. She shifted and he moved closer to fill his lungs with even more of her scent. Slowly, he pulled her up and turned her to face him. Their eyes met.

Permission was granted. For the first time, they understood the full meaning of mutual consent. It did not matter that they had only known each other in trauma. They did not ask about potential "someones."

They knew there was no engagement, she was not pregnant, and no one in this room would be suicidal about this in the morning. Tomorrow had its own issues. Tonight, they were here, fully present in this moment.

His lips explored her so slowly it hurt. She knew what static electricity must feel like when his tongue found hers. When he placed his hands on her cheek, she tried to pull away because the air between them was gone. She was panting. Brock leaned forward to stay connected to her.

Madison slid to the floor. He joined her. The fireplace was their witness and just like that their ride began.

As though extracting honey from a flower, he undressed her. He did not even know his life was deficient until he touched her. She turned in the firelight in an air of embarrassment. He was not having it and held her hands above her head.

"You are beautiful." "No, I'm not."

"You're not petite. I do not know why women feel men only find size sensuous. Men want a woman who knows she is and what she wants. You do. You are also exactly what I need. You are beautiful in every way my mind can comprehend."

He was not much taller than she. Brock was Mr. Clean minus the earring. He was clairvoyant. She was sure of it. How else would he know where to touch her? He kissed the bend of her knees, and she trembled with an ache deep within. She felt her body begin to drip when he licked her ankles and indulged in her toes. The strokes he applied aided her submission. She was willing; he was waiting.

Finally, she returned the madness. To simply touch him in return would be blasphemy. She pulled his shirt over his head and held his arms captive. He could not touch her, which activated his own torture.

He pretended to wrestle with her as she kissed his chest and suckled his nipples. Brock pushed her backwards with the weight of his body, and she unzipped his slacks and slid her hand inside.

Madison stroked him, and he moaned out her name in Morse code. Her mind could not process anything past the heat she felt in his loins. If she was nearly as hot to the touch as he, they were going to burst into flames any second. "Damn, he felt so endowed in her hands!"

A breeze rustled over her skin as he rose to discard the things preventing full skin on her skin. He looked deeply into her eyes as he split the vortex of her thighs. When she could focus, she was half lying, half sitting on the floor. What happened? Why did she hear noises outside? Oh shit, it was her; no, him; no, them moaning!

They pleased each other twice before morning. It was Saturday. Helen wanted to open the restaurant, so Madison took the weekend off. She stretched with the urgency of a feline, and Brock stirred next to her.

"Good morning." He whispered in her ear. "Good morning."

She suddenly felt strange and shy. She started to pull the covers over her breasts, and he protested.

"I've seen the most intimate parts of your body by firelight. Why can't I witness it by sunlight?" He pushed the covers down to her ankles, and she looked away from him.

"Don't," he whispered, "let me look at you. Watch how beautiful my eyes and body think you are. There is nothing about your body I would change."

"I'm thick in all the wrong places."

"You are a real woman, and I can assure you, men have no problem watching and wishing they were me right now. Let me show you what they think." The actions of the night replayed in real-time but in slower motion.

"Would you like some breakfast?" Madison whispered to his bent head. "Convenient. I don't even have to get out of bed for it."

Eventually, they did get out of bed. He savored her response to the way he luxuriously bathed her. They made breakfast together. It felt like he was trying to overflow her senses with the little things. It was working.

Brock read the paper while she clipped coupons. She did not expect him to stay. He had. He seemed genuinely interested in her thoughts about things she enjoyed and listened intently.

They were so comfortable observers would think they had been lovers for years. Lovers? Were they, or was he being polite? It was bad manners to leave immediately after the sins they had committed. There was a name for it and Madison did not like it."

Finally, as dusk crept upon them, he said he had to leave. She was both relieved and disappointed. Brock had been great company. However, she needed to check on Helen, and she to think. He kissed her in a long-exaggerated goodbye.

Madison heard him take the stairs two at a time. "Was he late or energized?" She closed the door and tried to stop her mind from racing. She was not the type of woman to bed a man and immediately began examining China patterns.

Last night was definitely the best fuck of her life; surely, she could keep perspective! She picked up her purse and headed over to Satyre's. She wanted to lay eyes on Helen, and she needed a change of scenery.

Helen was in the dining room when she arrived.

"I thought I told you to stay home this weekend. I ran the place without you before, you know. God knows you deserve some time away from here."

"You know me well enough to know I wasn't going to stay gone all day." "Yes, I do." Helen stared at Madison for a long moment.

" Have you eaten anything today?"

"No, I've not been very hungry. My stomach has been in knots."

"Well, Barney can manage out here for a while. I will make you some soup. Go into the office." Helen knew Madison was not going to take "no" for an answer.

Madison heated some cream of potato and brought it to Helen in the office. "Now, I'll be right back. I need to check on an order."

"Madi, wait. I need to talk to you for a moment. Close the door." Madison did not like the sound of the command but did as she was told.

"I had a long talk with Terry Morton today. I told him to come by the house early this morning. He took a long look over my assets and the financial picture of the restaurant."

"You're not in trouble, are you? I told you I could reduce my salary. There is only me, Helen, and I…"

"Wait a moment. First of all, you already don't take home your current salary, so a cut would definitely not be a discussion. Second, my bookkeeper let me know you did not give yourself the previous raise we agreed upon. But we will come back to that. Our financial situation is in better shape than it has ever been, thanks to you. Our debt is net 30 same as cash, with no outstanding bills. Our profit margin is 72%.

Madison, from the day I met you, you have been a daughter to me. When Vikki first brought you home, I knew you would stand by her until the end. You did. And moreover, you have stood by me, not something a parent ever expects from their children's friends. You oversaw the whole sordid mess.

"My intention was to split everything equally between you and Vickie," her voice trailed off. At my request, Terry drew up the paperwork to make everything yours. You are officially my soul heir and beneficiary except for the portion designated to St. Jude's Children's Hospital in Memphis, Tennessee.

They do fine work without scandal for those children. All parents who opt to have children deserve the privilege of watching them grow into adulthood. No parent should ever have to bury their child."

"Helen, don't do this to me. You are going to live longer than any of us. I don't want you to go and do something foolish."

"I am not out of my mind; I need to get things handled. There is no one in this world who means more to me than you. Likewise, Terry thought it was a fine idea, and you know attorneys don't outright agree with much."

"I don't know what to say, Helen."

"Exercise those manners I'm sure you own and say thank you. Now, get your butt out of here and enjoy the rest of your weekend."

"Thank you. I'll leave as soon as you have finished that soup."

Madison thoroughly enjoyed her weekend. She called her old friend Natalie. They spent Saturday night out on the town. Natalie went to college with her and Victoria. They had not seen each other since the funeral. Each woman tried to keep the evening upbeat after she told Natalie how Helen really was.

"Well, who else do you think deserves the honor Mad? You have been her lifeblood before and after Victoria died. I think it is wonderful." Madison got home around 3 a.m.

Madison went to bed and fell asleep instantly. The amaretto sours had a hand in it, she was sure. She rose the next morning and spent the day on her C.P.A. exams. She thought it a bit hypocritical to go to church with alcohol still permeating her pores. She went to bed early on Sunday night too.

When the alarm went off on Monday morning at 3:30, she jumped. "Okay, okay." She showered, as her mind reminisced on the night with Brock. She would see him in less than an hour. What would she say? They had not spoken since he left at dusk on Saturday.

She arrived at the restaurant early. Brock was already waiting for her. She let him in through the back door. Not hanging around for small talk, she went to the front and turned on the lights and the grill. After counting the tills, she went into her office and sat down.

"So, we're not even speaking to each other this morning? I guess my idea of sexual etiquette needs to be updated."

" Good morning."

" Why can't you say it the way you did the last morning we were alone?" "Because we're not about to be alone much longer."

"But right now." He took her in his arms and left no room for questions. His desire smoldered below the surface.

"I missed you yesterday." He whispered as he inhaled the smell of her hair. "I was studying most of the day." Was that her voice barely audible?

"I wanted to call you, but I didn't want to press my luck. All I have thought about is being inside you and hearing you call out my name."

"Brock, please."

"Please, what? Say my name again the same, breathless and sexy way." "I cannot concentrate. I have to unlock the doors up front."

"When are you going to unlock the doors in here?" He pointed to her heart. "Brock, not here, not now. Don't do this."

"Meet me this evening. Better yet, I'll pick you up around 6:00." With another quick kiss, he was gone. Brock went out to his truck and turned on the radio. "No Ordinary Love" by Sade was playing, and he began to hum. "How could this younger woman sweep him away so quickly? What was Helen going to say? How could he make this work?"

Day Three

Madison awoke from her dreamy state. She could still feel him as though it were this morning, not twelve years ago. Whenever she thought about those early days with Brock, it stirred her emotions like a good concert from back in the day. "Be honest St. John, the issue was not his skills as a lover. It was his character as a man."

She poured herself a glass of wine. On second thought, she grabbed the bottle. Her mind continued its journey into the past despite her attempts to focus. Why not? She was home alone, so she indulged the memories a bit longer. "Silly me, I went with him that night. He made me happy to be a woman. Hindsight is 20-200, not 20-20."

Brock picked her up and she left her car at the restaurant. They went to dinner at this nice little Italian place that catered to lovers. One of his friends owned the restaurant, so they got a private room all to themselves.

"So," other than you prefer your coffee black and homemade croissants with cream cheese, I really don't know a lot about you, Brock."

"Well, you know I love Helen like a sister. I have an all-consuming passion for this lady who is young enough to be my kid sister with the initials M. St. But you tell me, what would you like to know?"

"Are you originally from New Haven? What are your parents like? Do you have any children? When is your birthday? Have you ever been married? What are your hobbies? You know the basic stuff."

He smiled at her and said," No, Kansas City. My father died last year. My mother died when I was a child. No children. December 11th, yes, divorced about 20 years ago. I like to lift weights, cook, and make love to you. Did I get everything?"

She was breathless. Hell, she did not remember half of the questions after the last part of the answer.

He continued, "Now for the things you didn't ask. My father's house is still in KC but on the market. I went to the military for six years straight out of high school. I was deployed to Italy which explains my passion for Italian food and friends.

I spent a year in Germany. I came back to the States in the mid-1970s and got a degree in Physical Education. A friend and I were going to open a gym, but it never materialized. Consequently, I have been doing this for the past eight years. I have no siblings, only two fantastic aunts who live in Chicago; they are my father's sisters. My middle name is Julius. Now, it's your turn."

"Brock Julius, it sounds like a drink of some kind." "It can be."

Once again, he rendered her speechless. "I am originally from Alabama. I have been here for about four years. I met Victoria when we both attended Memphis State and decided I'd come here and give it a shot. Helen talked me into staying.

My degree is in Business Administration, and I am studying for my CPA exam. I have never been married but engaged three times. I was more flattered than committed, so I called them off before the monies got spent. My parents both died when I was in college, separately. Helen has helped me cope with the void of not having a mother, and Victoria was the sister I never had."

"How do you feel about what happened between us Madison?" She took a sip of her wine.

"Well, we're both adults. We both consented. I don't have any regrets."

"Perfect and politically correct answer, but Madison, how do you feel? For instance, he took her hand, dipped her finger in his wine glass, and licked the excess liquid off her fingers when I do this?" A chill ran down her spine.

"Well, I...I... I don't want you to stop."

"Then let's go someplace where I don't have to."

She guessed he paid the check; she was not quite sure. All she remembered was his hand up her skirt and pulling her panties down along with her mind when he opened the car door. Right in the parking lot, in front of God and the people parked next to them, he began to kiss her thighs. She trembled when he said," I've wanted to do this since this morning in your office."

"Brock."

"What's a little embarrassment when it can lead to this?" His tongue found a crevice she did not even know she owned. She moaned so loudly the couple getting into the car next to them started to fondle each other. When the woman became a little shy of her surroundings, she heard the man whisper, "If he can do that in public, surely..." Madison was completely delirious.

By the time they reached her door, she thought she was dead. She could not feel her legs or her lips from the intense pounding within her. He kicked open the door, and she never withdrew her keys from the lock. They tumbled inside the door and continued their journey to ecstasy.

Later, as they lay on her sofa, she got a comforter from her bed. "One day, we are actually going to start this in bed."

"Is it a requirement? I cannot help it if your bedroom is way back there, and making love to you deserves an immediate reaction. You excite something unexpected in me. All I have thought about from the first night we were together is the way you smell. The way you taste and that Southern drawl as you say "yes" while I'm inside you."

"My Southern drawl doesn't come out, does it."

"Yes. It is only apparent when you say things like "yes" in an enthusiastic moment or the number 9. Otherwise, it blends in."

"So, you listen to me during sex?" "I listen to you, period."

She remembered closing her eyes and envisioning the days they shared. He was attentive, passionate, and complimentary. Brock was the kind of man who made you rejoice in being a woman. She felt glad to be in her own skin. The way he celebrated the trivial things in life was extraordinary.

There were objects present her whole life she had taken for granted until she saw them through his eyes. He pointed out the sunrise was more blood orange than yellow. Ants travel in a straight line down a sidewalk. Brock noticed the different chirps of crickets or when a set of squirrels moved to a new tree. He was special, plain, and simple. He made her feel like she had waited her whole life for the way he loved her.

They drifted through the summer and into the fall with the same rhythmic sensation. He came by the restaurant or met her at her place since it was closer to town than his subdivision in Station Point. They went to dinner or to a play and made love every time like it was their first experience. Sometimes, he stayed. Other times, he left when she fell asleep. He would use his key to lock the door if his day began earlier than hers.

During those times, he would leave little notes in the bathroom shower or on the coffee pot. Once, he even left her a note on her tampon box because he knew menstrual cycle time should be close. He was thoughtful.

Lost in her thoughts of Brock one day at the restaurant, someone said, "Excuse me."

When she looked up, cashmere grey eyes were staring at her. Damn, I bet my toes would feel great rolling around in those. He had olive skin, a small dash of salt in his black hair, and a dimple slightly covered by a morning shadow. He wore a black turtleneck and a pair of Levi 501 jeans. "The Lord sure does make some beautiful things!"

"Yes?" She responded.

"My friend and I were wondering how many meals we have to eat here in order to find out your name. My friend says three more. I said you would not be that cruel because we would be regulars and know by that time. So, which of us is right?"

"My vote for the weakest line I have ever heard goes to both of you. But because you had the nerve to walk over here and say it to me, I'll say neither you nor your friend are correct." Thinking back with a smile, Madison recalled Joshua was the friend.

Ashley looked surprised at Madison's dismissal of Zeus. What the hell? Damn Mad, the twin brothers of Roman Reigns and Idris Elba are trying to find out about you, and you cannot recognize it because you're dating a look-alike, Jim Brown?

Shit, the room is always open for potential members of The Silver Fox Squad! Why in the hell didn't I wear any makeup today? If either is looking to meet someone…

The mystery god walked away, shaking his head.

Ashley sprang into action! Hell, he was clearly interested in Madison, but the sidekick was fine as hell, too! They checked all the immediate boxes from where she sat. Fine, check. Sexy, check. No rings or tan lines on the important finger, check. Beautiful smiles, check. Impeccably dressed, including shoes, check. Professional men with jobs, check and check!

"May I refill your drinks, gentlemen? Her name is Madison St. John. She is the manager of this fine establishment. She is single, with no children, and working on her CPA exam. She loves music of any kind! Most of the time, she is here from 5 a.m. until… Helen, the owner, makes her take at least two weekends a month off. It happens to be this weekend." Both men started laughing. Each handed her a $100 bill as a tip.

"Thanks for the intel!" the god said. They began to walk away. She raced over to the door.

"Anytime, and by the way, my name is Ashley. I am her assistant. I may need a job if she finds out I told you any of this!"

"Come see me if you do. There is always room in the D.A.'s office for a woman who knows how to get things done." Added the sidekick with his gorgeous chocolate eyes.

'You like her already, don't you, P."

"Are we talking about me or you?" Joshua smiled in a coy way. "Ashley, hmmm…"

The next morning, the god came back in for coffee. This time, he was alone. "Good morning, Ms. St. John."

"How? Never mind, Ashley. Good morning, sir. Would you care for anything else with your coffee?"

"As a matter of fact, I would." "Okay, let me get you a menu."

"Actually, what I would like is to tell you my name, Pedro Santiago, and ask you to have dinner with me."

"Well, Mr. Santiago, if Ashley was as thorough as I believe, she told you I am seeing someone. So, I will respectfully have to decline." "God, I must really be in love with Brock because I turned down Perseus."

"I was actually informed your status was "kind of seeing someone," so perhaps the next time I ask, you will be kind-of-not. Have a good day, Ms. St. John." He picked up her hand and kissed it softly goodbye. As Pedro walked to his car, he thought, "I just officially met my wife. Thank you, God, for allowing me to find my good thing!"

"ASHLEY!" Madison ran after her into Ashley's office.

"Before you start, are you insane? He is a gorgeous, employed, and interested man. He did not ask to stop by and holla. He didn't ask what you are cooking. He didn't even ask to put his bill on credit.

Do you have any idea what is not out here in these streets? The only thing I am sorry for is his fine-ass friend did not come this time!" Ashley did her best imitation of a pouting child, and Madison cracked up.

"You know I am trying to figure out what is going on with me right now." "The heavens sent you a hand-delivered gift and you sent it back without so much as a sampling? Whatever Brock is laying on your ass make mine a double. In the meantime, since God knows your name and address, could you put in a word for a sista?" Both ladies erupted with laughter.

Helen witnessed the whole exchange and was not the slightest bit amused. She had been afraid of this very thing happening between Madison and Brock. Madison noticed the crease in Helen's brow. "Well, we did not want her to find out this way, but now she knows.

She is going to worry about the outcome of another young woman in love. Victoria died over the very same thing. But she was not Victoria, and Brock wasn't Stephen by any means.

Brock called later and told Madison he was not going to be able to keep their date. "Brock!"

"Sweetie, you know I wouldn't cancel unless it was a necessity. I promise to make it up to you."

"Oh, all right. I won't ask what is more important than me. But know I am extremely jealous, and you owe me big time."

As he hung up the phone, Brock was glad she had not asked. He did not have an answer although he had a strong suspicion. Helen called and said it was of the utmost importance and Madison was not to know.

They met at a quiet little restaurant on the outskirts of town. He had trouble finding it and he had lived in this city for years. He knew Madison would never be out here. Helen was seated at a table in the back when he walked in.

"Good evening."

"Brock." He sat down and Helen did not mince words. "I'll get to the point, and we can enjoy our dinner."

"Okay."

"I have known you for over twenty years. When Victoria died, the only way I survived that horrible ordeal was because of you and Madi. You are the two most important people in my life. I trust you with my life. I will not trust you with Madison's! She is in love with you, Brock! You know something must be done.

I have lost one child to heartbreak. I will not stand by and watch another sacrificed! The two of you cannot continue this farce. Settle for a friendship to sustain some type of relationship with her. Lust comes and goes. I expect you to act swiftly or I shall.

She is stronger than Vickie. Life has made her that way. Madison will recover with time. Continue to betray my trust and you will not. Now, I will order for us. You will have a double scotch. The filet mignon is excellent also."

Brock sat back in his chair. Helen was right and he knew it as he stared at her across the table. She just destroyed his life with a single promise. Madison might recover from walking away from him. He was not sure he would. It was more than lust. He loved Madison. It should not have happened but dammit they were here now.

There was so much he could not explain. Yet, there was so much he needed to explain. Unfortunately, Helen only knew part of the details. He could not tell Helen how much he longed for Madison in the middle of the night. The mere thought created an erection as he sat here now.

No one would understand his side. He did not plan to be captivated by her smile. Those cognac eyes stirred him in a way he had never experienced. Her sense of humor and timing were impeccable. She was brilliant and ... No, he had not planned to love her, he simply did.

She was kind and loving. She gave from her heart and asked for so little. Laughter had returned to his life because of her. Madison accepted his failures and flaws without question. "We all have baggage, Brock. We must condense it as a carry-on for the overhead bin and not keep keys to storage lockers." He smiled as he thought of her words when he tried to explain parts of his life to her.

Her eyes made him want to drown near a life jacket. The smell of her and the smoothness of her skin pacified his pain with the tranquility of sailing. Her response to his touch made him ache for her. Although there was an intensity to the desire he felt, they were more than a variation of David and Bathsheba.

He was in love for the first time in his adult life. He was not simply accepting his fate after a failed marriage from his youth. Brock desperately wanted to run to the end of Europe with Madison and leave no forwarding address. Why couldn't life really be easy? Free will has failed so many of us.

Realizing his elongated silence, he finally said, "I love her, Helen. I love her more than I could ever make you understand. She deserves complete honesty even if it means I must lose her. You have my word. However, if she chooses to stay, I need you to respect it."

"You have my word as well, Brock." They spent the rest of the meal chatting about mindless things. They caught up on events and talked as two friends who cleared the air.

Brock walked Helen to her car and waved goodbye. He got into his and sat there. How was he going to do this? Break his own heart.

Helen had his word so avoiding following through was not optional. How had he gotten himself into such a son-of a-bitch predicament? Of all the things in his life, why did he have to potentially sacrifice her? He and Helen both knew why.

JoAnne. Her name was JoAnne. They had been together for five years. She was ten years his senior. They never married but lately she was pushing. She felt she was losing him, and she was right. Walking away was becoming more of a thought inside his head. Their new house was less than a year old. They moved in two months before a tsunami named Madison made her presence felt in his life.

They had mutual respect he and JoAnne. She was in love with him; he loved her. Looking back, he knew he had never been in love with her. After a certain age, love seems so secondary compared to the quality of life built with someone.

His last romance was twenty years prior. They married and quickly realized it was not the best for either of them. The divorce was painful but necessary. Being in love stopped being a prerequisite to being satisfied. Before JoAnne, he dated without the interest of anything more. Sex and limited companionship were his only offerings. It suited his lifestyle and needs.

JoAnne would walk over hot coals for him. Sex between them was an act of fulfillment. It did not move him. It was a means to an end. Lately, he could not even focus on her when they did. How many times had Melissa Etheridge's "Similar Features" played in his head while they made love? He was ashamed that in their most intimate moments he could not concentrate on her. JoAnne deserved better.

His feelings for Madison would be summarized as a midlife crisis. He did not feel so at all. He genuinely enjoyed her; making love was extra. He expressed it to a friend this way. "Loving Madison was like winning the lottery. The first purchase would be her devotion. Whatever it took to make her stay." He was too old to believe in obsession, but he had lost himself to her.

Sometimes, after making love, he watched her sleeping in his arms. Those were some of his most treasured memories. He honestly tried to feel that with JoAnne after he and Madison were together for the first time. It did not happen.

JoAnne did not deserve to be hurt. He knew she sensed something because one day he came home, and she was playing "Girl Crush" by Little Big Town. He saw her peep out the window to time the start as he walked into the house. She had been through so much since he had known her. He should be ashamed for being torn.

Three years ago, her son Mitchell was diagnosed with leukemia. Remission came and went twice. Each time, the cancer returned more aggressively. The past couple of months had been touch and go. He was so weak and frail JoAnne spent countless hours at the hospital with him or at his apartment.

Brock used to go with her until it became too much to see him struggle for the right to live. Watching the ordeal made him feel helpless because he could not do a damn thing for either of them. He felt like an intruder in their precious moments as mother and son. It took so much out of JoAnne. Lately, he tried harder to support her because Mitchell was not doing very well. He reduced his days with Madison and blamed it on a heavier seasonal workload.

JoAnne was at the hospital on the nights he stayed with Madison. Guilt plagued him over his deception of them both. Most of all, he was deceiving himself. JoAnne was by his side when his father passed away. She deserved the same respect from him now. He wanted to be friends with JoAnne and husband to Madison.

Right now, the only person who had what they wanted was Madison because she was unaware of it all.

He and Madison never talked about other relationships. She had to know in the beginning there was someone. "Hell, everyone has someone." They may only qualify as a drive-by lover, in which case the door to a new relationship is always open to opportunity. By now, Madison believed any previous relationships he had were in the past, like a developed and cataloged Polaroid film. Why wouldn't she?

He spent countless nights in her bed and endless hours on the phone with her. Her security was more important than his own. The thought of Madison being with someone else disturbed him. The same images of JoAnne brought relief.

Brock laughed aloud. Who was he fooling? He was nineteen years Madison's senior. JoAnne was twenty-nine when she was born. For goodness' sake, JoAnne should be enough. In essence, he had promised Helen she would be.

Across town, JoAnne sat down on the sofa. Her again, she thought. "Who is this woman between us? Brock is not stupid enough to walk out on what we have. Financially, he would have to start over.

Finances, is that all we have between us now? She loved him. If hers had to be enough for both of them, so be it. She was not starting over without a fight. Fifty-four was not the age to date. She refused to throw away five years of her life because he was "confused."

It was about 9:30 when Brock arrived at Madison's apartment. He sat outside and stared up at her window. He found himself doing battle with "a case of should."

"I should have never let this happen. I should not have to step on my own heart and break it. I am forty-four and should have known better! I should take my memories of Madison to my grave because I will never feel this way about another woman. I should be home. I should be holding the woman who loves me and lives there. I should have been able to fight this.

There is a woman willing to sell her soul for me and here I am. The thought of smelling Madison's hair made him tremble. JoAnne will love me when we share strained potato soup, after our prescriptions are filled, and when the biggest grocery bill items are

82

matching boxes of his and her undergarments. He started his car and drove home. He took JoAnne in his arms and made love to her like she was the only woman in the world for him. Madison.

The next day, he called in sick to work and asked JoAnne to stay home as well. She agreed. She would help him purge his soul. They spent the day talking about dreams and taking long walks by the pool and in the park.

Dinner was a joint effort. Afterwards, they took in a movie. They made love and she felt like her man was finally back with her. Nestling her head on his shoulder, she drifted into a contented sleep. Brock's eyes never closed the entire night. Daylight always comes.

Brock called off work again the next day, except this time, he did not tell JoAnne. He called Helen and requested coverage for Madison so they could talk. She agreed.

It was 5 a.m. when he arrived at her apartment. When she opened the door, it felt like his first breath of oxygen after suffering deprivation for the past two days. How in the hell was he going to get through this?

"Good morning."

"Good morning to you. Helen said you wanted to talk to me." Madison had visions of how he was going to do it. Would he propose on one knee like a Southern gentleman? Would they make love first, and then he would pop the question? She was ready to be a wife now, unlike the times before. If Helen was in on this, he must have asked her for her blessing.

"Yes." Thank you, Helen, he thought, for making sure I didn't lose my nerve.

"All right, let's talk."

"I need you to promise me you won't interrupt, or I swear I will lose my nerve."

"Promise." She was almost giddy with anticipation.

He began. He told her about JoAnne and the life they shared together for the past five years. He told her about Mitchell and his situation being touch and go. He explained why he was able to spend all those days, nights, and endless hours of conversation with her while JoAnne was at the hospital.

Brock tried to explain not hurting JoAnne, but it was difficult because it meant hurting Madison. He expressed his guilt for deceiving them both. Finally, with his promise kept to Helen, he braced himself for impact. It did not happen. Instead, she sat quietly.

Her face slipped back into the mask he had known before he knew her. It made him uncomfortable. Madison did not say a word. She got up, walked over to the window, and peered out into the darkness becoming daylight. Brock ached to touch her. He wanted to hold her and say how much he loved her without sounding like a hypocrite.

He wanted to say he would figure out a way to make it all okay. Instead, he waited. Had he said any of it aloud? Finally, when the silence was playing tricks with his mind, she spoke. She turned and looked completely through him.

"Was it real? The feelings you shared with me, I mean, were they real? I am a big girl, Brock. I can handle the truth. Was everything between us simply a way to pass the time until you knew what was going to happen to her son?"

"No. You are everything I have ever wanted in a woman. Only it is five years too late. Everything I said, felt, and still feel for you is real. I love you. God knows I have no right to.

I did not mean to fall in love with you, but I did! Damn, that makes it sound like I set out to play some type of game. On our first night together, we were helping each other unwind. I never meant to touch you. But when I did, I never wanted to stop. I love you, Madison. Please believe me. I have spent the past few days trying to reassemble my life without you. I cannot. I don't want to."

She continued to stare through him. He got up and crossed the distance between them. When he reached for her, she turned her back to him. A dagger through his heart would have hurt less; he was sure of it. Brock paused for a moment. He had to reach her.

Something inside him snapped. He touched her again and she pushed his hands away to cross to the other side of the room. He followed, grabbed her forcefully, and took her in his arms. She refused to touch him in return.

"Madison, please! Do not shut me out like this! He buried his face in her shoulder, and she stood there, unfeeling, stiff. He had successfully done the one thing that kept him up about this unveiling of the truth. He deserved it, but damn it hurt.

She took a step back and looked him in the eye for the first time." On your way out, close the door. Leave the key on the table."

"Madison, talk to me, let's work this out." She walked into her bedroom and closed the door behind her. He heard the lock click. It was the loudest sound he had ever heard. As he walked toward his car, he glanced up at her bedroom window. She was staring down at him. He turned to fully face her, and she closed the blinds. Brock spent the rest of the day in a bar across town.

Three weeks later, Madison called Pedro and asked him to dinner. He was at the restaurant having breakfast when they spoke. Helen overheard the conversation. "Proceed with caution, because Madi would be a bit down," she told Pedro. Later, Madison arrived at the restaurant.

She looked at Helen's face and maintained her composure long enough to go through the kitchen and out the back door. She spent the day in the park with a bottle of brandy she snatched off the shelf. As she sat on the bench, she understood why ducks fly south for the winter. Being this cold on the inside is a bitch.

Pedro was quite charming. He was a beautiful man. It was not superficial for someone who had been on the cover of a magazine. He was soft and subtle, with a dynamic sense of humor. The perfect man for any woman in the world, except Madison. Good people do not deserve to become victims of someone not emotionally ready for a relationship.

Any other time, she would be thrilled to be with a man of his caliber. Tonight however, she was agonizing over a broken heart. No one should be the "first" person after a bad breakup when there are still unresolved emotions. She needed to apologize, excuse herself, and go home to finish the date she started earlier with her bottle of brandy.

She tried to reason the pain away. How could Brock have faked everything? Why had he risked it all? How could she figure a man like Brock was unattached? Madison sat and envisioned JoAnne with a son only a few years younger than her. She thought about Brock touching her and choked on her wine.

"Are you okay?"

"Yes, I swallowed wrong. "Dear God, she forgot he was even there! I am feeling a bit worn out. I'm sorry I'm not much company tonight."

"It's all right, Madison. After everything, I am not surprised. The hours you put in are incredible." He was making excuses for her. He truly was a remarkable soul.

"I'll tell you what, how about we make this another time? How about next Tuesday? I will concentrate on getting some rest to clear my mind, and maybe you won't regret going out with me."

"I don't regret it now; however, I would like a chance to know the focused Madison. What type of food do you prefer," she smiled at him.

"I'll cook dinner for us?" He smiled. He was handsome.

He walked her to the door and kissed her cheek. Surprisingly, she was stunned and pleased. On the drive from the restaurant, she tried to figure out how this moment would not be awkward.

"Get some rest because I am holding you to next Tuesday." He flashed a quick heart-wrenching smile and was gone.

There was an immediate knock on her door. "Did you forget... Why are you here, Brock?"

"So, this is how you've been healing yourself? At least he did not kiss you. I would have walked up sooner." He pushed past her and stood inside her apartment.

"Why are you here? You know what, I don't even give a shit. Get the fuck out! Go home to that old ass bitch you do not want to hurt and leave me the hell alone!"

"Not until I say what I came to say. Madison, I am sorry I hurt you. I do love you. I truly do. I have tried to let you sort out your feelings. It is killing me to stay away from the restaurant until I know you are gone. I have made a mess of things. I will fix them somehow. I will."

"You are assuming I give a shit what you do! What is it baby? Did she forget what an orgasm was? Did it dry out all those nights alone and the lubricant isn't strong enough?"

"Madison, shut the fuck up! Do you think it is easy telling you I can't make love to her without seeing your face? Do you think I am proud of what I've done to all of us? Believe me, if I could've sport-fucked your ass without any emotion, I would have. No harm, no foul. Besides, you cannot get used when you're using, can you, Sweetie!"

"Brock, stop. Do not do this to you or me. You made a choice; help us both honor it. Do not come by here again. Do not call. Ashley is opening now, so we do not have to see each other. Just let it be! "

"I can't let you walk out of my life this way.'

"You had me sign on as the side whore without my knowledge, and now you don't want me to walk away? You do not have a choice. Goodnight, Brock." She was tired. She also wanted to touch him. She would betray herself if he stayed much longer. He grabbed her arm as she tried to turn away.

"Don't throw us away, Madison. There is so much we can have together. I know how good we are, and so do you." She opened the door and slammed it closed after him. Bourbon did not help her with the battle. She spent the rest of the evening with the worst migraine she had experienced in a long time.

The next morning, Helen stopped by to see her.

"Cat still dragging things in I see. Let me put on a pot of coffee while you shower."

"Helen, I really don't feel like this right now."

"I will make some waffles to absorb some of the liquor in your system. Where is the waffle batter?" Helen completely ignored Madison's words.

Helen was insistent so Madison decided to do as she was told. She did feel slightly better afterward her shower. She put on a pair of sweats and came out to the smell of homemade waffles and "the talk" she knew was brewing.

"You have known about JoAnne the whole time, haven't you?" Madison recalled the scowl on Helen's face the day she and Ashley talked about Brock in the office. She saw the concern on her face.

"Yes. I did not know they bought the house, but I did know they were together. I met her once a few years ago. They came to the restaurant for dinner. So, yes, I knew. The night I told you to get some air, I did not mean to sleep together! A soda or an ice cream used to be sufficient in my day."

"Do you think I wanted this? Hell, I have not slept in days. I feel him everywhere. In my bed, in my head, I cannot even shower without feeling him touch me. I sacrificed a portion of myself to him, Helen. Last night, when he burst in, his smell nearly drove me over the edge!

I told him to get out. At the same time, I wanted him to stay. I could not fall asleep because I ached for him so badly. I cried until my eyes felt like potting soil. I have seen him outside my apartment and called someone to keep from running out into his arms. The bank teller thought I was crazy because I kept hitting redial to keep from answering the door when he knocked. He won't stop and I don't know how long I can either!"

I feel like I am obsessed with this man! This unavailable goddamn man who knew his fucking predicament from the beginning! Son-of-a-bitch! I am sorry. I didn't mean to use that kind of language in front of you." Helen's eyes widened at her outburst.

"You use it with somebody else?" She smiled to lighten Madison's mood. It did not work.

"My God, Pedro is a beautiful man. He is intelligent, funny, sensitive, warm, and kind. Most importantly, he is available! I should be worshipping the ground he walks on. Instead, I could not even concentrate long enough to have dinner with him! What has Brock done to me?"

Helen stared at Madison as if she were seeing a ghost. Victoria was coming back from the dead. How many nights had she listened to her rave in this same fashion about Stephen? She walked over to Madison and touched her hands to her cheeks.

"He's made you love him. Bastard. You are not obsessed with a man. You are quite badly whipped, but that will subside. You need to ... "

"Helen! Helen!" Madison yelled as Helen slumped to the floor.

"How is she?" Brock asked as he raced to Madison's side.

"I don't know yet. The doctors are still with her. "Ms. St John?"
"Yes, I'm Madison St. John."

"I need to speak with you about Mrs. Cromwell."

"Can I see her?"

"Yes, but I need to speak with you first about her condition.
"Condition? What condition?"

"Come on, Madi, let's sit and hear what the doctor has to say."
Brock escorted her to the private waiting area.

The doctor began with the stress Helen had been under since
Victoria died. It started with an aggravated bleeding ulcer inside the
lining of her stomach. She refused surgery, so they prescribed a series
of antibiotics. It partially healed and Helen stopped taking them. The
infection returned and formed a larger abscess, then tumor. Now, it's
become malignant.

That is why her appetite has fallen off and she has been in such
pain. "Pain?" She did not know Helen was in pain. She had masked it
well. The doctor continued. It also accounted for why she has been so
weak and tired lately. Madison dug her nails into Brock's arm.

"There's a chance for Helen if she allows us to operate and remove
the tumor while the cancer is still confined to her stomach. They could
perform a procedure like a gastric bypass. If she would give consent,
her chances were optimistic.

"No," Helen said vehemently.

"What do you mean, no!" She and Brock said jointly.

"I have lived my life, Madison. I want to be buried with everything
I was born with. Everyone knows once air hits cancer, it spreads.
Leaving me where, chopped up and dead? No kids, I will make the
most of the time I have left. I am tired now. Let's allow that insurance

I pay for to afford me a good night's sleep. I'll be ready to go home tomorrow."

"Helen."

"Good evening, children." Madison and Brock walked out of Helen's room and down the hallway. Neither of them spoke until the evening air hit them in the face.

"Do you want to go for a walk to process this?"

He was being kind and Madison understood, but somehow that hurt even more. She could not think. He could not even tell if she was breathing. She ached all over.

She could not even imagine her life without Helen. Attempting to process it with Brock beside her was unbearable. When she finally found her voice, she realized she was staring at him.

'I do not know, Brock, right now I can't think. He touched her cheek and wiped away the pool of tears.

"We will get through this Madison together. I know there are a lot of unresolved issues with us. Helen is as much a part of my life as she is yours. I will not let you do this alone." He pulled her into his arms, and she resisted.

"Damn you, Madison! Do you always have to be so damned stubborn!

Why are you the only person allowed to feel anything? Why is pain designated to only abide at your house? You are not the only person who loves her.

Maybe I need to hold you for both of us! I have not tried to kiss you or strip you down in this parking lot have I? No! Damn you!" He stormed off toward his car.

Something inside her broke with his rage. "Brock, Brock!" she screamed as she ran across the parking lot to him. "I'm sorry, I'm sorry.

I... I'm sorry."

She could not tell him she felt like her world was spinning, and she wanted to get off and go home. She could not say this was too painful for her to manage alone. Hadn't she told him to stay away from her? Yet, he was the first person she called after 9-1-1. He looked at her and understood it all.

"I'll follow you home." It was a simple statement that balanced her world for a moment.

She opened the door to Helen's house. She stood in the doorway. How many times had she come home to this place and Helen? How many times had they folded laundry on that sofa? How many meals were burned because they were engrossed in a film?

Madison swayed against the door and Brock caught her. "Oh no, you don't! You will not give up hope yet." She turned and put her arms around his neck and wept.

"Your shirt is completely drenched. I am sorry." She noticed as they sat on the sofa. It was two hours later. "It does not matter. Sometimes, one must sacrifice a new shirt for the cause." "Oh, Brock." She smiled through her tears.

"Now that was worth a whole wardrobe," she smiled. She should have moved but it felt good to be close to him. He cared about the same person she did. For now, it was enough. She needed to feel something other than pain. She knew her rationale was insane, but she could not face Helen's mortality right now.

Madison needed confirmation there was something beyond the pain she was feeling. He understood. He turned to kiss her. Reality kicked her in the head like a frightened stallion.

"Brock, don't, please. You may want to do this, but I will regret it tomorrow when I am thinking more clearly. I cannot bear anything else right now."

"I am not leaving you alone tonight. I will sleep here on the couch if I must but leaving you is not an option. Madison went and retrieved some covers and a couple of pillows from the hall closet.

She went into her bedroom down the hall and locked the door. She was not sure if it was to keep Brock out or herself in. All she knew was if she had sex with him tonight it would be another log on the fire of devastation. The sound of the "click" was the second loudest rejection Brock had ever experienced. Both came from her.

"Are you ready?" Brock squeezed her hand as they sat in the hospital parking lot. Helen was waiting for them. "No. But if this is what she wants I cannot override her decision."

After she signed her own against medical advice (AMA) and the "Do Not Resuscitate" (DNR) forms they checked Helen out of the hospital. She was ready, so they had to be. They got her settled at home and found themselves back at her apartment in the same timeless situation. He wanted to comfort her, and she politely refused.

"Brock, please," she said, if you have ever loved me, let me go. I am doing my best to walk away gracefully. All our mutual attention needs to be on Helen. If you cannot honor my decision, I will tend to her needs alone. Do you think we can convince her to have the surgery?" Madison changed the subject as a distraction from the way he was staring at her.

"I hope so." He said it for Madison's sake. Brock had known Helen longer, and when she decided, she meant it. Look at what she decided about them being together! He already tried on separate occasions to talk to her about the surgery. She stood firm.

"Brock, I know I should honor her choice, but it's so selfish of her. I guess she could say the same thing about me. I have already lost one mother. You said your mother died when you were a child. You have no idea how blessed you were in a sad sort of way.

You missed a mother's love, but you also missed the heartbreak when memories replace where they used to be. The phone calls for advice you didn't think you wanted until you needed it. They have hedge of protection prayers that go directly to God on your behalf. Sometimes my mother would laugh uncontrollably until it brought tears to her eyes.

They have an eagle-eye for character that recognizes your new crush is "a piece of shit in waiting." Finally, nothing compares to hearing your mother say, "It's gonna be alright." Those few words can calm the roughest storms in your life. I am having to do this twice. The second time is not easier."

"Sweetie, let's not think about this now. She will probably outlive us both. The hospice nurse is getting her settled tonight. We are honoring her wishes by leaving. She was right, it keeps us from asking the poor nurse a million questions. Tomorrow morning first thing, we will go over and check on our archangel."

He did not have to stay with her. It was actually more for him. Same couch, same lock, and the same click. He was watching two women he loved fade from his life simultaneously. Helpless. It was not an emotion he wanted to get use to feeling.

Madison made Helen promise to rest while she oversaw everything at the restaurant. She closed her bedroom door and made lunch. Brock fidgeted around the room as though he needed to say something yet did not quite know how.

"You have to go, don't you?"

"I was just thinking I needed to check on some things."

"Brock, thank you for being available the past few days. I really appreciated it. You do not have to stammer around. I know you need to see JoAnne. It is okay. Remember, we promised each other honesty. I'll call you if something changes with Helen."

Madison busied herself with monthly paperwork. She had

schedules to complete, vendor appointments, weekly specials to post, bills to pay, and menu items to sample. She did not want to think about anything else. She would bide the amount of time remaining with the second mother in her life and not look toward the future.

The future was for people with certainty, and she was definitely not one of them. She needed stability, so she took a break and picked up the phone. She called the one person in her life who had always provided it, Rozalyn Crenshaw.

"Hello?" A very sleepy voice on the other end answered.

"Are you asleep?"

"Well, it is 3 a.m., Madison."

"Oh God Roz, I'm sorry! I forgot about the time difference between the States and Germany. I'll call you back later this evening my time."

"Oh no, you don't. You have already got me up now. It will be this evening before I get back to sleep. You have an excellent memory Mad, so if you have forgotten time zones, it means something is terribly wrong. Spill it, I'm not asking, by the way."

Madison told Roz about everything bothering her. She talked about Helen. She told her about Brock. "You have always been fascinated by the unobtainable." "Thank you for your words of encouragement."

She could share all her emotions with Roz. Roz was always blatantly honest with her opinions. They were based in a sort of transactional realism peppered with a hint of sarcasm. Madison was more of a transformational optimist until it was time to "shit or get off the pot" They had been friends since they were children and supported each other through some awful times.

Roz covered for her when she used alcohol to cope with her messed up teenage years. She also covered for her when she vanished on one of her risqué rendezvous or nights she chose not to remember. Madison often wondered if she returned the support she received.

They were freshmen in college when Roz's first child, Samantha, was born. Roz dropped out but Madison bullied her into returning. It took some additional years, but she graduated college and law school with honors despite having three children in tow. Madison quizzed her long distance, which helped her with case law and review. Roz passed the bar on her first attempt. She was academically brilliant.

She met Ted in law school, and they got married shortly thereafter. He was in the military and had orders to deploy to Germany. He was a Judge Advocate General. Their three-year stint allowed Roz to study foreign policy and keep herself abreast of U.S. relations with Germany, Russia, China, and Japan.

"Mad, you know you are the eternal optimist. God loves you for it. This man probably does love you but how happy would you be knowing he is banging someone else? We will not even discuss the health issues involved with that sort of tryst.

As you know, I myself have made a few exceptions when good sex is involved, but Lord knows a faithful husband is hard to find. No pun intended." Both women burst into laughter. "There is a reason I call you Mad; you know. Sometimes, I do envy your enthusiasm to walk on the wild side. It generates a certain excitement one can vicariously count on."

"Well, vicarious on bitch! And I have not, then again…"

"Remember when you dated the guy who liked to drink "Big Mouth beers"? Your sacrificial lamb stories always keep it interesting, to say the least!"

"Oh, shut up! You have been well laid over the years, too! Remember, you do have three kids! Seriously, though, you keep referring to mediocre performance. Is everything with you and Ted, okay? Is he slacking?"

"Ted isn't slacking he's just lacking, period! Sex has simply become sex which ranks right next to not getting any. Not sure which scenario is worse. At least not having sex leaves the imagination open to adventure. I am bored and have been for a couple of years.

I realized how bad it was the other day when I actually considered an offer I got. However, you know how I feel about other people and their legal entanglements, not to mention my own. For a split second, I had a "what would Mad do moment."

I remembered I do not have your "black-it-all-out" ability so, I opted instead for your back-in-the-day theme song and took my Black ass home to my husband and let him "stand-up-in it."

"Which song? You know, depending on my mood, the genre changes to this day."

"Your Place or Mine" by The Bar-Kays." They both laughed.

Madison knew by that admission Roz was unhappier than she said. Roz was always the trooper for fidelity. "Hey, you know my place is always available for you and the kids. Hell, we have lived in dormitories; it doesn't get much tighter. I would love to see the kids anyway. Merely a suggestion."

"You never know. Now, about you and Mister. What are you going to do? I know the answer, but I am going to let you toy with the element of surprise?"

"Shut up! I will take pictures for you next time!" Madison got off the phone with Roz and thought moving to a new country held lots of appeal.

She was bombarded with questions about Helen when walked out of her office. Madison scheduled a staff meeting at 2:30 so everyone could hear the news firsthand. She was going to need help from everyone before this was all over.

During the meeting, she tried to be as upbeat as possible about

Helen's diagnosis. Reassurance was the thing she promoted. She assured everyone their jobs were safe; therefore, no resumes needed to be distributed.

The best way they could support Helen, for now, was to keep this restaurant open and thriving. She would expect nothing less. Customers will have questions, so feel free to answer them. Most of these people were very dear friends to Helen, and she would want them to know.

Madison explained her schedule would be very unpredictable because she would have to accommodate any arising needs for Helen. She gave everyone her cell and home numbers. It was an update for most. She promoted Ashley and Jesse to co-managers, and they chose two assistant managers to fill their spots.

She held a 5:00 meeting with the management staff. They discussed their new responsibilities, training plans, concerns with personnel, vacations, etc. She stressed her confidence in their abilities. Madison told them empowerment and communication are how they win this battle.

She trusted them to make decisions as a team in her absence. She set spending approval limits and assigned each a certain group of vendors. If she was unavailable, the final say belonged to Ashley and Jesse. Only when they could not agree should she be contacted if she were unaware of the situation. They accepted their new charges with excitement. Each swore they would not let Helen or Madison down.

"Do you need anything?"

"No, you've done what you always do, Madison, taken care of everything. I am sitting here reading the paper and drinking a carafe of grape juice. Call "Entertainment Weekly." I am so excited! How is everything going?"

"They're all worried about you otherwise, all is well. She told her about the personnel changes. I informed them about your routinely scheduled beatings, so I will be in and out for a while." Helen roared with laughter. It sounded good.

"May I at least choose my weapon of throttling? By the way, how's Roz?' "How did you know I called Roz?"

"You are quite dependable and transparent, my dear. Now, how is she?"

"She and the kids are physically fine. I do wonder about her emotional health. She dropped a lot of hints about the romance home fires not being all they were cracked up to be these days. She, sort of, has the blues about it."

"Hell, she's married to a man, sweetie, which entitles her to free therapy. They are useful sometimes if you tame them properly."

"Oh, Helen, you sound like Roz! I have to go; I'll call you later. Madison hung up and continued laughing. One is never too preoccupied, old, or ill for thoughts of great sex!

She was exhausted. This had been a day. The phone rang as she turned off the lights in her office.

"Hello Madison."

She felt exposed and subconsciously touched her throat. She knew his voice anywhere. Oh Lord, she had not spoken with him since everything happened to Helen. He did not know anything about it.

"Hello Pedro."

"I was wondering if you have plans for dinner. You do owe me a meal, remember? I am starving."

"Oh, Pedro, so much has happened since we spoke. However, if you allow me to go check on Helen and shower, I will be happy to feed you." I will even pick you up if you want. We might as well do this properly. Can your stomach hold out that long?"

"I'll expect you about 7:00. He provided his address. Maybe it was the conversation with Roz about her trip to nowhere with Brock, but Madison looked forward to seeing Pedro again.

She saw expensive homes with beautifully manicured lawns as she entered his subdivision,. Yep, 13951 Cherokee Lane, this was the right place. She looked around and took a moment to absorb her surroundings. This was a long way from Humphrey, Alabama.

Back home, you were privileged to have indoor plumbing and a car. This place was spectacular with its circular drives on two-acre properties. A teenager with a Lexus Coupe sped past her. She worked 70-hour weeks for hers. Now, somehow, it felt very underachieving. She was twenty-five. She should own a Lamborghini by now!

She rang the bell at 7:00 sharp. "Here we go." Anticipation pounced on her as she awaited his arrival at the door.

"You came. I was half expecting the phone to ring." She earned the sarcasm. "We Southerners take our word very seriously, she smirked as she walked through the door."

"So, are you ready, Mr. Naysayer?" "I made reservations for 7:30."

She admired the artwork and the color scheme of his foyer. She was lost in the original Ansel Adams when he took her arm.

"I have waited a long time for this moment, Ms. St. John, after you."

She started toward the door, and he said, "Oh, I forgot to tell you. I have no intention of sharing you with anyone. Dinner is now being served at SHAY PEDRO."

"You are kidding me?" He led her into an elegant dining room with seating for twelve but a place setting for two.

He pulled out her chair to ensure her comfort and poured a glass champagne. "Why, Ms. St. John, I do believe you're speechless. I surprised you, didn't I?

"Yes, you most certainly have."

"Good. It is my mission to keep you interested. I hope your appetite is as great as your smile. I slaved all day over a hot stove, and I hate a woman who is afraid to digest more than salad."

"I'm from the South. I like everything in my life robust. My appetite is no exception." Her blunt statement caught him off guard.

Watch out, Santiago; she may have just one-upped you. "You can wash up in the third room to the right. I'll be right back with our appetizers." Looking at him had done it for her, but okay.

He returned with a mixed platter of cream cheese-filled crab cakes, portabella mushrooms drizzled with hollandaise, and bacon-wrapped shallots with a honey strawberry sauce. She raised her hand to take an hors d'oeuvre from the platter, and he swiped it away.

"No. You take care of people every day. Tonight, let me pamper you." He held a crab cake to her lips. She took a bite, and he ran his thumb across her lips as she closed her eyes. "Delicious." She opened her eyes, afraid one of them melted from the heat in the room. "A penny for your thoughts."

"I was thinking this is exceptional. Did I taste a hint of cinnamon?" She lied through her teeth. Her honest thoughts made her burn with shame. She was locking herself away from Brock two weeks ago! Sexy and available is one hell of an aphrodisiac.

"Yes, a pinch of cinnamon and a hint of strawberry." He let her escape with an unchallenged lie. She sampled one of everything.

"Are you ready for our next course?"

"Yes." He returned with a potato julienne soup served in an eggplant shell for presentation. He sat down and spooned it into her waiting mouth.

"Um, this is delicious with a hint of spice. Tell me again why you dine with us when you can do this?"

"I like the atmosphere." His smile held a devilish undertone. The main course was blackened sea bass with persimmon and rosemary stuffing, and creamed baby carrots with a tarragon pineapple glaze. Dessert was a sinful chocolate custard drizzled with fresh cream, almonds slithers, and topped with a red rose made of white chocolate. The meal should be photographed for Bon Appetit, not eaten.

With each course, he wiped her mouth and held a glass to her lips, taking his own bites while she chewed. Madison thought, Dear God when this dream ends, please don't let my hangover be horrible. She knew reality had a cruel way of laughing at you when you were not in the mood. This was one of those times.

He was intoxicating, and she decided to inhale deeply and pay later. She sat back and contemplated whether he could be gay, maybe bisexual, or pansexual? Otherwise, he would be married with eighty-five babies by now. The idea that he was single was a sacrilege.

"Would you care for seconds of anything?"

"Huh? Oh no, I just need to walk off some of this poundage you added to my body. Dinner was scrumptious. I have never enjoyed a meal or being pampered so much in my entire life."

"Thank you. Let me replace your shoes, and we'll walk."

When did he remove her shoes? Hell, her wisdom teeth could be missing. She would not have known. He returned and slipped them on as easily as they must have come off. Pedro extended his hand and they stood there for a moment in silence.

Damn, she was beautiful.

He was most assuredly a direct descendent of Zeus.

Pedro opened the French double doors to reveal a wondrous courtyard more magnificent than the grounds in front of the house. The proper name for these luscious greens had to be grounds. It was splendid and vastly different from the lawn of Helen's home and a lifetime away from the yard where she grew up.

In Humphrey, grass was a luxury, and seedlings were an unheard oddity unless it referred to a garden out back. Intentionally growing grass was an attempt to prolong the cotton-chopping season. Yet, she tried to retain some modicum of class and culture as she fought the urge to sink her bare toes into the green velvet beneath her feet.

They walked and talked for hours. She found out he was the youngest of three siblings at thirty-five. His mother was still alive and well, living in Rhode Island. She was anxiously awaiting the birth of his older brother's first child. His sister was a well-respected fashion designer who worked alongside Stella McCartney in New York. Their father passed away shortly after moving his family to the United States.

His mother was a registered nurse and put him and his siblings through college. Pedro was always fascinated by law, so he majored in criminal justice with a minor in culinary arts. People need to balance high-pressure careers with a stress reliever. Cooking relaxed him.

His undergraduate degree was from the University of Michigan. He attended Yale Law School and had reciprocity to practice in fifteen states. He was the current Assistant District Attorney with the ambition of removing the "assistant" from his title one day. Right now, the guy who held the job was his best friend, Joshua Thomas. He was who accompanied him to her restaurant the first time they met.

"Correction, the first time I introduced myself to you, dear lady, you did not return the hospitality in kind."

"Wait, let me apologize right now. I was rudely preoccupied, and you were a guest."

"Uh-huh. Ashley definitely saved the day."

"Let me stick a pin in that. I owe her something for her intrusiveness." She laughed and asked him to continue.

He was divorced after a brief marriage of two years. One year for her and one for him, to play let's pretend. She was an architect and lived in New York. He bought the house two years ago with plans to remarry one day and start a family of his own. He answered the question plaguing Madison. He said they should never have married. They were always better friends than lovers.

They shared the passion for their careers that most people feel for their spouses. Their divorce held no demands except well wishes. She remarried last year. He walked her down the aisle in place of her estranged father. All their friends thought it preposterous yet typical of the relationship she and he shared.

He was thrilled to do it. It did not seem strange to either of them until they saw the wedding photos. Most people do not have a wedding picture with two husbands in it! Both thought of it as one best friend escorting the other down the aisle to the wedded bliss she deserved.

When it was Madison's turn to speak, she was more open than she had been to anyone except Roz. Yet, she found the exchange comforting with the newest person in her life. She talked about growing up in Humphrey, a small, impoverished city. Cotton chopping was the employment for teenagers and those with lesser skills. It was hot, dirty, and gratifying in a strange way. A date with a hoe provided a lot of time to think.

It allowed time for reflection and dreaming. It takes a special person to "make a day" and transfer those skills into an air-conditioned career. Some made it, others did not. Her mother was determined she would get out of that small town with no opportunities except as farm laborers.

Madison explained parenting required too much effort from her father, so he walked away when she was a preschooler. Abandonment is a hard emotion to recover from. It leaves a hole inside always begging the question, why weren't we good enough? Low self-esteem stays inside and manifests in multiple ways with no regard for a person's level of success. Some symptoms are toxic relationship choices, addiction, imposter syndrome, workaholism, control issues, depression, etc.

Her mother worked as a nurse's assistant at a hospital 45 minutes away on the night shift. Madison spoke of the desire to move away to a safe place that plagued her when she lived in Humphrey. Pedro learned about her path to self-destruction as a teen. She also expressed the heartbreak and loneliness she suffered after her mother's sudden death her senior year in college.

When that happened, leaving her past behind became a priority. So, she moved to Connecticut after college, turning down a more lucrative job offer in Alabama. She spoke about her relationships with Roz, Victoria, Ashley, and Helen. Her dreams of becoming a CPA were manifesting nicely. She already completed the goal of an MBA.

When he asked her about a love life, she was honest. She and Brock had connected through a series of tragic events. What they shared would never be more. They loved each other in an unhealthy crippling way.

Their emotional investment in the same people made him her safe place to land during traumatic situations. Their sexual relationship was over because there was nothing connecting them except pain. He thought she was referring to Victoria's death. She explained that was only part of it and explained Helen's illness and decision not to fight.

Madison tried to maintain her composure. He listened without pressing her beyond her capacity to speak about it. In his mind, Pedro thought, Brock will not miss this opportunity to try and reinsert himself. You think he has accepted it's over, as a man, I know he has not. I would bide my time too for the woman I wanted to need me again.

She told him loneliness is a state of mind, not a physical technicality. In some ways, she had been alone her whole life. When her father died, she explained the out-of-body experience his funeral was for her. She felt more regret over having no regrets than children should feel over losing a parent. She recalled how it finalized the fact she was not going to see him tomorrow anyway, so the loss was very miniscule.

For the first time in her life, she told someone about her mother's depression. She loved someone in her youth who never quite returned the depth of feeling. In a way, she never recovered from the pain. Unhealthy relationship decisions, including marrying my father, started her spiral into depression. It went untreated and fueled by a combination of self-neglect and ill-managed diabetes.

Madison admitted to Pedro she struggled with some of her mother's generational curses in many ways. She had a constant fear of reliving her life. Growing up, she was unsure she had ever witnessed a balanced and healthy romantic relationship. Consequently, she did not know how to have one. Brock was further proof.

Her stark admission made Pedro halt. "Madison, you are too loving and caring a person to feel unworthy of being loved. I see how you are with Helen. Do not ever voluntarily settle for less than you deserve. As for Andrews, men do not end relationships they enjoy.

They might make stupid decisions while the relationship is in progress, but they do not end them. When a man is involved with more than one woman, there is something gratifying about both for him. He may eventually yield to one, but he will not end it with the other. The yield is because he stopped enjoying time in the previous spot. He will begin to spend time elsewhere.

He will always check-in on the "other" woman if she allows the door to be revolving. Andrews is not finished attempting to be in your life. He enjoys being with you." There he had said it. He continued quickly because he did not want to lose her to that bulletin.

"Women end relationships because "it's the right thing to do." Men do not think that way. Take my divorce, for example. I did not end our relationship; I ended the marriage. Gabrielle and I are still friends because the relationship was the most enjoyable.

You have endured a magnitude of loss in a fleeting period of time, which proves the abundance of your strength. Love does not always have to hurt. It can bring enormous joy when it is demonstrated and given properly." She did not appear to get sidetracked by the thought of Andrews. His optimism began to grow. He paused in hopes she would continue speaking.

She continued and told him of the dream haunting her. She could not understand what she was supposed to learn, and it was beginning to create anxiety for her. She tried to connect the dream to a particular emotion or relevant event in her current life but found nothing thus far.

After pausing for a reflective moment, she said, "My, I didn't mean to ramble on."

"You describe reviewing your life as rambling? A description of the defense mechanism you have put into place perhaps, but not rambling. Your preference for mystery intrigues me. All this time, I thought your intimacy boundary was for us outsiders. Tonight, I find you have designed it for yourself."

"No, Pedro, my boundaries have been crushed and violated many times. I understand pain. We have a special connection. When I have been away too long, it always finds its way back to me. It is an exotic dance partner who will not allow me to take a break and sit one out.

I survive through detachment. Being me is so exhausting most days. People are comfortable not really knowing others. Anything requiring attachment like love takes time and patience. The whole concept terrifies me because I have never been good at it.

Consequently, I make choices I can walk away from at any time. I have a propensity to gravitate toward men who are unavailable on some level, either emotionally, physically, or legally. Which is why I cannot believe I came here tonight. Maybe it was to discover whether you had five kids in private school and a wife who traveled the world curing dementia or something."

"Do you believe you deserve to be loved, Madison?"

"I don't know what that means, Pedro. Maybe one day I will find someone willing to show me an honest love, so I have some frame of reference."

"You are very much worth the effort, and you don't even know it yet." He looked into his eyes and caressed the side of her face.

"It will be my pleasure to accompany you on this journey of self-discovery. "

He pulled her into his arms and held her like she was a frightened child. The touch made her feel like a slow dance with your date on prom night. Maybe it was the champagne or his attentive demeanor, but she was comfortable in his embrace.

He was pursuing her, which sent a chill down her spine. He was single, emotionally available, and unattached. Had she ever experienced this trifecta in a man before now? She took a step out of his embrace and Pedro searched her eyes for a sign of peace.

"Thank you for allowing me to invade your personal space. That felt nice."

"Yes," she replied as a shiver escaped her.

"Are you cold?" He placed a protective arm around her and

escorted her back inside quickly.

"Oh, my goodness! It is almost midnight. I must go and check on Helen. Pedro, I had a magical time. You are the most thoughtful man. You seduced me into talking about my most repulsive subject, me, while keeping the evening light and tasteful. We must do this again."

"Most definitely. He walked her to the car and kissed her forehead. Drive carefully and let me know you arrived home safely."

"A true gentleman, " she thought as she drove away from Eden.

It was hard to believe her first real date with Pedro was twelve years ago. The best word to describe it was enchanting. Those were the moments that made her love him deeply. He met her in trauma and focused on keeping her balanced. She knew she wanted to marry him again.

This time she wanted to be sure their expectations were aligned. She had learned all the questions to ask unlike before. He taught her that. They were exceptional parents and lovers but that did not save them the first time. She wanted to be sure there was nothing left between them that would undermine their relationship and shatter their marriage again. Hopefully, they would have a chance to discuss their status after the masquerade ball.

Madison decided to watch a movie. She remembered "Wuthering Heights" was coming on and she could never resist the temptation of Heathcliff and Kathy. She decided popcorn would be a nice accompaniment. As she entered the extensive kitchen, she gazed at her surroundings. This was the home she always wanted with the family to love residing within it.

Pedro had always been a wonderful man. She had not always known how to appreciate it. She found herself looking forward to the masquerade ball on Saturday. He really wanted to go if he was willing to dress as a skunk! Although Pepe Le Pew was not just any skunk, he was the love of Penelope's life, even if she didn't want to admit it.

While the popcorn was making its debut, she glanced into her closet. What would she wear to pull off the "purrfect" Penelope? She would figure it out, she already felt the appropriate emotions.

Transition, she thought as she walked back to the sofa. She experienced a lot of it throughout her life. Her thoughts circled back to Helen and Brock. That was one of the most difficult journeys. It ranked right up there with the death of her mother and life without Pedro. Somewhere in the distance, she heard the microwave singing.

She left Pedro all those years ago with an unusual sense of peace. She was unaware the powers of the universe had been voting during dinner. The draft cards did not align in her favor. The calm before the storm was brewing.

The clock read 1:00 a.m. when she arrived at Helen's house. She crept in and found her fast asleep. After a gentle kiss on the cheek, she closed the door, walked down the hall, showered, and crawled into bed. It was the first peaceful night's sleep she had known in a very long time.

She awoke to the sound of cabinet doors slamming. She pulled on her robe and found Helen in the kitchen, fully dressed with dishes in her hand.

"What are you doing?"

"I thought I would make you breakfast. I was trying to be quiet, but you know that is when you are loudest."

"I'll finish," Madison said as she took the dishes. "Madison, I'm not dead yet! I know you mean well, but you are treating me like fine dinnerware, and I will not stand for it any longer!" The look on Madison's face registered her hurt. Helen never yelled at her.

"I'm sorry."

Helen walked over and touched her cheek. "No, I am sorry. I am going stir-crazy. If I stay in this house one more minute, I swear I will start needlepointing! They burst into laughter. Helen always mocked older women who sat for hours and made booties and Afghans.

"All right, I'll have two eggs over easy and a piece of Canadian bacon with two slices of toast. The grape jam is in the fridge."

"My tip better be a good one!"

They finished breakfast and headed to the restaurant. Helen told her to take the weekend off, she was quite capable of running things for a few days. She assured her Ashley was only a phone call away. Jesse also encouraged her to vanish for the weekend. Madison decided to go to her own apartment and clean.

"The only problem with cleaning is one has to be around long enough to dirty something." She took off her gloves, pulled out some of her favorite CDs, and sat down in front of her stereo. The doorbell rang immediately.

"I have a delivery for Ms. Madison St. John."

"That would be me."

"Please sign here."

"Oh, wait a minute." She found her purse and gave the man a $10.00 tip.

She worked in an industry where tipping was crucial. "Thank you, ma'am. Have a nice day." She opened one large box to find two smaller boxes inside. One contained two dozen long-stemmed roses mixed with orchids. The other contained a beautiful black three-quarter-length cocktail dress with matching shoes and a bag.

"Oh!" The card read: "Only the best for a princess. P.S. I got your shoe size from the other night, and Helen was only happy to oblige on the dress! I will pick you up at 8:00! "P."

She could not believe it. When she moved to put the flowers in water, she noticed a dazzling sparkle amongst them. Tucked snugly inside the paper were two stunningly beautiful 1-karat diamond earrings.

"The gentleman does think of everything." She could not wait to try everything on immediately. The dress could not fit any better if she stood in the designer's studio while he made alterations. It slit and dipped in all the right places.

Her hips were beautifully accentuated which exposed the curvature of her spine in the most tantalizing way. She looked phenomenal if she did say so herself. Standing in the mirror made her nauseous. Quickly, she stepped out of the dress and rushed to the toilet. She threw up violently. This always happened when she assessed her appearance positively.

She glanced at the clock when she was finished, it was 6:15! She brushed her teeth twice and plugged in the curlers as her bath water began to throttle into the tub.

"Well, this is as good as it gets." It was 7:59. The doorbell rang. She opened the door to expose Perseus in the flesh.

"Good evening." His smile sent chills down her spine. Amazing how he had that effect on her.

"Are you ready?"

"Yes, let me get my purse."

"You look exquisite. The designer could have only hoped the dress would have such a radiating effect. Simply beautiful."

"Thank you. You look quite dashing yourself, sir." As she stepped over the threshold, he pulled out a long black satin scarf.

"Do you trust me enough to let me blindfold you?" She hesitated for a brief second, "Hell, she could always ransom the outfit to get home."

"Okay," he placed the scarf over her eyes.

"This evening is about the uncensored ability to feel. You think you've lost it, but I intend to show you it's only been ignored." He planted a small kiss in the palm of her hand and guided her down the hallway. He could have been leading her to slaughter, and she would have made sure her mani-pedi was on point for the occasion!

After she was securely fastened into her seat, she was handed a glass. Instinctively, she sniffed the contents and placed it to her lips, "Mmm."

"You like it?" "Oh, yes."

"Good, it's the perfect accompaniment to this, open wide." He placed a small skewer between her lips. It was a tantalizing display of peaches, kiwis, strawberries, and chocolate. She moaned as though she were making love to the fruit.

"I hope one day you make that sound for me." Her embarrassment was evident. "Pleasure should never be an embarrassment, Madison. The shame is to withhold it." She felt the car stop.

"Mr. Santiago, we're here."

"Thank you, Jacob." Pedro escorted her from the car and up some stairs. "Relax and watch your step." She heard a roaring sound." Pedro, May I take my blindfold off now?"

"Not quite yet." She felt them begin to move. "Pedro!"

He removed the blindfold; she was inside an aircraft preparing for take-off. "You're being kidnapped for the next four nights."

"What! I cannot leave Helen. I must... "

"Have a life of your own again. I am under strict orders and conspiracy with Helen. You may call her to verify if you wish.

"I, what in the world, give me that phone!" When Helen answered the phone, she could not stop laughing.

'This is absolutely marvelous, dear. I would love to have a man take me on a cruise around the French Riviera for four nights and three days. See if you can get a sneak peek at Tina Turner's house while you are there! She is simply the best you know. Have a glorious time!

"Goodbye!"

"She hung up on me! I do not even have my toothbrush!"

"Madison, please don't underestimate me. Of course, I have taken care of the minute details such as wardrobe and toiletries. Helen and I went to the store via the Internet and had everything delivered to my house this morning. You have no excuse not to enjoy yourself unless you would prefer other company."

"There is no one in the world I would rather be with than you." He kissed her quickly. She was slightly disappointed it had been her cheek. Down slut, down! She whispered to her dampening undergarments. She sat back and followed the flow of the evening. They landed and boarded the largest cruise ship she had ever seen.

"The captain's table is this way, Sir, Mademoiselle. We are seating guests promptly, and the captain will join you in one-half hour."

"Merci beau coup," Pedro responded.

Dinner was divine. Fresh lobster bisque and tails, scallops with butter cream sauce, asparagus and water chestnuts with garlic mousse layered atop chopped endives, and dessert was hand delivered by the resident-certified chocolatier. Scrumptious! She tasted things she had no clue how to pronounce.

Pedro watched her. She was glowing with joy. Dear Mary Mother of God, let me keep this woman in this moment for the rest of our lives. I have fallen for her, and she is torn between possibility and the insanity of her life. I can make her happy if she would only let me. Oh, yes, thanks, Helen, for recognizing how good she and I could be together, with one exception.

They walked out to the deck of their private balcony and watched the serenity of the water. There was a slight breeze, and Pedro draped his dinner jacket over her shoulders. She stood near him and breathed in his scent. She could not imagine being any happier if she had been granted her wings.

"Forgiven?" He asked her as he turned to face her. 'Absolutely," she whispered.

"Well, we have several stops tomorrow where we will get off and see what Nice and Eze have to offer. So, let's put a cap on this evening, shall we?" He handed her a key as they walked back inside.

"What is this for?" Madison looked confused.

"We have adjoining rooms." Pedro kissed her cheek and told her to be ready early. We have a big day tomorrow.

She stepped into the shower and smiled. He had thought of everything a gentleman would. He spent an excessive amount of time, energy, and money to make her feel worthy of being someone's desire. She felt like a princess.

When she came out, there was a miniature sailboat on her pillow with a note attached. It read: You were captivating this evening. The epitome of grace and elegance. A true heart's desire. Sweet dreams, "P." She scribbled on a linen napkin from the bedside table and slid it under his door. "I had a Renaissance man as my escort. You were breathtaking. M."

The next morning, she woke to the smell of vanilla cappuccino, cream-filled croissants, over-easy eggs, juice, and strawberries. The day took on a life of its own. They docked in Nice and toured little shops in Old Town and Castle Hill, then hustled over to admire the art of the Chagall and Matisse museums.

In Eze, they toured Jardin Botanique d'Eze, located in a former medieval fortress. The panoramic view of the French Rivera was spectacular. By evening, she was in awe of the beauty she witnessed, including her escort.

After boarding, Pedro ordered a bottle of champagne. On the balcony, they sat quietly for a spell, absorbed their surroundings, mindlessly caressed their flutes. He poured another glass for both. She took the opportunity to snuggle closer to him, placing her free hand on his chest.

Music flowed freely through the ship. Suddenly, "Feelings (Live)" by Dre Scot and his band sailed in with the perfect words to express the mood. They both paused and listened to the lyrics. Madison shivered at the accuracy.

"Chill?"

"No, I want to be closer to you. If that is okay, Monsieur?"

"Mademoiselle, you are already a part of me. You don't know how deeply."

He looked into her eyes. Searching. He must have found what he was looking for because he kissed her. Madison thoroughly enjoyed the moment. Finally, their lips separated. His eyes swallowed her.

"Oh, lady, you have no idea what you are doing to me, do you?"

"I hope it is close to what is happening over here. You have patiently waited for me to respond. It is priceless to me. I was not the most receptive to you when you met me, as you put it." She chuckled.

Pedro laughed, "Do not act like you rolled out the red carpet for me. Joshua laughed at me halfway back to the office."

"Well, what would Joshua say now?"

"Damn, P, you got it right this time." He kissed her again, and she could tell their natural instincts were taking over. Suddenly, everything went from soft to hard. Her nipples were aching, and he was shifting uncomfortably.

"No, not now." He whispered in her ear. "What?" Madison was dazed and confused.

"I want you; heaven knows I do. But I do not want you to feel obligated or pressured because we are here. There will be a time when we are back home, and you have a chance to examine your feelings. If you still want to make love to me, I will leave the door open. Having you regret this is not something I want. So, let's go back inside. There is a shower I need to take."

He did not wait for her to respond. He pulled her up and escorted her to her room. As she unlocked the door, he placed an extended kiss on her forehead. "Oh, Madison, if you only knew…" He walked away.

The next morning, they had coffee and beignets for breakfast before they docked in Villefranche-Sur-Mer. The local artwork was a brilliant display of corals and gold-toned buildings. Niçoise anglers were roaming about the village with their wares and catches of the day.

Madison and Pedro walked along the alleyways holding hands as they enjoyed visiting the 16th-century Saint-Elme Citadel. A display of luxury yachts rivaled their attention. Afterwards, they stopped off at an outdoor café for a light snack.

"Pedro, this is breathtaking. Thank you so much for knowing I needed this more than I did."

"You're welcome. But my motives were not entirely pure. I wanted you to myself without distraction so you could have private fantasies of me when we get home." He cracked up at the look on her face. Refusing to be outdone, she clapped back.

"How do you know it wasn't happening before we left?" Pedro's eyes smoldered. She did not miss the dramatic effect.

"Touché' Mademoiselle. Touché'."

They spent the final day of their excursion in Saint-Paul de Vence. There, they walked and talked with local artists about their works and inspirations. They ate at La Brouette's, which featured Scandinavian-inspired cuisine. They sampled korvapuusti (a cinnamon pastry), pyttipanna (Swedish hash), julskinka (ham), and lussekatter (St. Lucia buns).

"Pedro, can you imagine the reaction of Satyre's customers if I changed the menu to this?"

"Yes, they would never go home."

"Better stick with tradition and maybe offer samples of these. I already work crazy hours."

"True. I do not want to roll out my sleeping bag in the office to see you." She laughed and thought, "Well, if it will fit two…"

As the ship headed back towards the States, they enjoyed their last night on board by a fire in one of the restaurants. Pedro was unusually quiet. Madison wondered what was on his mind. The cruise had been wonderful, at least she thought. Finally, she could not take it anymore.

"Pedro, is everything okay?"

"Everything has been perfect. That is the problem." He saw her confusion, so he continued. "Madison, I care very deeply about you. These past few days have been spectacular. I have seen you laugh, relax, and enjoy being with me. I am trying to envision us when we return home. You still have to interact with Brock.

I do not know what I am supposed to do with my feelings while you sort yours out. I am not trying to pressure you, but the thought of you in his arms after what we have shared is already gnawing at me."

"Pedro, I have been thinking too. The cold showers were not only for you. We discovered something here together. I want to see where it leads. If you are willing to open yourself to me as messed up as I am, I am willing to let someone as magnificent as you love me. Brock and I were over before you and I had dinner at your house. We got together in tragedy; we never had a start.

The sudden impact of the trauma is over. I am smiling from the inside because you invested in my ability to heal. I do not know what tomorrow looks like, yet I know I want you to be in it."

"I accept." He reached over and kissed her hands. "Wait, did I just propose?"

"Not yet." His eyes twinkled, and they burst into laughter.

As they boarded the plane headed back to Connecticut, Pedro touched Madison's hand.

"Was it worth sacrificing a few days away?"

"You can have me anytime," she replied sleepily. She had no idea how much his heart accepted her words. The thud of the landing gear against the runway woke her. "Where are we?"

"We are almost at the gate."

"Oh!" She sat up and bolted to the bathroom when the plane stopped. She ignored the evil look from the flight attendant because the "fasten your seatbelt" sign was not turned off. She reappeared with a fresh mouth, a mint, combed hair, and freshly applied lipstick. Pedro had taken care of his hygiene incidentals while she slept.

"Are you ready?" "Yes."

The ride to her apartment was relatively uneventful, with chatter about unimportant things like the differences in weather and upcoming events.

Pedro opened the car door, and she brushed against him. They both froze. He wanted to kiss her, but he refrained and let her step past him. When they reached her door, she turned to him, "Come in."

"No, the driver is waiting, and I..." "Come in."

He ran his finger along her lips. "You have no idea how much I want to take you up on that offer. I want to make love to you until you beg me to stop, but you have experienced that before. I want you to relate to me! Feel me from the inside out. Want me with your mind Madison.

Anyone or thing with the necessary anatomy and need can have sex. Animals do it all the time, it is chemical. I want you to have an orgasm from thought when I am nowhere around. When you can capture a moment, internalize it, taste it, feel the difference, only then will you know how much I want us to be together.

If it happens for you, too, I'll be out here. Find me." He did not wait for a reply. He turned and walked away, leaving her in the doorway in complete dismay.

For the first time in over a year, she actually entertained the idea of being with someone for love. Brock was only capable of physical displays of affection. He listened for her moments of weakness because it was all he was free to provide and control.

Pedro swept her off her feet and had only kissed when they were on the cruise. He was waiting for her to come to him with a real possibility of creating something more than a physical reaction. Hell, he made her restrain herself from the attraction to him! She never considered "free will " an aphrodisiac; she had been surprisingly mistaken.

Madison did not want to end her fantasy thoughts of Pedro when Monday morning reared its ugly head. She realized the message light on her answering machine was blinking furiously, on her way out of the apartment. She paused, and pushed the button, "You have 16 messages it shot back."

"I don't have time for 16 messages. I'll listen to you when I get home."

She dashed to the front door and hit the alarm before Ashley appeared to make sure she was who she was supposed to be. "Good morning," she stated as she rushed past Brock. A cold silence met her greeting.

"Well, fine," she thought as she headed back to her office. He acted like she had been missing and unaccounted for. He would not disrupt the pleasure of her past four days!

Ashley came in, and they began to discuss the weekend and the restaurant books. Finally, she said, "Okay, spill it! Helen told me you went on the date of a lifetime. Four days, you never have known how to date! Tell me everything."

Madison obliged as Ashley squealed with delight. She told her about dancing in the narrow streets overlooking the French Rivera, the cobblestone buildings, the amazing cuisine, the champagne dinners, and the strolls through the museums while conversing with the local artists of those regions of France. Ashley purred with envy.

"See, you tramp; you didn't even want to give him your name! So, in essence, you could say you owe your newfound bliss to me and my "blabbermouth," I believe you called it." They both laughed.

"All right, let's applaud Ashley's mouth for its overactivity and extreme boldness." Both ladies burst into teenage laughter. After regaining composure, they heard the back door slam. Brock overheard the whole thing! He got into his truck and drove off.

"Well, my mother always said eavesdroppers never hear anything about themselves they want to." "Yeah," Madison responded halfheartedly. She knew it was over with Brock, but they still had to maintain a civil relationship as Helen's caregivers. Their personal involvement was over. That did not mean they had to be adversarial.

She had 17 messages when she finally got home and listened to everything from the time she was away. She heard Helen tell her to have a wonderful time, someone selling siding and window treatments. There were several hang-ups and wrong numbers. Then the onslaught began.

Six straight messages from Brock plastered her machine. He was alone for the entire weekend. JoAnne went to visit her sister in Wisconsin for a week. He came by twice, but she was not home. He left numbers where she could reach him. The last message was doused with acid.

"I'm sorry someone like me can't afford to have a private jet at his disposal. All I have to offer you is love. My priorities are all fucked up. You were the one who asked for honesty. Apparently, respect is not mutual. Let me ask you Madison, does your new exotic lover with his pedigreed standards have an issue wading through my leftovers to get... "

The space ran out. She stood there with her hand stuck on the button. She could not believe… What the fuck! Was that an attempt at hurt? Did he call her puss "leftover? Oh baby, you will rue the day you…!

He went home to Doan's pill popping, SSS Tonic, Father John drinking cunt every night they had been together, and he had the audacity to talk shit! Damn him! And why was he angry? It struck her like a Charley horse cramp. Ouch!

In the beginning, he used her emotional turmoil to rescue her with sex and sympathies. He latched on to the power she surrendered and took her ass down a winding road to nowhere. She took it back along with control of the situation. His insults were because he did not want to relinquish it without a fight! "Well, bring it!"

When the initial brunt of his anger subsided, Brock was furious. He calmed down enough to realize he had no right to treat her the way he did. He was the one involved with someone else.

He was the one who should be satisfied at home and able to just be her friend. If he were honest, it was not her going away for a few days that infuriated him. It was the fact that he wanted to be the one who afforded that for her, with her.

She was a vibrant woman with dreams to fulfill and life to pursue. She was unattached and could see whomever she chose. He was the one with "an obligation," as she always coldly referred to JoAnne. He should be honored for every moment she let him touch her, not in some jealous rage because she found someone to temporarily ease her desires.

Oh, Latin lover did not know he was temporary, but he would. Brock knew Madison loved him and the new fling was not going to keep them apart. If he knew nothing else, Brock knew that! When she awoke from this fantasy, she would replay his voicemail messages. Pissed off! That is what she will be after she hears them combined with his "damn you" attitude this morning. "Not a smart move, Andrews."

Brock knew what he had to do. He needed to see her. Right now, he did not know what he would tell JoAnne and he could not give two-shits about it. He was losing Madison. He had to make her remember the way they were together. All they needed was some time in each other's arms. She would forget this temporary infatuation. She had too!

Madison checked on Helen then sat down to study for her much-neglected CPA exam. About six hours into it, her head was pounding. Numbers and formulas poured out of every orifice in her body. She desperately needed some pain reliever and a stretch.

The sudden pounding on the door did nothing to ease those needs. She snatched the door open to reveal Brock nervously waiting. "I'm sorry." He belted out before she could speak. "You think that is sufficient for the shit you said?"

"I didn't think. Any attention you give me is more than I deserve. I lashed out because of my own inadequacies, and it was not fair. As good as we are together, you do have the right to find your own happiness. May I come in?"

She stood cautiously and watched him grovel. "It is killing me slowly and painfully, Madison. I need you, which is not a luxury I can afford. Please let me come in." She stepped aside. There were so many emotions inside her. Damn him for provoking me! Damn him, period.

She stood back and fully analyzed him. He was quite nicely stacked. He had one of the firmest butts she had ever gazed upon. His chest was rippled and massive, and his lips were exquisite. The pleasure they created was illegal in all fifty states and several continents, she was sure.

If there was a single part of his anatomy to hold onto forever, it would be his mouth. Instinctively, she ran her fingers over his lips. The Lord sure does make some beautiful things! She would miss them.

"Go home, Brock Andrews. Your lack of emotional capacity is not my fault. You insulted me for actions I did not commit. You treated me like I broke our marriage vows because I spent time with someone I deeply respect.

Every night you curl up with a warm body. If it no longer fulfills you, again, not my problem. Our days of penetration are over. Finally, I realize I do not play well with other people's toys."

"What?" He looked at her with puzzlement on his face. Madison acknowledged their relationship headed downhill weeks ago at Pedro's house. It took a moment, but the Brock chokehold broke somewhere in the waters off the coast of France.

"You are kidding, right? This is bullshit. If you did not want to make love, why did you let me come in? Say not tonight, Brock. What you are proposing is fucking cruel. We are more than this, Madison. We are more than some game of sultry teasing like teenagers in the back seat of a goddamn car with fogged-up windows!"

""First of all, every time my door opens my puss does not need to be let out to piss. Second, you are 100% correct. I am worth more than a fucking backseat tryst. You are acknowledging exactly what I thought was true; you only want me when you want me. I am sick of this.

You ignore me, treat me like shit, then think you can waltz in here and fuck me whenever you want! The party is officially over Brock. You taste-tested the new specialty ice cream when old-fashioned vanilla got boring and spent the gift cards. Now you want a refund. Get out! If I ever require your services again, I know how to find you."

He walked out and slammed the door. "Well, I guess he didn't get what he asked Santa for this year."

Unbeknownst to either of them, Pedro was sitting outside in his car. He saw Brock go upstairs to Madison's apartment. Apparently, the magic wore off quickly. He was about to drive off but something inside him made him hesitate.

Exactly seven minutes later, he saw Brock storm out of her building like lava was hot on his trail. He snatched his car door open and sped out of the parking lot. Pedro smiled. "Now there goes an unsatisfied man."

Upstairs, Madison got ready for bed and walked through her apartment turning off the lights. She made the best decision. Now, let's act like a woman who knows her worth St. John. She dialed Pedro and the phone went to voicemail.

"I wanted to hear your voice before I called it a night. Guess your answering machine will have to suffice. I also wanted to tell you again what a magical experience I had with you in France. Talk to you soon."

She eased onto the side of the bed, pulled back the covers, and fluffed the pillows to create a head indentation. She heard a knock and paused before going to the door. "Ugh, Brock, I am not in the mood for this tonight!"

She snatched open the door and found Pedro standing there. "Hi."

"Hi. What are you doing…"

He rushed her like an offensive lineman protecting their quarterback. He grabbed her head to keep it from hitting the floor. He ripped her nightgown open and forcefully bit her breasts. He shredded the rest of her gown until she lay naked on the floor, trembling.

He devoured her with his eyes. His hands ravaged her hips and spread her legs apart as he teased her with his mouth. His fingers tormented and played inside her as she squirmed.

Pedro lay on top of her and simulated a slow grinding motion. She moaned and thought she would lose her sanity. He turned her over and began a tormenting rain of kisses over her back and hips. She cringed as he stroked her and ran his hands along her thighs and calves until she was pulsating.

"Tell me you want me, Madison? All I have thought about since that night at my house was this moment. Do you want me? Can you feel what you do to me? Can you give him up for good?" Madison had to think for a moment. Who?

"Tell Andrews I am taking over your adventures now. I'll match him breast for breast. In fact, I will raise him a thigh!" He ran his tongue along the inner side of her leg, which separated her thigh and left cheek.

Madison was in so much shock and pleasure she was barely coherent. Was this the passive and demure Pedro? He had an aggression that would have frightened her any other time.

"Can you give him up?" "I did."

"Say my name." "Pedro."

"Again."

"Pedro."

"Tonight, I am going to love you like we both deserve. When we are finished, you won't be able to recognize Andrews in a lineup!"

"Wait, is this about your desire for me or your disdain for him?"

"Both! Let me show you what happens when you stop settling."

Her phone was ringing somewhere in the distance. Madison gave zero-damn!

Pedro was a very methodical lover. He refused to be rushed. His touch was deliberate on every part of her body. His movements were like feathers moving down her spine. She was commanded to lay still and take it. He whispered things to her in Spanish and French. The combination of phrases and sounds drove her wild.

He satisfied desires she did not know she had. When he knew she was on the verge of erupting, he rolled over.

"Get on top! Concentrate on me, Madison. Demand I treat you better. Dare me to stand by you. Dare me to love you. Show me you want me in your life, in your bed. Damn words, show me."

She stared into his eyes and climbed aboard while whispering, "The expectations. Do not make me regret it!" She rocked him like a plane experiencing heavy turbulence. Her arsenal of whore tactics came out to play. Madison knew she had been successful when he screamed her name as they climaxed.

Somebody was trembling from the force, but she was unsure who. She collapsed on his chest. Sometime into the night, they nestled beneath the covers. Dawn was peeking into the blinds when she stirred.

"Good morning, sleepy head,' he whispered into her hair. "Good morning."

"I hope I did not hurt you last night. I controlled my emotions as long as I could. When you called me, I was outside in your parking lot trying to decide if an unannounced visit would be okay." She sat up in horror.

"How long were you outside?"

"I saw Brock leaving, if you're wondering." "Pedro...." He placed a finger on her lips to silence her.

"I saw him when he drove up. I knew he would come by when we returned. What I did not know was whether you could handle seeing him. I knew nothing happened to his satisfaction by the way he stormed out of the building and slammed his car door. It will not be his last attempt. Thank you for demonstrating France meant something special to you, too."

"You mean something special to me. The patience you have shown through all the madness I call my life is priceless. I know this is not easy for you. I will do everything I can to avoid Brock. I do not want you to wonder whether my feelings for you are real."

"Madison, I do not want you to avoid Brock. I want you to stop fucking Brock. Not for me, but because you want to stop. It is easy to stop doing something you don't have access to. It is a challenge when it's in your face and you must choose not to give in to it. I want you to be able to see Brock every day and be okay with it because you chose a life with me." His bluntness stunned her.

"I understand." Was all she could say.

"Do you? The past week has been indescribable for me. I hope you feel the same way. You and Brock have a history we have not built yet. You scare me because I have never felt this before. When I married Gabrielle, it was not because I felt this.

I want a future with you, but only if it is what you want too. The decision is yours to make. I cannot wonder if you are still involved with your trauma battle buddy every time life shows up." He sat up and went into the bathroom to shower.

Madison sat on the bed and thought about his statements. He was right. He was asking for something only she could give him: commitment. Pedro opened his vulnerability to her. It was time to put her "big girl panties on" and be the woman he was asking her to be. It was time to break the generational curses of self-destructive choices and infidelity and step out on faith.

She walked into the bathroom and opened the shower doors. She stepped in behind him. Pedro was wet and slippery as he turned towards her.

"Let's do life." The way he kissed and made love to her left no doubt. They could have easily been replacements for Olivia Pope and Fritz in an erotica scene from Scandal.

Later, they ate breakfast, and Pedro left for the office. Madison was not too far behind him. She remembered the answering machine beeping last night when she was in a "do not disturb" moment with Pedro. The flashes of them together brought a smile to her face. He was a beautiful human.

She pressed play as she grabbed her purse and keys.

"Are you sure you want to continue this game, little girl? No, I do not have the right to be upset, however, neither do you. You have known about JoAnne for quite some time. And you are pretending this thing between us is only physical. I am a grown-ass man Madison. If all I wanted was sex, I knew how to get that before and after you. Shit, it is at my house always readily available! But I will tell you what…

The next time we are together, and I know there will be a next time, you will have to come to me. I'm not sure what tricks lover is using with you, but I know I got to you first. I made a statement! We do exchange something when we make love, and it is not merely biological fluids! It is called love. You may never admit it, but we love each other. Otherwise, this shit would be insane!

Whatever fascination you have with your new toy, it will not last. People like us only have room for one. I am yours, and you are mine. We pass the time and keep security with everyone else. JoAnne is the latter for me, and I know lover is the latter for you. You will come back to me. End this shit with him now!"

"You bastard!" She slammed the phone down and deleted the message.

She felt a migraine in progress. The slamming of the door only accentuated the throbbing between her eyes. She got to her car and the drums beat louder. The pain was excruciating. Madison called Ashley to let her know she would not be in today.

"Another migraine, it sounds like."

"Yes, I cannot even pull out of the parking lot. The sunlight is making me nauseous.

"Would you check on Helen for me?"

"Absolutely, honey. Get some rest. Everything is under control over here." "You're the best." Madison stumbled back upstairs, holding tightly to the banister railing, took some medication, and went back to bed.

Later, she turned over in bed to hear the most pleasant of voices sitting beside her in a chair.

"I hear you have an awful headache. How long ago did you take this stuff?" He was examining her prescription medication on the bedside table.

"How did you get in here?" They both chimed in, "Helen."

"Lie back while I make something that always works for me when I have one of these unwelcomed visitors." A little later, he returned with a cup of chamomile tea.

"Here, sip this slowly. My mother says migraines come from

suppressing emotions or feelings needing to be expressed." She coughed and nearly spit the tea in Pedro's face. His mother was too accurate. She never met the woman, so there is no way she could know the tension created by Brock's voicemail. It did not fill her with pride that a few things he said were true about "people like them."

"I have been so worried about Helen these past few months." It was not a total lie. "Well, Helen sent me to try and ease some of your stress. I would have come anyway when I found out you did not feel well. It really was sudden because when I left this morning, you were right behind me.

Would you like some more tea?" When he looked at her with the softness in his eyes, he could have talked her into being a circus clown. "Sure. Too much fun last night combined with a direct hit from the sunlight this morning, I guess." He smiled.

What is wrong with me, Madison thought as Pedro left the room? I feel like I am living outside myself. This is not remotely close to how I should be acting or feeling. I am falling for one man and cannot handle the irrational behavior of another.

Why do I keep listening to the bullshit Brock is spewing? She answered herself, because I am afraid of how I am going to handle it when Helen is gone. This new relationship with Pedro is easy now, but will he stay around when this gets bad?

Brock wanted to control her. His high-strung emotions were because he felt her slipping out of reach. Her whole life, she avoided relationships for the toll they took on her soul.

As she sat waiting for Pedro to return with more tea, she wondered what it would be like to wake up next to the same man for the rest of her life. She smiled as she realized she wanted it to be Pedro. Relax into it St. John. Do not lose the affection of a good man because you are scared to reach for a love of your own.

"Okay, let's take care of your muscles now. We need to relax them, so let's head into the shower."

"Pedro, I hardly think that is necessary. We were in there earlier, and showering was not what happened. Seriously, bear with me a few moments."

"I'm well aware of your morning activities, ma'am, but I intend to wash your hair. As tempting as you are when you are wet, I would never take advantage of you when you don't feel well. Now healthy Madison in the shower …, he winked, so come on." He put her arm around his neck and guided her into the bathroom. Madison followed instructions. The way he cared for her; she would let him insert her tampon if he wanted!

He stood in her shower and took off her robe. Gently, he took off her bra and panties. He took off his clothes, and she watched as he adjusted the water temperature. The water streamed down her head and directly into her face. He smiled at her and told her to keep her eyes closed as he moved behind her. He ran his fingers along her temples first.

"Relax, Madison, or it defeats the purpose."

Hell, she was trying! Every woman in the world would agree she was doing well to be naked in a shower with Roman Reigns' body double and had not fainted yet. Shit, she was applauding herself! Tense was an understatement for what she was feeling.

Pedro began to lather her hair and massage her neck by running his fingers over every inch of it. He felt himself begin to pulsate. He pushed her head forward as he repeated the massage technique on her shoulders. He felt her muscles begin to relax and become more supple. He let her shampoo engulf them in the smell of honeysuckle and jasmine. He was on fire!

She is so beautiful, Pedro thought to himself. She does not feel well, yet she smells wonderful. The water running between her breasts created an erection he shifted to keep it from touching her.

In this delicate position, he could mold her wet body the way he had this morning. There had been other females throughout his life, but none made him want to take care of them this way. He did not feel this virile and unashamed about the longing in his loins.

She was intriguing and incredibly sensual. The way she licked her lips when she thought no one was watching. She let food linger on her taste buds and thoroughly enjoyed it to the point of changing her facial expression. He loved to see her eat something she enjoyed because it drove him quietly mad. She was the subject of many daydreams and nocturnal emissions.

His mind drifted to the image of her in that black evening gown from their cruise. She was spectacular. She was naturally lovely. He watched her sleep for hours on the return flight home.

Her body was soft and warm as she let her guard down and lay on his shoulder. The way she laughed and attempted to hide the slight crowding of her bottom teeth when she did. She had no idea what she considered a flaw drove him to oblivion when she suckled him last night.

He did not know much about Brock's character. He only knew he was unavailable. How could a man who has access to this woman and her heart choose another?

Helen warned him to go slowly. Pedro promised her he would. But last night, he had to release part of what he felt for her because it was killing him softly. Brock was slowly getting the message from his reaction last night. Now, it was time for Madison to share those same words with her heart.

Still, he could not stop himself from wanting her now, migraine and all. She smelled like jasmine and honey. Her skin was drenched from head to toe.

Delectable. Her broad, sensual hips would be excellent for bearing his children. His erection was larger as she started to turn and face him. He intentionally ran a hand full of water over her face.

"Pedro!"

"I'm sorry. Why did you move? Here, take this towel and dry yourself off.

I will turn off the water and clean the shower. Go lay down."

She stepped blindly out of the shower with his assistance and went to dry herself and replace her robe. He ran chilly water over his hands to diminish the results of the steamy scene he and his mind had witnessed. His hands were not the only things soothed by the chilly water.

"Does your head feel better?"

Surprisingly, it does. "Tell your mother she should bottle this remedy." "Ancient Cuban secret," he mocked. "However, Ms. St. John, you still have a lot of rest ahead of you, so back to bed with you." "Oh, all right. Will you stay and read to me until I fall asleep?" "It would be my pleasure."

The book she chose was a collaboration done by Maya Angelou and Iyanla Vanzant. It was clips from each of their finer works compressed into one volume. Sultry and refreshing would be the words used to describe them because it was not something he would normally read.

He wanted to sit in a chair, but Madison was not having it. She insisted he lay beside her so she could use his body as a pillow. Pedro read intently, actually finding himself embracing the heroines. Their words poured from his lips like dewdrops.

She laid her head on his chest. The silk scarf tied around her hair caressed his shoulder. He felt like they had been married forty years. Her body fit perfectly against his, and he drank in the moments. He realized she was sound asleep.

Pedro knew he should ease away and go back to the office, but she felt so good. He let several more hours slip by before he tore himself away. She made him want to protect her from anything bad in her life.

"It has been my pleasure, baby. I will not leave you when this gets harder. I know that is part of your anxiety." he whispered as he kissed her forehead.

The streetlight suddenly popped on and became an annoyance to Madison. She stirred in protest. She got up and splashed water on her face before walking down the hallway.

Fast asleep on her sofa was a beautiful creature. She smiled and admired the view for quite some time. His briefcase was open on her dining room table with stacks of files everywhere. He stayed and worked from her apartment.

"How long are you going to watch me sleep?" She nearly jumped out of her skin.

"You nearly scared me half to death." His eyes opened, to reveal her favorite-colored cashmere sweater yelling. Touch me, touch me! She was staring and could not help it.

"Did I drool or something?"

"No. Pedro? Why isn't there someone in your life? I mean, you are an extremely attractive, funny, caring, sincere, successful man. You are the kind of man women spend their entire lives in search of. This would be the part where you finally tell me you are bisexual or gay. As long as you haven't tested positive, I will do my best not to fall apart."

"No. Madison, I am 200% heterosexual male. Somewhere a game began with relationships, and we got chosen to play whether we wanted to or not. I know the kind of relationship my parents had, and I want one as close to it as I can find. Unfortunately, most women today do not. It gets old Madison.

My family is wealthy, aside from my career. My father worked his ass off to provide for his family, and it paid off. My mother managed our assets well. Upon my father's death, she divided everything into trust accounts for my sister, brother, and me.

My parents agreed their children would establish themselves before they gave us a dime. Work ethic takes you farther than trust funds. To answer your question, I get tired of the tirade of women who want me for weekends in the Swiss Alps, a Telluride getaway, or Sotheby's platinum account." He swung himself into a sitting position.

"I decided long ago I would see women on my terms. If I found one interesting beyond the first or second date, I would pursue it. Only then would I allow my emotions to be accessible. Anyway, who says there is no one in my life?"

"Well, I assumed there wasn't." Fuck she thought. Here we go again!

"Well, you know what they say about assumptions!" Her embarrassment was tangible. He delighted in it wholeheartedly until he saw her begin to emotionally retreat.

"Madison, I was joking. The only woman in my life is this dynamic beauty with cognac eyes. She stands about so tall, with this incredible shade of dark auburn hair. She has this fascination with cuisine and loves to snuggle on my chest as she falls asleep. She gets these migraines that wipe her out for hours. And guess what?" He moved closer to her.

"What?" Her eyes were brimming with tears at the thought he was seeing someone else.

"I am positively infatuated with her and would not change a damn thing. If I had to spend all my coins on migraine medicine, I would. She lets me take time out of my schedule to read to her until she falls asleep which was very calming for me too."

'Oh, Pedro."

"If I thought I could be gentle, I would make you say my name the way you did last night! However, I need to go to Joshua's. He has some questions about a case we are prosecuting next week."

He kissed her softly on the cheek. "I'll call you later."

"Okay. While I am not seeing double, I need to go check on Helen. I am sure her refrigerator is running low. I will most likely spend the night over there." She bid Pedro farewell with a hug and a real kiss as they got in their respective cars.

Madison drove to Helen's house to make a list of things to get from the market. This had become her routine since Helen's diagnosis three months ago. Helen attempted to hide it, but signs of fatigue were beginning to show more readily now. Madison spent most of her free time between the restaurant and Helen's house.

She and Brock had not spoken in nearly two weeks and hadn't been intimate in almost six months. Her relationship with Pedro had progressed, and she felt comfortable and secure for the first time in years with the direction of her life.

She was cramming as much study time for her exams as she could. She fell asleep in her books every chance she got. The exam date was less than three weeks away. She refused to think anything but positively about the outcome. After which, she and Helen should take a much-needed vacation.

Perhaps the doctors would clear Helen to fly to Germany to see Roz. If not, maybe they could take a quick drive up the coast to Nantucket for a change of scenery. There had been no dreams lately of the mystery weekend with her mother. Yes, Madison dared to say she was feeling peacefully optimistic… happy.

She was lost in thought when she opened the front door. Her terrified shriek sent the neighbors running across the lawn. Helen lay face down on the floor. Madison rushed to her and found she still had a pulse, but it was faint. She called 9-1-1 and cradled Helen's head in her lap. "Dear God, no, not now, not now!"

Day Four

The doctor came through the door and told her Helen was extremely weak. The cancer spread, and it would be touch and go. Madison called Brock's cell phone and got the recorded message he would be out of town until Friday. She called Pedro. He was at Joshua's and did not answer. For hours, she waited alone. Her mind began a journey backwards to the last time she sat in a hospital and was told the prognosis was "touch and go."

She was a senior in college. A friend finally convinced her to go home with her for the weekend. Back then, cell phones were a luxury, not a necessity. When she returned home, she had numerous calls from her mother's neighbor Kelly. Get to the hospital now!

Kelly had a key in case of emergencies or deliveries, etc. He had been a trusted family friend for years. Madison always thought he was a little sweet on her mom, but she was not having it. He had an urgent sensation to visit her mom that morning.

He found her mother passed out on the floor of her bedroom. She seemed to be getting dressed because she did not have any pants on. He rushed her to the closest hospital. Humphrey did not have a resident ambulance or hospital of its own.

Madison called her roommate's boyfriend to tell him what happened. They came over and rushed her to the hospital. When she arrived, Kelly was waiting. The doctors in intensive care worked frantically to save her mother's life. Finally, Dr. Virginia Matthews came out and advised her mother had been neglecting herself and developed complications with her diabetes. It would be "touch and go."

Obviously, Madison's mind knew she needed a break. The shrill of a siren made her realize she was safe and sitting on her sofa at home. The memories of her mother and Helen's illnesses caused the same pain as they had years earlier. The heart did not consider time a useful instrument for minimizing heartache and loss caused from losing a loved one.

Tears flowed down her face. Some pain does not subside. Well-wishers said it would get easier with time. Time must not know her address. She tried to stop the travel backwards. Her mind was saying, "you started this, so we're going all the way to the end." It forced her back to the scene at Helen's bedside.

She was allowed to see Helen. Madison prayed she would not see any similarities between Helen and her mother. There it was the same ashen sheen on Helen's face her mother had. Having worked in a hospital as an aide, her mother explained the ashen was "death's calling card." When it appeared, loved ones were officially being put on notice." She never saw any patient recover from it. Sadly, neither had her mother.

Now, it had served notice for Helen. Time escaped her as she sat by her bedside. She laid her head down on Helen's hands and silently wept. Helen used her non-intravenous hand to touch hair.

"Hey there, Sweetie." Helen's voice was so frail Madison could barely hear her. "Don't you sweetie me! How could you not call me? You scared me half to death! If you have any plans of not seeing me pass my CPA exams, you can forget it.

You have to advise me on the restaurant and if I am handling this Brock fiasco correctly. And Pedro… Oh God, yes, Pedro. You know I am terrified. I already lost one mother, and yes, I am selfish, but you cannot leave me, too!" Madison became hysterical.

"Madi, Madison Elise St. John, you stop bawling right this instant! Do you hear me? You are an intelligent young woman with your whole life ahead of you. I am so proud of the woman you are, and I speak for all your mothers. You have not let anyone down. I will always be with you, guiding you, chastising you, and loving you. I have lived my life, Madison.

I have buried a husband and a child. I am tired. I have been battling this cancer for a long time. Longer than you even know because I swore my doctor to privacy and made her abide by that patient confidentiality clause.

It is winning, and I don't care any longer. I have fought the good fight. I have finished my course. I understand what the Apostle Paul meant now. You are my Timothy.

You will finish your exams, and you will pass. Promise me! Promise me! You have worked too damn hard, and I will not let you throw it all away on grief and pity. You are an extension of a lot of women's sacrifice and efforts. I am leaving you in the best hands I could have chosen.

Pedro loves you, Madison. He has from the very beginning. I have watched him build his career and settle himself away from the unnecessary spotlight. He is a good man, and he'll take good care of you if you let him. Brock is like a brother to me, and I accept him for his faults and flaws. I love him, but you do not have to. I love him for the little lost boy he is.

He is not a good love for you. That is why I was so against your relationship when I found out about it. You love him for the man you want him to be. He has a good life with JoAnne. The only reason he is withholding the love she wants is because he thinks there is a chance with you.

He will straddle the fence until one of you is woman enough to let him go. Let him go. Men like Pedro do not come along nor wait forever. Brock will settle for whoever is left. He has a restless spirit. Let JoAnne wrestle with the heartache. She has more experience with it than you do.

I am not trying to hurt you, baby; I just don't want you to stake your heart on a man who throws knives for a living. I am tired now. I am going to get some rest. I will be here tomorrow, I promise. I am going home soon, though. God and I have worked out a compromise. He will let me see you are protected if I promise to come home this year."

"I'm not leaving here tonight."

"God keeps his promises, Madi." Helen closed his eyes, and Madison held her hand until she fell asleep. She left the room and walked down the hall to the chapel.

She sat there and tried to imagine her mother's thoughts years earlier when she made her agreement with God. Was her heart so shattered by unrequited love she gave up on ever attempting to know it again. Did she make peace with settling? She was fifty-nine when she made her pact with God.

Madison thought of the mother she had known as a child. Reverse psychology was her rearing tool of choice. She always believed the marriage to her father was a mere formality. She had surrendered by that time. She married him in a black dress!

After he left, Madison listened to the rants, insults, and degradation of him for years. It was as if her mother's self-fulfilling prophecy rewarded her expectations. Sitting here processing it all, Madison wondered if the dreams were a warning. Neon sign flashing "Stop! Wrong choices ahead. Choose differently."

She remembered her mother's expression when the rumors of her father's numerous trysts made it to their doorstep. When the "street talk" was delivered, sometimes her mother went into another room and never spoke of it. Other times, she expelled such hateful and profane things it was hard to listen to. Then, suddenly, she would change the subject.

Looking back, Madison realized her mother's lost expectations of love had taught her to do the same. Pain and heartache were for weak women and men. It was to be internalized.

Madison often wondered if her mother would still be alive if she had sought treatment for her depression. She also recognized they were poor. Finding a doctor to render a diagnosis for a woman of color is not easy these days. Back then, it would have been virtually impossible.

Prayer was constant in their lives. It kept her mother balanced between "lonely spell," as she referred to them. Her mother was the poster child for "I love Jesus, but I cuss a little!" Research taught Madison her mother suffered with undiagnosed depression that included mild bipolar mood swings. Did it all stem from a broken heart?

Who teaches children coping skills? How do they develop when parents have not had the lessons either? Today, we have the phrases emotional intelligence and cognitive restructuring. The terms acknowledge you need to figure some stuff out. It is okay to be a work-in- progress.

She loved meeting Victoria and Helen. They seemed to have a strong grasp on support, affection, emotional and mental health. Now, she wondered if her novice eyes saw what existed or what she wanted them to see.

Victoria obviously still had some things to work out because her distress ended her life. Maybe her area of development was prompted by the question, what happens when entitlement doesn't yield the expect result? Maybe, in its own way, self-destruction comes for all of us at some point. Maybe, she had been Victoria's Timothy too. She left Helen in her hands and expected her to continue the legacy of being Helen's daughter.

How many times has history shown us the fate of unrequited lovers? What were the odds for children whose parents stayed together compared to those society labeled dysfunctional through divorce, poverty, or broken homes? Victoria's father stayed and passed away only a few years ago. Victoria still suffered anxiety and self-worth issues when processing betrayal.

What is healthy love? Helen told her Pedro loved her. What does that mean exactly? Is it deed, bill paying, sex, or honesty? What expectations are there in return? Were there ever discussions or only assumptions? Who teaches healthy love? A person can learn to love unhealthily in any environment.

Her mother settled. She was an intelligent woman who made sound business decisions. Her moral compass was grounded in faith. However, she took the life her father offered until the day he rescinded it. He swapped it out like one exchanges a vehicle. Stayed in one spot until the maintenance costs exceeded oil changes and tire rotations then, went in search of another.

Her father left a trail of used tires and broken parts strewn behind him. Maybe that is what Pedro meant when he said men don't end relationships. They stop enjoying them. Madison's parents never divorced. They remained separated until her father died years later.

Had her mother held onto the pain as Helen, long enough for it to be too late for treatment? She surrendered once she believed her daughter would be okay. Like Helen and the Apostle Paul, perhaps her mother felt she "fought the good fight and finished her course." Was Madison her mother's Timothy, too? Do something, be something, break these generational curses. Carry our legacy forward.

Madison sat in the chapel for hours, turning thoughts over in her mind. "God does not put more on you than you can bear," The Scripture was quoted often when she was a child. "Well, He definitely takes the weight down to the last ounce, doesn't He?"

She walked back to Helen's room and found her resting peacefully. The pain medication had taken effect. Peace, she thought, is the goal of life. Helen reached it. She decided to go for a walk. Watching someone fade from your life was much more painful than being informed they had suddenly been wiped away.

The sun beat down like a warm caress. She looked over at him as they strolled along the Magnificent Mile. It was named quite aptly JoAnne thought as she glanced at Brock. Finally, she could put her demons to rest. They had been through a lot together, and this time alone secured the feelings they shared.

He loved her. He had proven it over and over in the past three days. Whatever "she" meant to him was finished, finally. Brock came to his senses and recognized no one in the world would ever love him like her. He had survived his midlife crisis, and she was still by his side.

She snuggled a little closer to his shoulder. Heck, it was a beautiful 80 degrees, and she was happy and completely in love with this man who strolled by her side. His fingers were tightly and protectively intertwined with hers.

Brock was in a reflective mood too. He watched smiles cross her face these past few days. She was laughing at the little things in life again. Children laughing, murals on museum walls, lovers enjoying ice cream cones. JoAnne was back to the woman he remembered when they met. She looked ten years younger.

Yes, this trip to Chicago was the right thing for everyone. If he were honest, he would admit he was relaxed. Now, if he could convince himself he was happy, it would all be perfect.

The past few nights were the only times she came to him. A moan escaped his lips last night as he made love to JoAnne. She squealed with delight. Brock was relieved he had not said her name. He was making love to someone with milk chocolate skin and cognac eyes, not the lover beneath him with eyes of blue. He tasted fingertips with a hint of jasmine as they wrapped around his neck.

The breasts he suckled were laced with cinnamon and raspberry, not "White Shoulders" perfume. His Aunt Frances told him, "Sometimes we do what we must instead of what we want, and we find a way to make it work." In this case, he realized compassion called on him to make the most empathetic decision.

Madison was a fantasy, and his reality was JoAnne. In twenty years, JoAnne would still be by his side because that is where she felt she belonged. Madison would be in the prime of her sexual prowess. He would have to inhale Viagra and blood pressure medication to keep up with her.

If he were honest, he would admit the past five years had not been bad ones. He and JoAnne spent a lot of time getting to know each other, which led to their decision to buy a house together. They vacationed, laughed, and shared tragedies and triumphs. All the things a relationship called for; they had. It was the perfect arrangement until he compared it with something else.

"Well, it's been three days. I need to check in with the office and see if they processed my request for five more days off."

"Okay, I'll run into Macy's and see if I can find something that will make you never want to get out of bed with me tonight." She kissed him softly and dashed off. You won't find Madison in Macy's, JoAnne, he thought.

The first five messages were the usual guys trying to find out where he was. He forgot to tell them he was going out of town. The next message stopped him in his tracks.

"Brock, this is Madison. Helen, she, well, she collapsed, and I am at Saint Joseph's. I do not know where you are, but she needs you. Please call me or come here when you get this message. I, I don't know if she will... I... call me, please."

She needed him. Oh God, Helen, what have you done! He was in a full sprint towards a taxi when he realized JoAnne was still inside Macy's! Almost annoyingly, he turned around and rushed back towards the store. She better have her ass in the lingerie department, I don't have time to search for her!

Pedro came to the hospital and found Madison asleep in a chair next Helen's bed. She is like a faithful dog, she will stick by her master until the end, he thought. He got her voicemail message after a long debate with Joshua about their strategy for an upcoming case. Reviewing the depositions of a murder takes hours.

He was headed home when he glanced at his cell phone and saw the voicemail. Expecting to hear something sexy, instead he heard the panic in her voice about Helen. He raced over to the hospital. God, please do not let the situation have turned for the worse. Also, let me beat Brock to her side; otherwise, I may have a fight on my hands, he prayed silently.

He and Helen discussed the devastation her death would eventually cause Madison. Helen told him, "Madison will need you. I am counting on you to be there for my child. If you fail, this is exactly the traumatic experience Brock will use to manipulate her feelings for him. Make no mistake, he will leave JoAnne if he believes Madison will take him back.

Do not interpret his feelings as merely the lust of a middle-aged man. Brock loves her too, Pedro, but you are good for her. You are what she needs. She loves you, too. She is afraid to trust herself to do it well. Unfortunately, she and Brock understand many of the same heartbreaks.

Madison thinks of herself as a fragile bird and does not recognize she is an eagle. She has endured a tremendous amount in her young life. She needs someone to step in and say, "Baby, I got this, and I got you," and mean it." Pedro knew that someone was him, and he had every intention of making her realize it as well.

He went to find the doctor and learn Helen's prognosis while Madison slept. Helen added his name to the list of "people to discuss her business with" as her condition grew worse. Pedro also figured he could have all the hospital expenses billed to him the insurance did not cover. It would be one less thing for Madison to worry about when this was all over.

Upon returning, he found a familiar face staring into his in the hallway. "I took the first flight back I could. I am Brock Andrews. I've been helping her with Helen." He extended his hand in a formal gesture. He thought Pedro was one of the hospital administrators.

"I'm Pedro Santiago, Madison's future husband." Pedro knew it was childish, but he did not give a damn in that moment. Get used to the idea you son-of-a-bitch is all he thought! Brock dropped his hand. So, at last, this is the mutherfucker in the flesh, they both thought.

Each man did a mental assessment of the other. They circled each other like vultures going in for the kill. He's Cuban, a real Andy Garcia type, Mr. French Rivera. He reeks of money and weekends in The Hamptons.

He's older up close. This is the guy who has her heart. It definitely wasn't his social grace. He had a debonair charm. Pedro could see why women would find him entertainable. He was brashly confident to the point it brushed against arrogance.

Madison is in love with him. They both thought.

"Where is she?" Brock demanded.

"Helen is in room 327," Pedro replied coldly.

Brock started down the hall. Pedro was in step with him. Madison would not wake up to find this bastard by her side instead of him. She stirred when Brock walked in.

"Hey sweetie, how is she?" Brock asked Madison as straightened in her chair.

"She's been medicated, so the pain is bearable for her now. She said it feels like Mike Tyson is using her abdomen to work out." "How are you?"

"I'm holding on." She almost asked him where he had been but decided against it.

"Oh, by the way, there is some guy outside, Peter or something. He knew his name was Pedro. Saying it correctly acknowledged his existence so he would not.

Madison jumped up and ran out into the hallway. Pedro was standing outside the door. The sign said only two visitors at a time. He decided not to be an asshole about it.

"Pedro, you came! Oh my God, I am so happy to see you! I didn't know you were out here." She stretched out her arms and encircled him.

"You were asleep, so I went to speak with the doctor and the administration staff. I figured you needed the rest. I saw Brock, and I thought he would get around to remembering I was out here," he said icily."

He pulled her to arm's length. "I am here for you, sweetheart; you know that don't you? You are not alone in this."

"Yes, Pedro, I know." She tiptoed and kissed him softly. "Do you need anything?"

"Please come inside with me. I know Helen will appreciate it."

"Yes, but Brock may not. The sign says only two visitors, which is the only reason I stayed outside. I don't want to make him uncomfortable."

"I wasn't aware you were here for Brock." "You know what I mean."

"Yes, I do, but I need you to be with me for a little while. The least you could do is come see Helen then buy me a cup of coffee. Afterwards, we'll let Brock and Helen spend some time together until we get back."

"If, you're sure?" They walked in, and Helen opened her eyes. She smiled at Madison and Pedro.

"There you are. Like I pictured it, taking care of each other. Pedro, my Madison is a handful. However, if any man can manage her, my money is on you."

"Helen, you have my word. I will do everything in my power to take care of her." He bent and kissed Helen's temple.

"I am counting on your love for each other to pull you both through the passing of this old body. I wish for you the love my Richard and I had. Disagreements will happen. Always choose love. Let me have some time with my old friend Brock, would you?" Madison hesitated because she heard how weak Helen was.

"I will not leave without saying farewell, Princess. A lady is never rude, only assertive. Do as I ask, please, Brock and I need to chat about a few things. He will phone you when we finish reminiscing."

"Okay, but we will be downstairs in the restaurant. Brock, we are going to grab some coffee. We'll be right back." The look Brock shot at her was cold and disgusting. She was not in the mood to play "Who has the biggest balls" tonight. She was tired, and she knew it was going to be much worse before this was over.

Helen made it through the night fine. The doctor said her pain had stabilized. She needed to rest. Helen wanted to go home, so the next morning, Madison and Brock took her. There was no reason to worry about it any longer.

They made her as comfortable as possible. Madison was exhausted, but she still needed to fill Helen's prescriptions. She left Brock with Helen while she took care of it. It gave her a few minutes to be alone and clear her head.

She drove the long way to the pharmacy. A familiar looking car made a right turn in front of her. She drove up next to the woman in the parking lot and noticed the license plate. She had seen Brock drive this vehicle from time to time. This had to be the infamous JoAnne.

She was a simple woman in her mid-50s, heavy-set and blonde. He said Pedro looked like a foreigner.This woman was a comedic sight for sore eyes. Did she really think no one would notice a cheap bottled hair color missing half her roots?

When she turned to give Madison the full-frontal view, she was not impressed. An average 1900 's teacher would sum up the look of the woman who caused her so many nights of grief. Madison tried to give her the benefit of being tired; however, even well-rested, she could tell this woman was quite unattractive. She was definitely a "her."

She had the facial lines of Clara "Where's the beef?" from the 80's Wendy's commercial. It was combined with the look of poor white trash who attempted to clean up. She couldn't help but laugh aloud! No wonder Brock clung to her the way he did when they made love. Was this the cause of his mental and emotional struggle? Madison now understood why for totally different reasons.

This was not about her ethnicity. Hell, Pedro was Cuban. Ashley's mother was white. Yet, she succeeded in teaching biracial Ashley, after the Jesse fiasco, you cannot allow yourself to go to shit because you have man trouble. No, this was about personal upkeep as a woman. Some basic preventative maintenance is available in any income bracket. It is not like she and Brock were poor besides, trashy is an equal opportunity hater.

She was a rag muffin. Madison would give her some grace because she remembered her son was battling for his life. Given the circumstances; she was still a C- in her younger days.

After getting Helen's medication, Madison returned to Helen's. Brock was having a drink. He needed one if Rag Muffin was clouding his judgment. She should pour for him! She checked on Helen and saw she was sleeping. Brock gave her the sedative-pain reliever the doctor prescribed so she would be asleep the rest of the evening.

Madison sat down on the sofa with a "thud." Brock handed her a drink. She guzzled it and extended her hand for a refill. He obliged. She sipped this one with more patience and thought. She asked if he had any trouble connecting Helen's catheter. Outside of violating her dignity, he shook his head no.

Slowly, he began to massage her feet. She vividly pictured JoAnne as she allowed the drink to relax her. Laughter overtook her. Tears formed in her eyes because the image would not leave. He was looking at her and laughing, though he had no idea why. Which made it even more hilarious.

He leaned over and kissed her cheek. The look on his face let her know he was a little plastered. She had no idea how many drinks he had before she joined him. Pain has a way of making one lose track of minor details. He looked at her again, and the laughter subsided.

The fear in her suddenly wanted to connect with something in him. He was the only one who would feel this as deeply as she would. Helen was the binding force keeping them together against their will yet forbade them to be together.

"Avoiding him is easy. I want you to stop fucking Brock," she heard Pedro's statement in her head." She jumped up suddenly and called Pedro. "Hey, is Helen…"

"She is asleep. I really need you to come over." "I'm on my way."

"What the hell? Am I not here? Do I not understand how you feel, yet you call him? You really are a piece of work, Madison." Rejection is sobering like coffee and water will never be.

"How many trauma/ sympathy fucks do you think you're entitled to Brock?" "Oh, that's what we are now?"

"We have always been. I wanted it to be more." "So fucking Juan Valdez has given you clarity now?"

"No, watching Helen die has. Brock, do you enjoy being with me?" "What kind of question is that? Of course, I do."

"Do you enjoy making love to JoAnne?" "Where is this coming from?"

"It is a simple question. Do you enjoy making love to JoAnne?" "Sometimes. I mean, it is not us" "So, you enjoy both of us?"

"Yes, but for different reasons. I do not understand what this has to do with your calling Mr. Valdez over here to be with you tonight."

"Your maturity is astonishing! Are you really attempting to incorrectly insult his heritage? He does not have to split his emotions. I know you like the blues so try this one on for size Jodie. Pedro's got your girl, and you are the one going home!"

"What the fuck! You have it all figured out, do you? "Not all, but definitely, this. Good night, Brock, he will be here any minute." "Is he supposed to be my replacement?" Madison remembered she owed him a response for his "leftovers" comment.

"No, Brock, I wanted a model with less mileage and more cargo room when I decided to upgrade." Almost on cue, Pedro rang the doorbell. Brock snatched the door open with such force Pedro took a military fighting stance. He blew past him and peeled out of Helen's driveway. She closed the door behind him.

"Was it something I said," Pedro smiled sarcastically.

"No, he thought we might try our hands at trauma fucking again, but I called you instead." Madison turned and walked to the bottle of liquor Brock started and poured herself another drink with a cold, matter-of-factness. She was tired of these battles with him. Yet, she could not ban him from Helen in her last days. However, it was wearing her out.

"Sweetheart, what do you need?" He could tell she was hurting and humorless right now. He wanted to hold her but was unsure whether he was there because she wanted him to be or merely to piss Brock off. She read his mind.

"I did not call you to irritate Brock. I could have put him out fuckless and accomplished the same result. I called because I need you to help me do one of the hardest things in my life. When it is over, I need your strength to hold me through the aftermath.

I want to go lay in bed with Helen, but I am afraid to. I do not want her to suffer which is why I know God is coming for her very soon. I am afraid to be there because I can't trust myself not to try and keep her here. She has trusted me to be her Timothy so, I cannot let her transition home alone."

Pedro took her hand and led her into Helen's room. The bed was king-sized and custom-built with railings on each side so Helen could not fall out. Helen was only in one-fourth of the space. She had lost substantial weight and was a fraction of her former feisty self.

Pedro let the rail down on the side farthest from Helen. He bent down and took off Madison's shoes and his own. He helped Madison crawl in next to Helen, and he crawled in next to her. He held her as she held Helen's hands. She reached over and kissed Helen on the cheek.

"I love you so much. You loved me when I was a broken, motherless heap. You told me I was brave, and Victoria always needed a sister and you another daughter. I have no idea how to let you go, but I know I must. You are staying here for me. I do not want you to suffer any longer. If God says it is enough, do not fight it.

You have fought the good fight, Helen. You have finished your course. Pedro is here with me. I will be all right because we love each other, and you and I trust his God-given strength to get me through this. He also knows you will not take your eyes off him. Tell Victoria and my mother I said hello when you see them. I love you."

Pedro held her tightly as she wept. Her body was shaking as she tried to do it silently. Eventually, she drifted off to sleep. Only then did he allow his own tears to quietly roll during the night. He would not fail them.

Madison and Pedro woke to a gasping noise. The sound was coming from Helen. Madison jumped up in a panic and raised her head. Helen squeezed her hand, looked at her and Pedro, and smiled. It was over. Madison looked at Pedro like a lost child. He tried to take her to another room, but she would not go. Pedro called 9-1-1 and Helen's doctor.

"I will not leave her. I must see her all the way home. Only when they get here." She laid her head on Helen's shoulder until the EMTs arrived to carry Helen's body away. The hardest phone call Pedro made was to Brock. He had a right to know.

The doctor tried to calm Madison as Brock came into the room. Pedro convinced Madison to let Dr. Matthews give her a sedative. The doctor asked him to notify friends of Helen's passing. He called JoAnne and told her he would be home when all the arrangements were made. She asked him for Helen's address. He pretended not to hear her and disconnected the call.

Dr. Matthews assured them Madison would sleep well into the afternoon. "Are you absolutely sure she will not wake up in the next three hours?" Pedro had to be in court and would request a continuance before he let Madison wake up only to find Brock there.

"Gentlemen, I assure you she will be out like a light. She is exhausted, and the sedative is used to help patients rest who are recovering from abdominal surgery. It will be well into the afternoon before she stirs." Dr. Matthews thought, I'm not sure who is winning the testosterone fight over Madison, but she is one lucky woman either way!

Pedro gave Brock the look of a scorpion and left for court. He did not trust that bastard at all. So, he hedged Dr. Matthews' bet.

The court proceedings were running longer than Pedro's patience, but he had to wait for the jury to return. He had all types of visions in his head until he got a text. He calmed down and waited.

Madison was beginning to rouse when she heard the doorbell. As she attempted to focus, she heard voices. Brock was telling someone to keep their voice down, Madison was asleep. Still a little groggy, she came down the hallway and froze.

"Hello Madison, I am JoAnne. I wanted to make sure you did not need anything. I know Brock is overseeing the arrangements. I knew Helen and wanted to pay my respects. Do you have an outfit already picked out, or are there any other arrangements to be made?"

If the situation weren't tragic, it would be comical! Box Blonde came to help Brock move these arrangements along so he could get his ass back home. Do not you come to collect your man, like the past due rent! Realizing she had not spoken, Madison smiled.

"Hello JoAnne. Actually, Helen and I have already made those decisions. At this point, it is a matter of notifying everyone and setting the date. Yes, I do recall Helen mentioning you." Madison moved towards the kitchen and stopped suddenly. "Did you visit Helen often before she became ill?"

"No, I usually saw her at the restaurant when Brock and I ate there." "How did you say you got the address again?"

"Well, I did not. Pedro Santiago called me and told me I might be able to assist Brock with some arrangements. You were sleeping, and two hands are always better than one at a time like this. He said he had to step out for court."

"Santiago is quite effective in handling things." Brock's sarcastic tone was not lost on either woman.

Madison continued to the kitchen with a smirk. JoAnne was unamused. This is her! Damn right, he should have called me!

Madison peeped over her cup of tea as JoAnne glared at Brock while attempting to remain calm.

"Brock, is there something else you need to take care of today? Otherwise, let's give Madison some privacy. Too many people around at a time like this can stress a person." She picked up her purse.

"No, I guess we've taken care of everything we can right now. Madison, call me if you think of anything we haven't covered for the immediate time being." He was pissed!

"Yes, Madison, we will check on you again tomorrow to see if everything for Helen is on schedule." JoAnne looked like; I am going to cuss you the fuck out as soon as we step outside this door! Mutherfucker, bring your ass on here!

Madison heard them as soon as they started down the driveway. "Who the fuck do you think I am Brock? A goddamn idiot! That was her! Your sleepover whore! You've been fucking around with her for nearly a year under the pretense of helping Helen! Fuck you! And the bitch is even attractive without any goddamn makeup on!

"JoAnne, get your mutherfucking ass in the goddamn car! I didn't ask you to bring your ass over here. Are you fucking stalking me now?

"No, I'm stalking the goddamn 5-year investment I made. I will back out, but you drive off first. I don't want to hear any, I forgot my wallet bullshit!"

No sooner than both cars probably reached the intersection, Madison heard a soft knock, and the door opened. Pedro walked in and saw her in the kitchen.

"Hey sweetheart, what are you doing awake? You, okay?"

"Your package came, special delivery. I hear you stressed the importance it did not arrive late." They both laughed so hard they cried.

"Seriously, Pedro Miguel Santiago."

"I was protecting my investment."

"Funny, that's the same thing I heard JoAnne say. Her explanation contained a few more expletives, but I'm sure "investment" was in there somewhere. The only thing missing was Aunt Esther and Uncle Woodrow. "Whoa, Glory!" Again, they laughed. Right then, they understood they could make it through this together.

Helen's services were beautiful. She was laid to rest in an exact replica of the casket and attire as Victoria. Madison felt she would appreciate it, and it was also easier. She was an Air Force veteran in her youth, and they did a beautiful 21-gun salute. Her casket was draped with an American Flag given to Madison before she was interred.

As they lowered Helen to rest, Madison sat there. If she moved, she knew she would pass out. In her mind, she kept hearing Helen say, "I'm okay now, Madi, really." Still, she sat until Pedro took her arm and led her to the family car, where Brock and JoAnne waited. Madison insisted they all ride together; Brock was not so adamant.

She was even pretty in grief, JoAnne thought. She could see why Brock was so taken with her. His resistance when Madison demanded they all rode together in the family car let her know this was the one. He told Madison to list him on the obituary collectively with "friends" who mourned Helen's passing and not by name. His way of not acknowledging JoAnne.

He couldn't even look at Madison as she lay on Pedro's shoulder. It hit JoAnne like a bitch slap. Brock is in love with this woman!

When they arrived at Helen's house, Madison did what she could to be a good hostess. She tried to make sure everyone ate, mingled, and knew how much Helen would have appreciated their presence. Everyone could see she was sincere as she tried to remain calm. The bond she and Helen shared was closer in some opinions than Helen and Tori. The landing was going to be a hard one when the medications wore off.

Rita Parsons came into the restaurant often. Madison recognized her as she approached. "It was a lovely service. How are you holding up, dear?" Madison only smiled at her.

Rita continued." I haven't seen some of these people in a while. Of course, I saw Brock and his wife last week at their wedding. I was surprised you weren't there. It was the day Helen went into the hospital this last time, so I guess she was too ill for you to leave her side. You were a true blessing to her life, you know."

"Excuse me, Brock got married last Saturday?"

"Oh yes, dear, it was a nice ceremony at St. Anne's Catholic Church over on Maurer Boulevard. It must have slipped your mind. They looked quite happy. I heard they were honeymooning in Chicago because JoAnne had never been on the Magnificent Mile.

I am fairly certain that is where they received the news about Helen. He interrupted their wedding night to rush back to town. With all the stress you must have been under, I'm quite sure he will understand you forgot."

Forgot! "Excuse me, won't you?"

Madison made a beeline out the back door. She ran to a nearby tree and threw up. Brock saw her go and he followed her. He handed her his handkerchief to wipe her mouth. She turned and slapped his face as hard as she could. They weren't aware there were people outside getting some fresh air, too.

"You bastard! How dare you? You had a whole week to tell me! We won't even discuss the amount of time before your wedding day! You tried to sleep with me the day after your wedding! No, wait, it was Saturday night when Helen got sick, it was your wedding night! She was screaming at him, but she didn't care.

I see you really took the forsaking of all others to heart, didn't you, asshole? I am so grateful I came to my senses and quit fucking with you. But even more grateful I am not the poor bitch wearing your name. Don't you ever come near me again!"

Madison ran back inside the house and left Brock with the pairs of eyes watching him squirm in shame. Two of those pairs belonged to Pedro and JoAnne. Pedro didn't know if JoAnne knew the extent of Brock and Madison's affair before, but she and half the town sure as hell knew now!

JoAnne was absolutely stunned. "He just demonstrated his undying love and obsession for a woman. It ain't me!" Pedro wasn't sure what she wanted him to say, and he didn't stick around to find out.

He left JoAnne to confront Brock and went to find Madison. He hadn't expected a standoff in the Town Square, but a standing ovation was definitely in order. He found Madison in her bedroom with the door shut.

"Madison, it's me, Pedro." He heard the lock turn. As he opened the door, she was standing by the window. Grief, agony, and anger were pulsating from her.

He walked over and stood behind her. He fought the urge to touch her. She stood there, still. Her breathing was barely audible. A long sob finally escaped her lips, and she began to cry.

She needed to release some of the devastation within her. To try and console her now would do more harm than good. She turned to him after a while and looked through him as she could sometimes.

"Why are you so good to me? I knew Brock and I were over. I thought we shared the same pain for losing Helen. Now I realize, along with a whole yard of people, we have never been the same. He really was using this travesty to his advantage.

160

He is exactly the little lost boy Helen said he was. I am sorry for all the things you have endured because of me. You don't have to honor any promises to Helen you made about me. I release you completely. Go back to the life you had before I came in with my drama."

"I'm afraid you are not authorized to release me from promises between me and Helen. Was this foursome a mess for a while? Hell yes! But we are on the better side of it. I won't be having dinner with the bastard, but we are all adults.

Who amongst us hasn't messed up royally where love is concerned? Likewise, I made some promises to you too, and I have no intention of reneging on those either.

"The woman caught in the act of adultery from the Bible. That is what he would have turned me into had I not stopped sleeping with him."

"Well, they stopped stoning in this country some time ago. Furthermore, if Jesus forgave her…" Now, I'll go take care of your guests and goodbyes." He kissed her forehead and left the room.

He stayed long enough to let Jesse and Ashley know she was going to be fine and delegated goodbye duty to them. They told him to take care of Mad. Everything else would be a breeze.

Ashley and Jesse looked at each other in disbelief. "I've heard of four weddings and a funeral, but a foursome at a funeral is a new twist!' Ashley elbowed him.

"Obviously, you don't know Madison. She is the queen of "go big or go home"! "Let's get these people out of here."

When he walked into the room, she was in the same dazed position where he left her. It had been nearly an hour. Dr. Johnson told him about the sedatives he placed on her dresser. He found those, her slippers, and bathrobe.

Pedro quietly left Madison with her thoughts after she agreed to lie down and rest. Ashley told him she would take a tray of food to her a bit later. Madison must have dozed off because a soft wrap on the door awakened her.

"Come in." As she focused, she realized it was Roz. "When did you get here?" '

"Due to a horrific layover in London, extremely late this afternoon instead of yesterday. So, are you leaving this room anytime soon, or must I entertain myself with song?"

"You know dance is more your thing, Rozalyn Crenshaw."

"Well, somebody has to do both parts since our fans are waiting, and the other half of this duet won't get her ass out of bed! How many days have you been asleep again?"

"You bitch." Madison said through a yawn.

"You forgot it's Ms. Bitch to you mere subjects." Both women laughed. It was a beautiful sound.

"Now, Roz continued, I know how you hate to iron, so you are going to wear these clothes, right?"

"Where is Pedro? He was a much better partner; not as bossy, you know?"

"When you're in your right mind, I'm going to kick your ass, Missy. You didn't tell me Cuba was such a beautiful place. He is scrumptious!" She licked her lips." Hell, I'd move down there simply for the view!

Bronze skin, deep, dark grey eyes, 6'3, single. Did you say he has brothers, nephews, uncles, grandfathers, or something? I mean, those genes must not stop with him. Sacrilege!" Madison burst into laughter again.

"Damn, it is good to see you, you lunatic. I'm glad you have a new admiration for Cuba, but that son is taken. Perhaps you'd like to see if there is an heir to Fidel available."

"So, is the view as good from the sheets as it is from this side?" "Only ventured there twice so far, but better!" Madison smiled.

Roz glared at her. "You would be rationing puss for what purpose? Virginity only comes along once, my dear. Yours hasn't responded to that missing person's report we put out from what, twenty years ago?"

"Age has not made you less annoying, has it? Seriously, Rozalyn, I am happy you came."

"Yeah, you have me. However, there isn't a damn thing I can do for you in the "couchie coupon" area except wish you well. Although I am a fan of width, I require a little more length from my partner than you are capable of.

"Pedro went home to get some clothes and shower. He refused to take me. I told him you wouldn't mind if I saw him naked. Somehow, I don't think he bought it because he laughed and rushed off. He is beautiful. If you cannot make more time to explore those orifices, I will!"

"No."

"I'll tell him we've been friends since dirt. I will even say your name during sex to ease his guilt!

"Okay, okay. You have succeeded in torturing me from this spot. Now, where is my brother-in-law?"

"Oh, we were having so much fun apart we decided to make it permanent. He has the kids while I'm getting settled here. I'll get them at the end of the summer. Don't look like that. Close your mouth. It brings moisture." Madison's was stunned.

"It's been platonic for a long time, Madi. At least we can accept it and move forward with our lives. Now, do something about covering your ass so we can get out of here for a while."

"Roz, I really don't feel like going anywhere."

"Who said this was about you? You've been the star of this stage play too long. Get your ass up! You have 10 minutes! No matter what condition I find you in, we're leaving this house!" Madison was ready in eight. You just can't make old friends; she thought as she grabbed her purse.

The two went out and found some ice cream and talked for a while. Roz understood she was pushing Madison, but it was what she needed. Unfortunately, they had done this mother-connected grief thing twice before. She would keep Madison out only a brief time. They would reconvene tomorrow.

Day Five

"What do you have a taste for?" "Nothing." Madison's appetite was nonexistent since the funeral.

"You see when you ask a question, you get no response. Well, I feel like a chicken. It's hard to get good poultry overseas. You don't know if it's cat, rat, dog, seal, or what they may be trying to pass off on you, so I've abstained."

They went to Gloria's for the first time that day. Roz had her chicken with a feather on the side for validation and made Madison eat some greens and cornbread.

"It's good for the soul," she exclaimed.

After promising Gloria they would return, they drove around New Haven so Roz could get the official tour. They looked at homes and antique shops. They talked about growing up in the South.

"Remember the summer of 1980 when it was so hot people were passing out trying to "make a day?" Roz was feeling reminiscent.

Madison smiled, "Yeah, because they were not equipped with their bacon and egg sandwiches in their front shirt pockets, nor their Nehi peach sodas at lunch."

'We were on something back then. Only we didn't know it."

"Yes, it was called poverty row! We were fine without effort because walking passed the time and provided an opportunity to catch up on the latest gossip." Madison knew she could only have this "you had to be there" discussion with Roz.

"We were all fine back then. Remember when..."

Madison's spirits lifted, and Roz was grateful she knew her friend so well. Otherwise, she would have never pulled this off. They talked until they were thirsty. They grabbed some sodas and Roz decided she would drive them back.

"There is one stop I have to make before this evening is a complete bomb." Madison settled into the passenger's seat and buckled up. She remembered they passed a Krispy Kreme shop earlier. She was not a doughnut connoisseur but would not scoff at anyone else who needed a fix.

Her eyes flew open as Roz turned on Cherokee Lane. "I should have known something was brewing when you wanted to drive! Shame on me for thinking you were being considerate!"

"I am, but it's not confined to the two of us, dear! I think there is someone else who deserves a little consideration from you."

"You've taken up where Helen left off," Madison whispered.

"Great minds think alike. You've been much more appreciative for less respectable reasons! Now, go inside and be really "nice to him," as your mother used to say. I'm sure a resourceful woman like you can find a ride home. Your car will be at my house. Tootles!"

Madison got out. Roz locked the doors and shifted the car into reverse. She cracked the window and yelled, "Make me proud!"

"Well damn, I think my puss unofficially has an agent."

Madison rang the doorbell and waited. She didn't even know if the man was home! At least she was given her phone and purse as a parting gift.

Pedro came to the door in a pair of jeans and a tee shirt.

"Hello, this is a pleasant surprise. Come in. I was on my way back to you."

"Well, I got dropped off by a whirlwind named Rozalyn Crenshaw, so here I am. I came by to say thank you. You have been an outstanding presence in my life, and I don't think I ever said thank you. I know I wouldn't have made it through these last few months without you. The Brock thing at the repast was such a fiasco. I..."

"Shhh...," Pedro placed his finger to her lips and silenced her. "I knew about Brock when we met. Ashley was most generous. I must admit, as a member of the audience that day, I did not expect such an explosive ending, but it is definitely something I would watch again. In the words of the late Siskel & Ebert, "Two thumbs up!" They both laughed.

"Love is the freest element one has to offer Madison. We mere mortals make it complicated by stifling or betraying it. We are not in control of who we love. We are in control of knowing when it no longer serves us well and begin letting go. You told me your journey with Brock was over, and from where we all stood, it was crystal clear when he got booed off stage Live @ The Apollo." She cracked up at the visual.

"Yes, and I have no regrets about the decision."

"That's all the thanks I need, Madison. He moved over to the table and poured a brandy. Would you care for one?"

"No, I should probably call Roz and tell her to come back and get me."

"Why? Do you feel uncomfortable being here with me?"

"No. I came by unannounced, and I shouldn't have. "I'll call you later." She moved toward the door.

When she pulled, he pushed, and the door obeyed him. Pedro stood behind her and inhaled. She felt naked after her moment of brutal honesty. It was so sexy to him. He pulled her against him. He wrapped her fully in his arms. She didn't turn around.

"I have loved you for months." He rubbed her arms and lingered on the curve of her hips. He used his index finger to gingerly scan the column of her neck. She moaned from somewhere deep within her throat and started turning towards him.

'No," he whispered. "I have waited and hoped for the time we could be together again. Rushing this moment would be an insult to it and us. I want us to enjoy each other. His fingers searched for hers. I have watched these hands give care. They are strong and sturdy." He raised her fingers to his lips and kissed each tip.

His other hand brushed her hair aside and allowed her to turn. He put her head between his hands and stared at her without speaking. His eyes were asking hers. See me. See the intentions behind this soul. See the sincerity in this heart. See the honesty in this love. It was by far the most tender A capella moment sung from his heart to hers.

He was open to anything she wanted. They could stand here for eternity if it meant being together. He smiled and any reservations she had dissipated like a puff of smoke. She touched his face. Her fingers stroked the faint morning shadow peeking through. Right then, she knew what healthy love was.

"Let me love you back." She kissed him with all the apologies she owed love for ever doubting its existence. She was begging love to forgive her for the expletives she cursed at it while it made her wait. Pedro was worth it.

She kissed him with intentionality. He needed to know this is Madison signing on for whatever comes next. She began to love him and demonstrate she was "all in." It was slow and deliberate. Monitoring, sensing, and creating impulses and reactions.

Pedro was touching her in precise, timed movements. Making love was a paced exploration of spontaneity. It was finding the hidden treasures on a familiar road home. The way he touched her made her feel like a tourist inside her own body. He memorized every line in her neck and tasted every drop of dew on her lips with his tongue.

"Oh yes," she moaned as he shifted her again to let her forehead rest against the doorframe.

When he bent down and removed her shoes, she almost fainted. He lifted her feet and began an assault on her Achilles heels. He licked and nibbled them with soft little bites. She grabbed his hair when he ran his tongue over her toes at the pace of a snail.

She was dead. Madison was sure of it. There was nowhere on earth where it was possible to find this kind of man. God made retribution to her, and Pedro was her repayment.

He took her hand. "Come with me. There is so much more I need to experience with you here in my personal space."

Pedro led her out to a sunken Jacuzzi on his patio. There, the main course was served. He undressed her as he had the second time, they made love. He started an attack on her breasts. They were tasted, fumbled, fingered then, devoured like chocolate truffles.

He peeled off her slacks and hose. She stood clad only in her lacy underwear. He ran his mouth down her hips and persuaded her navel to stand erect. His tongue was warm as it traced an outline of her panties. Somewhere in the distance, she swore she heard Maxwell and Alicia Keyes singing "The Fire We Make."

When he dropped to his knees and let his tongue slip inside the opening he created, her bud of pleasure erupted, and she fell forward. Pedro caught her and began a slow, rhythmic assault on her pleasure source leaving her panting inside his mouth.

"Oh yes, Pedro! I can't ... hold back! You must... move!"

"Never!" He drank from her repeatedly. She made sure he felt like the Gatorade cooler was emptied over his head after winning the Super Bowl! He finally raised his head and smiled at her. He let her lick the dew from his lips as an added bonus.

She couldn't let that type of pleasure go unreciprocated. She took her time as she ran her hands down his body. It was his body's turn to feel like a traitor.

When her hand dipped lower and found an erection too large to hold comfortably, she grabbed his head and kissed him with such passion the sound he made was deafening.

"You are... oh baby..." He was incoherent when she let her hips slide up and down his thighs. Madison felt like fingers with free reign over a bowl of collard green pot liquor and hot water cornbread. Her tongue traced his beautifully chiseled abs. She dropped down and put her mouth where her hands ventured earlier.

She tasted him from end to tip, and her tongue made a note of every vein and sampled every drop of drizzling passion. When he began to tremble, she lifted her head quickly and rammed his shaft inside her. He was clearly incoherent. "Let me take care of you tonight," she whispered and took control of their rhythm.

"Pedro!" She needed him to know she was fully aware of who filled her. She tightened her pelvic muscles and locked him inside her like a vice grip. "Yes! Oh, Madison! I...Ooh!" Pedro buried his face in her shoulder, and she cradled his head.

A while later, he began to patiently wash them with soap making little champagne bubbles the more he lathered. His fingers found their way in and out of her body.

"You have this power over me I cannot fight. It's addictive. When you're around, I am helplessly out of my mind. It's the damnedest thing." Pedro drizzled more water over her breasts.

"I feel so fortunate you didn't run out of patience with me. You could have anyone, and yet you... "

"Waited for the woman my heart deserved. I know how you feel about music and lyrics. This one is perfect for us. Ours. He located a panel behind a tile and "Powers" by the artist TEEKS began to play through surround sound speakers.

He kissed her slowly as the lyrics lingered over them like a warm blanket. "This is a lifetime commitment we're doing here. Ease into the journey, remember?" He turned her around and entered her from behind before she could do anything other than gasp from the forcefulness with which he took her.

"Oh Pedro, I didn't know it could get..." He started and stopped.

"Better than the first time." He finished the sentence for her. She almost pulled his hair from his head attempting to keep time with his thrust.

They made love so many times she felt like the layers of her vagina were a flaky biscuit. Finally, when they almost drifted off inside the water, he helped her out, dried her off, and led her upstairs to his bedroom. He held her next to him as sleep took over.

Reality brought Madison back to the present with a smile. She was flushed all over again. She still felt the excitement. They had to find a way.

The phone rang, interrupting her thoughts of reconciliation. "Hello."

"I would really love to take credit for the pink roses, but they weren't from me," Dominic admitted. "I thought you hated pink."

"Oh, you have no idea how much!"

"Yes, I do, but obviously, your newest admirer doesn't." "Bye, Dominic Charles!" She laughed at his annoyance.

The phone immediately rang again. Madison didn't look. She grabbed the receiver. "Hello." There was silence. She continued. "Dominic? He and his butt dials." She smiled as she hung up the phone.

The caller smiled, too. He wanted to hear her voice. It hadn't mattered, she thought he was someone else. To feel her breathing on the other end of the line was enough. No, he wasn't pathetic Dominic

Charles. He was pleased to hold the title of her greatest love.

He'd come too far and searched too long to be detoured by the likes of Dominic Charles. From the way she looked today, she was worth every effort and deed it had taken to accomplish his task. She may resist at first, but once they were together again, she would remember. People would never understand how much he loved her.

All the attempts to substitute for her ended in extreme disappointment. No, she was an original. He could still feel her warmth after all this time. "In due time, my love, in due time." He kissed the photo he'd taken as she and Roz stepped off the curb and into the street. She was as magnificent as a sunrise.

She called to check on Grayson. She was out horseback riding with Melissa. Pedro seemed rather preoccupied. She found herself feeling jealous that it was not with her! "Snap out of it Madison Elise, you've got stuff to do today."

Madison was on her way to the restaurant but thought no; she would stop by the florist first. She wanted to place flowers on Helen's and Victoria's graves. She called Roz and asked her to meet her at the restaurant. She wanted them to have cocktails with Ashley. It was so much easier to discuss woes and joys when your two best girlfriends were also friends on some level too.

Over the years, she tried to cultivate a friendship between Roz and Ash. Somehow, neither seemed overly interested. Roz always made a reason to be busy. Ashley could never quite make it or stay exceptionally long if Roz was present.

Pedro told her they were both used to being the center of her attention. She was asking two number ones to accept new roles as co-winners, and that wasn't ever going to work. When you're all together, it requires your attention to be split.

Normally, it's called sharing, and adults generally don't mind unless you've spoiled them. In this case, you will find yourself choosing the friend of the day! The beauty is they love you enough to vie for your attention.

Madison laughed at his analysis of her friends. They were both equally vital to her. Roz was around when growing up was a real bitch. Ashley was there when being grown wasn't all it was cracked up to be. They were two different friendships from two different eras of her life. Neither was more or less important to her.

Pedro also hinted there were underlying factors about Roz she would never accept. He refused to go into detail about those. He smiled and said, "She has always been lucky to have you."

Madison picked orchids and begonias before leaving the shop. A chill passed through her. "It must be 75 degrees out here. What is wrong with me?" She shivered and walked down the familiar path to the family she laid to rest there.

"The pink carnations, please. I'll need twenty-eight of them surrounded by seven red roses. Would you deliver them to 13951 Cherokee Lane? I'll pay extra if they can be delivered by 5 p.m. today."

"Not necessary, sir. We service the area on our afternoon route.

Cash or charge?"

"Cash. I don't need a receipt."

"It's me, Helen. You know, if you hung around a little longer, you would have gotten to see Pedro and I break up and begin an attempt at reconciliation. We have a date, well, a non-date, on Saturday, and I am nervous as heck. He looks so good these days, better than the last time you saw him, if you can imagine!

Every day, Grayson looks increasingly like him. Unfortunately, she has my red hair. It is a striking combination for a little girl because people are immediately drawn to those grey eyes. She has gotten so tall, she's almost lanky, but I wouldn't dare tell her.

She wants to be a ballet dancer of all things! I say every time I come here, I'm not coming back because I know you're not here. Your souls are residing in a much higher plane than this one. Yet, it's the only place I have to be alone with you without interruptions. And fuss at Victoria for denying me the rights and privileges of additional auntie-ship."

"Hey, girlfriend, how are you today," she asked as she turned her head towards Victoria's grave." She placed the orchids on her headstone. "I wish you could have met Pedro. You would tell me if he was really what I needed. Helen was a little biased because he liked her peach cobbler.

I miss you so much. No one else will sit on the floor with me and eat miniature Reese's cups, drink a 40 oz. beer, and listen to the blues. Roz doesn't drink, and Ashley says when one can afford better, one should do better. I drove over to Baltimore Avenue last week for some Church's Chicken like we used to when we were struggling and broke. Do you know the price of a two-piece and a biscuit has skyrocketed? The peppers you get now are so small they are really not worth the $.50 extra.

Your kids could be to Grayson what you were to me since they would be a couple of years older. Well, before I get all choked up and angry with you like I used to for missing out on the best part of this joyride, I'll say see you later, and I love you still."

Madison slowly walked away from the memories of her life. She would always come here, no matter how often she threatened to stop. She even purchased the resting place next to Victoria years ago for herself.

"Hey, you!" She hugged Ashley.

"Hey yourself! Long time no see. We thought you snubbed your nose at us little working people. You missed Pedro and Gray yesterday. They came in for lunch with his mom, Marisol. He asked if you'd been in lately."

"It's good to see you too. I see you are as informative as ever." Madison gave Ashley another hug.

"You know, I feel it is my primary responsibility to reunite the two people who are my marriage role models. Remember, I am the one who started this whole merry-go-round off in the first place."

"I do remember it was the $200 tip." "So, have you made any decisions about your future?"

"I am trying to sort that out this week."

"Pedro was talking about expanding and needing a new GM for those locations. Word is he is looking for someone with a CPA, divorced, tall, sexy, dark auburn hair, African American with the last name of, well, let me see, St. John-Santiago or something. Do you know anyone with those qualifications?"

"You truly are impossible, aren't you? Yes, Pedro has mentioned it to me several times when picking up Gray. He believes it is something I'm interested in but it's not. Becoming an international name was a way to preserve Helen's legacy. The locations in London and Montreal are profitable. I always intended to walk away into silent ownership once that was accomplished.

He bought this one as a security blanket for me because I refused alimony. Hell, I know it's still in my name for goodness sakes! Grayson has three streams for her trust fund. You have done a wonderful job here so there is no need for me to come back. These are the types of things we need to discuss. We've come a long way from the bitterness we used to share."

"It wasn't bitterness, Mad; it was pain. He never wanted a divorce, and neither did you. What you needed was separation to clear your head, cool your anger, and reset. We've been friends a long time, and I feel I can be this brutally honest with you.

Men make mistakes. Women make mistakes. When you find someone willing to stand with you through those times, you keep them. You hurt him; he hurt you. Now, stop worshipping the agony god and reunite my family.

You owe it to yourself, and you owe it to Gray. Face it; the man set a standard. How many ex-husbands buy their wives' investments to fall back on in case of regret? He isn't seeing anyone and neither are you. Now, my sermon is over. Pay your tithes." Roz walked in as the two of them were laughing.

"Looks like the party started without me."

The three of them sat in a comer booth and shared two glasses of Chablis as Roz held true to Sprite. Madison was fretting about the upcoming date with Pedro. She explained the nervousness increased with the ticking hours. Roz and Ashley listened as intently as they could while evaluating the other's reaction to Madison's angst.

She was quite plain in an unobtrusive manner, Ashley thought as she scrutinized Roz. The word tired came to mind. Physically, so, it seemed. Well, she guessed it was appropriate for someone with three children, divorced, and transferring her life back from another country. The smile she offered didn't seem as genuine as Ashley thought it should.

Madi talked about all the years they'd been friends and how much stability Roz added to her life. Sitting here with her made Ashley wonder if the support was rooted in something else. Jealousy was a bit too harsh a word for the emotion. Perhaps envy was better. She would like to think after all these years together, it would have reared its ugly head by now.

For her educational attributes, though, Roz seemed almost complacent, borderline lazy in Ashley's opinion. What had she applied all her accolades to? There was an underlying anger that always seemed to surface at all the wrong times. Was she easily provoked or that pissed off at being reminded all the odds had been in her favor, and yet the favoritism fell on Madison?

She was the one with the stable home life, Madison explained. She had stellar grades and earned herself valedictorian. She'd worn her chastity belt for years as a sign of insult for Madison until Roz dropped the key one day in college. Three times. What was the excuse? She didn't drink, smoke, or do drugs.

By all parental accounts, she was the "perfect child," yet her ex-husband hadn't contested their divorce. She never spoke of her children's father in any positive light. Huh, Madison held all the fascinating and adventurous memories; the last laugh is a mutherfucker, isn't it?

In all the journeys of teenage angst Madison recalled, Roz was always sort of the wheel rolling along on the back passenger's side of the car. At first, Ashley thought it was because she was guarded about her younger years. Then, she realized Roz had little to contribute.

Madison designed the situation. Roz came along almost as a chaperone to make sure she came home. Although from pictures of these adventures, Madi set her up with some attractive guys. Their interests didn't quite catch fire for Roz.

It was quite clear of the twosome who shined and who twinkled. Ashley always wondered if the friendship was true for Madison and convenient for Roz. Who wouldn't want to be attached to the brightest star in the little galaxy they grew up in?

Roz watched Ashley attempt to assess her as she always did when they had an occasion to be with Madison together. She seemed like a groupie of Madison's. She was a younger, less bold version. The glossiness in her eyes, as she listened to Madison, was written about in fan club magazines.

Her mouth almost drooled with "when I grow up, I want to be like you" shimmer. It annoyed Rozalyn. The good ones always end up as honorable mentions in life, don't we?

Ashley probably has no idea what being a friend of Mad's requires. Some days, it was downright exhausting. Sure, she loved her, but saving her had been a hell of a ride all these years. Mad made sure she was always protected and happily bore any brunt of frustration from the parents. She supplied the necessary excuses to disentangle her from the most uncomfortable situations, but many of them were Madison's own creations.

After a while, the binges and the breakthroughs became too much to manage. She happily moved to Germany with Ted because it gave her some physical space from the drama. Being around Madison all those years was like season tickets to the same production with different actors.

There was always a man of some sort accompanied by some kind of betrayal, be it from him or her. The thing that infuriated Roz was they all seemed to find the error of their ways, whether their fault or not and want her back. Why?

Why always her? Most people didn't know behind those big warm brown eyes was a volatile temper easily switched to sub-zero depending on how pissed she was. She could be downright polarizing.

Roz knew the frustration she felt deeply towards Madison came from the light she carried. It always seemed to work out for her, no matter what happened. She always landed on her feet in the end. There was no real longsuffering for her sins. After she shed a stream of crocodile tears, she moved on.

She'd be the first to admit Mad had been through some shit. Roz found herself over the years wishing just once the leftovers in Mad's life glanced her way first. Instead, she spent a lifetime listening to the excitement "as experienced by Madison". She was done with her time as a lookout.

Hell, even her own marriage fell apart because Ted told her to adopt some of Madison's explosiveness for life. Roz told him if she was who he wanted, perhaps he should have married her! Ted's response shook her to the quick. "If only I had met her first and thought I had an STD chance with a virgin, I would have!"

The man who promised to love her and her children for life only agreed to do so because it gave him access to the current blockbuster film produced by Madison Inc. The irritating thing was she seemed so oblivious to the whole thing. She didn't recruit men. They came to her.

Roz couldn't recall a time in the thirty years she'd known her she was without a man that wasn't by choice. Mad sat home and ate Ben & Jerry's on the weekends because she wanted to. She could go to the store in a baseball cap and a housecoat, and men would make advances.

On the other hand, in her best Donna Karan, she couldn't hold the butcher's attention long enough to get her chicken breasts filleted. It wasn't fair, dammit. Roz didn't possess Madison's shroud of mystery to hide behind, which made her even more pissed! She sensed Ashley perceived it.

Yet, here was Madison, rebounding from marriage to the perfect man to probably end up reunited with him again. It hadn't happened yet, but, as always, it was just a matter of time. And people like Ashley sit back in adoration of the woman they only know on the surface. Madison St. John-Santiago was a survivor, not a woman to admire.

The cocktail hour ended with pleasantries between Ashley and Roz. They were both excited to see Madison gaining her life and strength back. They also knew the "Three Musketeers" image Madison held for them would never make it past this stage. Madison knew it, too, but refused to give up on the idea. For now, it was time to concentrate on assembling the perfect Penelope to Pedro's Pepe Le Pew.

"Oh wait, let me run out to my car so you can give me your opinion of my Penelope catsuit. I'll be right back." Madison dashed across the restaurant parking lot.

"She is nervous," Ashley said to Roz.

"Hell, she should be. You only get so many chances to fuck up perfection before it moves on." Roz's statement caught Ashley off guard. Ashley thought, you will never get the opportunity to knock on perfection's door bitch. Over our dead bodies!

Madison went into Ashley's office and tried on the costume. She looked fabulous. Only someone with long legs could pull this off. A shorter woman would look like a character from "Harry Potter."

"I've got to find a ponytail like the wrestler Bianca Belair to pull off the hair. If I get it long enough, it can run down my back and serve as a tail."

"Well, I think even if you open the door in pigtails and a blackened front tooth, Pedro won't notice. Bitch." Roz commented.

"Well, it's nice to be surrounded by such love. Madison laughed at Roz's dig. Ashley smiled thinking, I know you really meant it and took another sip of her wine.

"I have a date on Saturday night with my husband, and I am scared shitless. I feel like it's a blind date. I know it's ludicrous. Hell, I was married to him for eight years. We were together for ten. Now, it's been two and I don't want this to go sideways.

"Yes, it's called love caused by sexual tension. But the wonderful thing is he drank the same sauce. He obviously loves your dusty ass too! Since you haven't eaten, come try this new shrimp penne with walnut and crème fraiche pesto, and tell me what you think. I need an unbiased palate. Roz, if you must run, I understand," Ashley shot back over her shoulder.

"And miss the opportunity for a free meal, never. What type of chicken do you have working on the grill back here?"

Madison got home at about 4:30. She decided to follow Ashley's advice and not wait until Saturday to calm her jitters about an evening with Pedro. She called his office.

"Mr. Santiago is in a meeting right now. May I tell him who is calling?"

"Yes, tell him it's Mrs. St. John-Santiago," she said it more for her benefit than the receptionist.

"One moment, please." She didn't know there was a Mrs. Santiago.

"Madi, is everything okay, are you hurt?"

"No. Everything is fine with me. However, I threw your receptionist for a loop. Anyway, I was wondering if you were free this evening? If so, could convince your mother to watch Gray so her parents could have dinner together?" She crossed her fingers and her toes he didn't have a date.

"My mom's taking the kids to the movies tonight. I planned to grab something on the way home. What time would you like to have dinner?"

"Is seven o'clock too soon?"

Yesterday was too late, he thought. "No, seven o'clock is fine. Do you want me to bring anything?"

"Only you. I'll bring only me, and maybe the two of them can get reacquainted."

"I'll see you then. Goodbye, Mr. Santiago."

"Goodbye, Mrs. St. John-Santiago." Damn, that sounded good on his lips. The doorbell rang about eight minutes later. "Madison St. John?"

"Yes."

"These are for you. Someone thinks you're pretty special. This isn't even the best season for these, so they spent a fortune."

"Twenty-eight carnations and seven red roses. "Yuck! Are you married?"

"No, ma'am."

"Are you seeing anyone special? Anyone you want to impress?" The kid smiled at her shyly.

"Yes ma'am."

"I'll tell you what, give these to her, and I'll say they were delivered in mint condition. Here's $40 bucks as a tip if you will."

"You don't have to tip me, ma'am. These flowers are worth a mint." "Remember now, you're setting a standard. She will expect you to live up to it. Women expect you to start out like you plan to hold out. Her mother used to say it all the time. Make sure she's worth it." Pedro was phenomenal. He just couldn't remember her name, wasn't Barbie.

As the clock ticked down, she was giving in to her nerves. She should be ashamed of herself. She had been intimate with this man, they shared a six-year-old child, and a history twice as long for goodness's sake! Surely, they could have dinner together. Pedro was more gorgeous at forty-seven than he was at thirty-five when they'd met.

She called Ashley and told her to send over the shrimp penne she had sampled for lunch. Ashley also threw in an appetizer creation and a dessert she whipped up between her squeals of delight. Pedro hadn't tasted anything she was sampling tonight except, well, maybe her. The dinner arrived promptly at 6:30.

It looked mouthwatering. The appetizer was potato and rosemary crepes with whipped bleu cheese butter, and dessert was a bowl of cognac soaked-ganache drizzled strawberries and peach slices. A note was enclosed: 'Do everything I would do twice!" Love Ash.

Pedro rang the bell at 6:50. He carried a bottle of Blanc de Blanc in his arms.

She envied the bottle. He looked decadent. He wore a red cardigan sweater drawing immediate attention to the hints of grey in his beard. Precisely the reason he was voted by women constituents (and perhaps some men) as the "Sexiest Judicial Presence in the State of Connecticut." The couchie coupons were squirting out of control, and he was on the doorstep! They hadn't been intimate in nearly two and a half years.

"Hello, Madison."

"Hello, Pedro, come in."

The sexual charge between them immediately sent off the "I remember when we did it over there" missiles. She escorted him to the dining room the same way he had done their first dinner together in this house. He paused to duck into the kitchen and grab a bottle opener from the drawer. Still the same, he thought.

The conversation was full of distant familiarity in the way they ate. Each tasting and tantalizing the other with food. He loved her still; she knew it. She loved him still, and now he knew it too. Their unspoken acknowledgments were larger than an actual elephant in the room.

They talked and laughed nervously about Grayson antics to break the silent stares. Could they go deeper and talk about expectations, obligations, ways to communicate before crisis, code words for "I need help and I don't know what to ask you to do. Just shut up and hold me?" Could they?

They hadn't shared so much as a kiss since their divorce, but she still knew him. Madison wanted to cling to him like a fresh pot of grits. The way he caressed the wine glass with his fingers gave her chills.

Those hands cared for her with the gentleness of a whisper when migraines used to take her out of commission for hours. He expertly pacified Grayson while simultaneously providing soothing comfort to her too. He was an outstanding father. Another baby would have been wonderful after the hustle and bustle of life slowed down a bit.

He was lost inside the auburn tresses she cut above her ears about three weeks ago. He noticed when she did it but dared not mention it to her. The light created a soft shimmer on her skin. He wanted to touch it. He wanted to touch her.

She was the mother of his child, and she was phenomenal in the role. He had known it from the night she wore that black evening gown on the French Riveria. She cared for Helen too well to be anything except an excellent mother. They had never discussed having more children, but he was definitely open to the idea.

He was more relaxed than in the years before they parted. Sitting here tonight was reminiscent of the way they used to be. Before, priorities and commitments overshadowed the most important commitment, the one they made to each other. Before was a lifetime ago.

"One Heart One Love," a Phil Perry song, played softly as the bottle of wine was ending. They stared at each other. It was their first dance as husband and wife. She knew the song was somewhere on this mixed CD. Madison figured, if he doesn't notice, then we really are only Grayson's parents...

"Dance with me," he whispered. She stood up with her wineglass and pushed the repeat button.

"You won't need that," he said as he took it from her hand and placed it on the table. Yes, I do, she thought, it's harder to assault someone with only one free hand.

He felt so good. Being in his arms made her feel like she was floating. How could she have ever divorced him? He tightened his embrace as if to respond, Hell, I don't know either. A soft sigh slid through her lips. Lost in her own emotions, she jumped when his fingers brushed the side of her neck.

"Where are you going?" "I've never been anywhere."

His eyes locked hers. He was as unsure as she. He glanced at her lips and back into her eyes. It was a flashback to the time Roz dropped her off unannounced at his house, this house. The moment she knew she was "all in on loving and being loved by him." He recognized it too.

"The road still leads to the same destination," she whispered.

"It has always been one of my favorite places."

The kiss was electric. She returned the level of heat she was dealt. When he ran his hand under her skirt, she went ahead and ripped the damn thing off. Teasing was not on her list of "favorite things." Her body knew what was coming next, and she was making damn sure it was not disappointed.

The buttons on his shirt were asking her fingers for instruction. At last, there was nothing between them but the night. For a while, they stood there swaying to the music. She crushed her breasts against him, and he ground his hips against hers. When he got down on his knees, she remembered why she never got over him.

She wanted to collapse right there. He needed to be home completely. They could discuss it tomorrow. She took his hand and led him to their bedroom. She was trembling. She parted her lips to speak and he placed a gentle finger over them.

He spoke with restrained passion in his voice. "Show me we should have fought harder to stay together. Let me show you why I should've never let you send me away."

She didn't know when her breathing began again. All she knew was he caught her when she fell. Madison knew she loved this man more than life itself. If he asked her to surrender it right now, she would do it for one more grind of his hips against hers.

Pedro never felt the range of emotions he felt for this woman. She made him safe and scared all at once. She created a hunger within him he hadn't found since her. This was the way ecstasy was meant to feel. It didn't matter what the court said. She was still his wife.

The way she let her teeth nibble on his nipples made him grip her head and cry out in satiated pain. She was exquisite. The way she smelled, the way she tasted. Her hair was on his abdomen as she let her mouth do almost unbearable things to his body. He tried to see her eyes. She refused to relinquish her hold. It was delicious torture.

Slowly, she crawled back up, and he drank the taste from her lips. He licked away every drop of passion between them as he flipped her onto her back. Pedro tried not to rush when he entered her, but it was impossible. From the moment he was inside that sweet, moist flame of hers, he felt himself being scalded. Pulling back was forbidden.

"Madi, I... not like this... not this soon! I don't want to stop! I love you so much! It's been so long! I... Aww!" His thrusts rocked the entire bed railing. She loved every moment of it. He was as out of control as she. The ride took them to new heights!

When he collapsed with her in his arms, she couldn't separate his heartbeat from her own. They lay entwined for a long while in silence. Each waited for the other to speak. Madison was once again intrigued by the physical contrasts between them. Grayson was a stunning combination of all their best features.

Madison's auburn hair was highlighted compared to Pedro's in black. Her chestnut skin gave a lovely backdrop to his in mocha and her cognac eyes to his grey ones.

Meanwhile, Pedro thought of only one thing: how perfectly her curves fit inside his frame. Their relationship was a cracked eggshell. Sure, you could find another half, but only one made you as whole as life would allow. God designed this woman, his woman. He was not going to disappoint either of them again.

Madison broke the silence. " So, do you have to leave?" "Is that a question or a hint?"

She rose on her elbow and looked at him. "A question."

"This was not a "drive-by" for me, Madison. When you agreed to go to the masquerade ball, I was overjoyed. I want us to fix this. If tonight was more about physics for you than emotion, tell me now while I still have enough pride to walk out the door." His stare was intense.

"I was nervous about you coming to dinner this evening. I felt the same exhilaration the first night I came here. I love you. I have always loved you. Filing those papers was the hardest and dumbest decision I ever made about us. I want us to figure out how to put us back together and end up here."

"Right here?"

"Well, maybe more in this spot. Stay with me tonight." "Are you sure?"

"Unless you don't want to. I realize this was unexpected, and if there is somewhere else you need to be..."

"Do you know 'until death do us part' meant forever to me?"

"Good because I have a temper, and I am not afraid to use it on some random woman about my..."

"Yours?"

"There is still some doubt?"

"Well, you may need to repeat of few of those things you did earlier to… aah!"

The next morning, as Pedro walked out of the shower, her heart stopped beating. They lived this moment a thousand times as husband and wife. Their eyes met. The doubt was equal between them. Pedro quickly crossed the room to her.

"No. Last night was not about loneliness. It was about correcting a horrible wrong. I love you, and that doesn't change with the time of day." The kiss he branded her with left no room for questions.

"Will you call me later?" She sounded insecure. She didn't care.

"No. I'll be home at 6:00 sharp. What's for dinner?" He winked at her. "Some things never change." Madison was relieved.

"And the problem would be?"

"Not one damn thing."

She walked over and gave him a kiss as he put on his pants. Of course, Pedro wasn't about to let her have the last touch. Madison finally got him out and to the office about 10:00. It gave her the time she needed to pick up a few more items for her grand entrance as Penelope.

He had watched the entire seduction play out. The French doors off her kitchen patio and the sheer drapes in her bedroom had been quite accommodating. His car was parked at the neighbor's house two doors down. He was furious when he saw Santiago pull up.

The uncontrollable rage overtook him, and it was unfortunate for the woman who was in her backyard gardening. It was approaching dusk, so the dimming light provided the backdrop needed to catch her off guard. Thanks to her sheers, she had become fertilizer for the roses she apparently loved. By the time she was found, they should be in full bloom.

The proximity of her house to Madison's along with the plates on the rental car gave him anonymity. Unfortunately, he saw more than his stomach could stand! He wouldn't tolerate another one of these nights between the two of them. Who in the hell did Santiago think he was? They were over and it was time they both fucking realized it!

Madison found a close parking spot by sheer coincidence and veered into it with precision. A passerby gave her a nasty look, and she smiled. She sat there because Tank was singing this beautifully written song called "Our Song." The lyrics began "life without you ain't never been right…" Nothing was going to ruin her day. She spent the night with her husband, and that was worth a million finger salutes as "Bitch of the week."

Madison moved through the mall in search of the stripe for Penelope's body and the black tights to complete the ensemble. Somehow, she couldn't shake this strange sensation. It was as though she were being followed.

She kept looking behind her to see if she recognized any of the window shoppers. It was a moot point inside a mall. She must be more exhausted than she thought. A smile crossed her lips as she sauntered down the aisles. Madison was monitoring her time because she wanted to get home in plenty of time to greet her man properly.

He was still agitated today. How dare he spend the night in her bed, touching her! When the lights went out in her bedroom, he squeezed his beer bottle so hard it cracked in his hand. Blood splattered all over the thigh of his jeans. He collected the bottle pieces as the beer oozed down his leg. He stood outside the entire time and watched them as they assaulted each other.

The image was etched in his memory. Her ass was exposed except for a pair of hi-cut royal blue panties. Her legs were draped in some fashion around Santiago's waist as he stood there, fully aroused. He could see his erection from across the room!

When he dropped down on his knees in front of her and ripped those panties off her in one swift movement, he glimpsed her cherry tree in full bloom. Santiago pried her apart and inserted his fingers. He let his mouth take the lead. The intruder could almost taste her, too. It was pure greed the way Santiago left no spot to chance. He should have blown a hole right through his fucking throat!"

This morning Santiago skipped his happy ass out of her house like he was the fucking cure for world hunger. The kiss they shared lasted so long they parted like asthmatics. "Cock-sucking, mutherfucker! How could you let yourself be reduced to slut status? You belong to me Madison! Your memory might be faulty now, but it is about to become labor pain clear!"

He dreamt of her yesterday before the atrocity took place. He thought of the way she would feel in his arms. The scent of her perfume as it lingered in his nostrils while he loved her. He should be the one devouring her mouth. The smile on her face should be for him. Him!

"Sir, sir, did you want to purchase this one as well?"

"No, I'll bring my wife back because I'm not sure it will fit."

"It's a beautiful hue of pink. I'll hold it for you if you like. What name shall I put on it?"

"Madison."

He watched Madison go inside her house. "Soon, my sweet, we will be together always. I've waited a long time; tomorrow is not far away." A broad smile crossed his face. How many nights had he dreamt of her?

The others disappointed him drastically. Madison remained true to their vow of silence. Their love was heightened by her resilience. The thought of her in his arms gave him an erection he hadn't felt in years.

Slowly, he stroked himself and relieved the tension building for far too long. Tomorrow night he would plant his seed inside the object of his desire. A small moan escaped his lips. He let the leather interior of the car absorb his passion.

When he drove past Pedro's house, he made an exaggerated pause at the stop sign. He looked back through the rearview mirror in awe. Grayson was beautiful. She had her mother's hair and body type but her father's eyes. Her two long ponytails were lighter in color than her mother's hair.

Her burgundy bows matched her skirt. The bows held her hair evenly on each side of her perfectly round face. Apparently, she was giving Pedro some sort of quiz because she was laughing at his answers. He was making funny faces at her. Perfection. Madison gave birth to absolute perfection even with flawed sperm.

His gaze drifted to Pedro. He didn't deserve his life. Madison was the only one who understood loyalty in their relationship. The opportunity would present itself between now and tomorrow. Mr. Santiago didn't see the end coming.

The only reason he didn't kill him now was the beautiful child laughing beside him. Besides, he was hungry. He never killed on an empty stomach.

Pedro called Madison at about 6:00 p.m. "Hi." "Hi."

"I've thought about you all day." "Me too."

"You were so warm and inviting this morning. I didn't want to leave you. The way you taste has always driven me crazy."

"Is this a prank call? I don't think my husband would appreciate this, mister." "Are you kidding? Your husband told me to call! He knows he's left you alone on this perfect evening."

"Well, he should have told me. My lover is on his way over."

" I guess I should get there quickly." The phone went dead. Pedro knocked on the door about five seconds later. He took her in his arms and smothered her with his kiss.

"How did you get here so fast?"

"I was outside. The beauty of cellular. Gray is at Jennifer's house for a sleepover."

"Pedro, you are terrible, pawning our daughter off!"

"I didn't pawn her off. She wanted to go. Anyways, it created the perfect event for her parents to spend the night together."

"Pedro, slow down. We have one part of our relationship worked out, but I don't want this to only work if we are prone. We still have a lot to work out between us. Two years is a long time to be apart."

"I love you. You love me. The rest is in the details. I know we have things to discuss. I know I'm pushing, but I have been without the woman I love for a long time. You do know I have loved you from the moment I massaged your feet and cooked your dinner here twelve years ago, don't you?"

"No, but I appreciate the dramatization anyway." She moved to look out the window and put some space between them. "Pedro? Was that Jaguar parked there when you came in?"

"Yeah, why?"

"Because I may be imagining things, but it seems like I've seen it in several places I've been lately."

"Madison, you may have your walk of this city, but you don't own it. It's probably a relative of the neighbors. Furthermore, how many Jaguars are there in this town anyway? Don't change the subject on me."

"I am not changing the subject. I am making an observation. Anyway, I made dinner, so let's eat." He watched her toy with her food the entire time.

"What has you so uneasy about our reconciliation? Is it me or you? I have shared my feelings and you have shared yours. Is there something else?"

He put down his fork. "Madi, I can't bear another stake in my heart. I know what I want. If you are unsure, I must accept that. I am forty-seven years old. Do you know what that means? In terms of my happiness, the day you married me was only surpassed by the day you gave birth to Grayson.

Everything I said to you upstairs, on the phone, in your arms is who I am. You are who I am. I don't know how to be anyone except the man who loves you. Make sure it's enough for you."

He walked out of the door and got in his car. He drove away as she stood in the driveway calling his name. Once again, he didn't listen to her explain. He wanted what he wanted and apparently, why she was nervous could wait.

Madison stood in disbelief. Why is it whenever she was sure about anything, the bottom always fell out? She walked back into the house and looked around. Her eyes rested on the newly finished remodel of her kitchen. She subconsciously added some of the things Pedro always wanted when she drew up the plans.

The contractor thought she was insane to request an island on the side of the refrigerator strictly to store her pots, pans, and gadgets to alleviate counter clutter. The idea was not surprising; it was the size and depth of the dual-doored ensemble. She wanted to stack pots up to seven high and eight wide with tiny holes in a corkboard front for hooks and handles.

In her mind, their lives centered around food. She owned a restaurant and was always testing new recipes. Pedro liked to cook to unwind. She wanted him to be comfortable when he came home. When he came home… She started to well up with tears.

This kitchen, along with the rest of her house, felt like a tomb. She'd been buried alive by self-doubt once again. She grabbed her keys before she grabbed a bottle of bourbon instead. A drive was desperately needed to clear her head.

She got in her car and eventually headed towards the shoreline. Eric Clapton greeted her with the lyrics from "River of Tears." Madison often drove to the shore when she was stressed or distracted. The sound of the water crashing against the rocks made an icy A capella accompaniment for her tears. She felt like she was enclosed in an ice-cold Coca-Cola.

"Where was she going alone in the darkness? Ahh, the shore." He loved water, too. It made everything clean and new. She was distracted tonight. Soon all would be right in both their worlds.

Damn Santiago! Why couldn't she see Pedro was not the man she needed? Couldn't she see every time she got close to someone it didn't work? As he parked, he thought, she should give up this ridiculous idea of loving someone else.

Madison sat alone on the rocks and thought of her life. How did she always wind up alone? The constants in her life seemed to be loneliness, erratic behavior, and pain. She remembered growing up and feeling isolated. It was like she watched her life from someone else's big-screen television.

Girl meets boy. Girl loses boy. Girl meets another boy. Another boy lost. Woman meets good man. Woman acts stupid. Woman loses the man. Woman ends up as alone as the girl who lost the boys. If she were honest, it was her fault. Something inside her needed to be reset, but what?

While the pain remained with her, happiness skipped off with someone else. Why was she so afraid to commit? The only person she ever fully gave 100% was Grayson and that was a biological. Why?

Pedro sat in his car outside and waited. There was anger inside him that he never lost. All those years, all those hours, all those seconds ticked by, and still, this madness could show up instantly. Something inside her was broken. Hell, something inside him was broken for still wanting to figure it out.

Karla wanted to have drinks with him tonight. She was an attractive woman. Why the hell shouldn't he? Couldn't he? Because Karla wanted more than drinks. Karla wanted him.

It was obvious when he spoke to her. She gazed at him when she thought no one noticed. The surprise in her voice when Madison announced herself as "Mrs. Santiago" on the phone was almost comical. She sounded disappointed when he declined her invitation for dinner and drinks. Although she was more than willing, Karla didn't deserve second place. No one deserved it.

Second. It was a profound word to be so short in significance. He wondered if it mocked anyone else in the world the way it seemed to enjoy torturing him. This was their second chance. He had fallen in love with her second.

Grayson was her second child. Madison didn't know he knew she miscarried Brock's child shortly before they met. Helen told him. He was sure Brock didn't know either, otherwise he would never have married JoAnne. The other second choice. At least he was the first between the two of them to know that! He and Mad had never discussed it. Years passed and still he felt second to something.

She explained her father had a fear of commitment. What else can I do? She loves me. I know she does. I'm not competing with another person anymore. My life is half-empty without her. It wouldn't be fair to find someone else because they would be second, too. Maybe the bottom of this bottle of vodka will reveal the answer if I keep searching.

"Good evening," he said. "Don't be startled. I didn't mean to scare you." "Hello."

"You look as though you've lost either your best friend or someone died." 'It's a combination of both except the "someone" has never been born. Me."

She turned to face the outline of a man. He seemed about twenty

195

years her senior from the sound of his voice. The overcast sky and the darkness made it hard to discern his facial features.

He wore a trench coat to withstand the breeze. If she were conscious, that same breeze would be chilling her to the bone. He stood about six feet tall. A slight limp was revealed as he moved closer to her. His action was very non-confrontational, so she remained in her relaxed state.

'So," he continued, "why do we spend our lives chasing figments of what the world imagines we should be? It seemed to be an age-old question. What keeps you from breaking free of the shell stalling your life?"

"I don't know. I know I am tired of the vicious cycle of love, mishap, heartache, and recklessness at my door."

"You sound as though you are echoing sentiments laced with testosterone. If he's what you need then, you would be with him now, don't you think?"

"I've been where he is. I didn't appreciate the view one damn bit. I understand his feelings; I don't understand my own. I would move heaven and earth for him. Yet, something I can't explain keeps us circling the bowels of hell."

"Maybe he isn't the one for you. I mean if happiness keeps eluding you there must be a reason. Is there someone else?"

"No. This man is the center of all that has ever been right in my life. He has always been the epitome of patience and compassion. I always find a way to fuck it up. There is some kind of darkness that won't release me. My apologies for emptying my mind and destroying your peaceful walk on the shore. I should be going."

"I understand the torture created by being torn away from something you would die. My advice to you is what I've decided for myself. No matter how many obstacles stand between you and destiny, your victory will emerge when the time is right. Never give up on love, no matter what you must do to win."

"Thank you, I will remember. Good evening."

Madison started back to her car and thought how personal the advice felt from the stranger. He spoke from experience. "Never give up on love, no matter what you must do to win."

The car radio said 2:20 a.m. She didn't realize she'd been on the shore that long. She passed two lovers strolling along the rocks headed toward the direction where she'd recently been. They should be her and Pedro. A shiver rushed down her spine. Maybe it was the angels agreeing with her.

She needed him more than ever, he thought. Talking to her now stirred something inside him. He almost called her by name when he spoke to her. That would have made her afraid of him. He waited too long to have her afraid. Yet, the thought of her in his arms was painfully arousing him.

He sat on the rock where she had been. He could still smell her in the air. His nostrils flared at the thought of her. She was beautiful and articulate. It was all he could do not to touch her.

Now, he sat alone with the scent of her perfume devouring his senses. It nearly drove him insane. She consumed his every waking moment. Everything he had done and would do was for her. There were no obstacles insurmountable.

Madison called Pedro on his cell. He didn't answer. She called the house number in hopes he had returned and waited. Although he never used them, he still had keys. No answer. She drove to his house.

They could not sleep with this between them tonight.

The doorbell rang, and she waited. There was no answer. She pressed the bell again. This time, her ears heard music playing softly. Her heart started racing. She banged on the door. Suddenly, there was silence, then footsteps.

The door opened, and Pedro stood with his shirt unfastened and an expression of exhaustion on his face. "What is it, Madi? It's 2:00 in the morning."

"I went down to the rocks to think about what a fool I have been and how I have never meant to hurt you."

"Go home, Madison. It's late."

"Not with this between us. We should be in bed planning our wedding, not fighting over my stupidity. I..."

"Pedro? Is everything all right?"

A familiar voice echoed from the background. Madison's statement froze on her lips. "Let me guess. You decided to promote her from legal assistant to head whore just this evening. No pun intended! At least let me be unfaithful before you pay me back in spades!"

"You come to my house in the middle of the night after telling me you don't know if your fear of NOTHING is something we can overcome and insult my guest! Twelve years Madison St. John, for TWELVE FUCKING YEARS I have tried to love you. I have tried to be everything you needed, even when I knew I was a fool. Why? Because I love your Black ass! Well, tonight, I decided to let someone else love me. And here you are fucking this up too! Go home, Madison!"

She knew he kept yelling at her, but all she heard was her maiden name. He hadn't done that in eight years. The sharp intake of breath from her was not lost on him.

She supposed he kept turning the dagger, but the first cut was the deepest. Oh hell, no! This was not over. She didn't fight him the first time they walked away from each other. But she'd be damned if that were the case this time!

Madison pushed the door and walked inside. There she was Ms. collagen-injected silicone implant herself.

"You almost had something of mine. I'll excuse your poor judgment this time. If I ever see you within two centimeters of my husband again, I will give you a whole new reason for plastic surgery! I don't know if your car is in his garage or not, but the only person spending the night under this roof with this penis is me! Get your shit!"

"Pedro! Who is this bitch? Who does she think she is talking to? I thought you were divorced. You brought me here and I'm not leaving!"

"Madison, stop it!"

"I'm talking to you, and, oh yes bitch, you're leaving here! Choose Uber or a body bag. It matters not to me! All I know is any penetration that didn't happen based on the smudge on his pants ain't happening with y'all tonight!"

He saw the wrath in her eyes. The only time he'd seen her this way was when she told him to leave two years ago. He wouldn't let her hurt Karla. However, he couldn't guarantee they wouldn't hurt each other after he got Karla to safety.

"Karla, I apologize. Get your things. I will take you home. I don't know what's gotten into my ex-wife, but you don't need to be subjected to this."

"Now you got shit all off-key, Pedro. You're not taking this bitch home. Oh no, baby, we will take her home. I'll drive. Get your shit, let's go!"

Madison made Pedro sit in the front seat with her while Karla occupied the back. Pedro rode sideways to keep an eye on both. When Madison pulled up to Karla's house, she put the car in park, turned and calmly whispered, "It's been nice meeting you face-to-face, Karla.

Let's not make it slit-to-throat next time, okay?"

Karla got out of the car and slammed the door. Pedro turned in the front seat with Madison. As pissed as he was, something twisted inside him enjoyed her territorial attitude.

The drive back to his house was made in complete silence. Madison was fuming. He brought some bitch to his house as retribution for her needing to think!

No, this was for all the times she punished him with Brock years ago. Pedro still thinks that man has some kind of hold on me. I haven't seen him since Helen's funeral. I will not lose my husband again! We've been through too much. I love him too much.

Pedro stared at her the whole drive. He was pissed! He didn't want them to have an accident so, like a wild animal stalking his prey, he waited.

She had stormed into his house and asserted a right she no longer had. What in the hell did she want from him? He was exhausted trying to figure it out. He was damned without her and damned tired with her. This torture ends tonight!

Madison pulled up to his house and sat still as Pedro got out of the car and slammed the door. He turned and realized she was still sitting as he unlocked the door to the house. Marching over to the car, he snatched the door open and yanked her out. He nearly separated her arm from its socket in her shoulder.

"Don't get all goddamn nervous on me now! I'm sure the gravity of what you did has finally hit you, hasn't it? Get your ass inside before we both wind up in jail!" He was furious with her and he had every right to be!

"Pedro, I…"

"Stand your ass right there and shut the fuck up! Do not say another goddamn word or I swear I will hurt you! How dare you come to my home and do what you did? I am so goddamn sick of your indecision Madison! You want me and then you don't! You see me attempt to move on with my life and then I'm the object of your desire!"

"I laid here for two years and pined for you! Two long-suffering years in hopes you would let me come home! Yes, I cheated on you with Tamara. Yes, I did, and I was wrong. But how quickly do we become self-righteous and forget? Two words for you, baby, Brock Andrews! Remember him?"

"Finally, when I'm about to lose my mind, and I break down and make the first move, you accept. What the hell were you waiting for if you wanted us back together? You put me out. I didn't leave you!" He was pacing in front of her like an angry rhino who had just witnessed the slaughter of its young. He continued.

"When all is going well, you drop the "I am scared and need us to be clear about things bomb! "What the fuck is there to get clear on? Huh?" His eyes were charcoal with fury. "I took a couple of hours to cool off and think maybe I've overexaggerated and should have listened to what your concerns are. I come back to find your ass gone!"

"I waited two hours for you and not one word! When you decide you have time for me, you come to my house and dismiss my guest like a goddamn hangnail in your $25 pantyhose. Now you're concerned about whether you went too far. Be glad you're a woman because I wish a man would…" his voice trailed off.

"News flash St. John! After the bullshit I've allowed you to put me through, if I decide to fuck the Easter Bunny on national television in Times Square on New Year's Eve, all you better ask is if the bath water is warm enough!"

"You have some kind of aversion to love. You respond to and respect pain, Madison. It's a sick obsession between the two of you. The only time you love me is when I'm hurting you! I can't live like that. I won't! I would fucking kill you and bury your ass next to Helen and Victoria if it didn't feel like suicide."

"You choose right here and right now! You either want the kind of healthy love I know how to give you, AND you get some therapy, or you get the hell out of my life!"

"I will pick a drop-off place for Grayson, so I don't ever have to deal with your crazy ass again! I am sick and tired of your bullshit! I am crazy as hell to keep wanting you in my life! CHOOSE!"

"What you should be thankful for is I don't hit women. Otherwise, I would beat the living shit out of you right now!" He stopped yelling long enough to notice she was trembling like a battered child. "Oh, fuck, now you're scared of me! I can't catch a mutherfucking break."

Her voice trembled as she spoke. "I'm sorry! I don't mean to hurt you; I love you! I love you in all the ways I know how. You are right. I feel like there is something inside me that won't let me be happy. I told you when we met, I'm self-destructive. I push when I shouldn't, and I fight at the wrong times. All I want is to be with you and Grayson."

"Lately, I feel like I'm losing my mind. I'm edgy. I feel scared when I shouldn't. I feel cold in 80-degree weather. I thought someone was following me the other day in the mall, of all places. I don't know what's happening to me. I have this sinking feeling; I can't explain it."

"When I saw that woman here, in your home, coming from… I knew what you felt about Brock all those years ago. I know you didn't believe me, but I never slept with him again after we made love. You were the only man in my heart when we married and to this day."

"I have never betrayed you when we were together. Never. I drove you into Tamera's arms because I was trying to "fix" things for us and Grayson. I understand that now. I should have let you come home. Hate me for what I do to you, scald your skin after I touch you, but please, don't leave me, Pedro. I will go to therapy. Please."

He stared at her. She was as vulnerable as she knew how to be. For the second time, in the twelve years they'd been together and apart, he felt like she needed him, too. Dear God, he hoped therapy would uncover whatever this thing was and kill it. He was going to make an appointment for her first thing in the morning. A friend owed him a favor.

When he opened his arms, she rushed into them and nearly knocked the wind out of him. Pedro didn't know who trembled more. A wall came down between them. Finally, maybe, they could love each other like normal people.

"Good morning." She whispered.

"I'm still angry with you. Don't think driving me to distraction in bed makes up for putting me through hell."

"Doesn't it ease the slightest bit when you picture my face after I heard that woman's voice coming downstairs?"

"You weren't really going to hurt her, were you?"

"I would've slit that bitch open like a loaded baked potato."

"She has a name, by the way. I'm sure I'll have to call the temp service and request a new assistant on Monday. If she continues this assignment, I'll never be able to face her again.

"I can type, and I take dictation very well."

What the fuck! She actually gave a damn what that asshole did! She was letting him cheat on her in her face after sitting on the shore and talking about devotion! You're being a fucking idiot, Madison!

It took everything in him not to light his ass up! The way he snatched her out of her car in the driveway infused his rage. Standing outside his doorway and hearing him scold her like a child was unbearable. The red dot of his scope was aimed directly at his head when she ran into his arms. This was the last time her love would save him. Santiago would pay!

He needed a release that involved someone other than himself and a memory. She would be his by this time tomorrow, but tonight, he needed warmth. A smile crossed his lips as he thought of the perfect substitute.

The slice of pie was smothered in whip cream. He slid the fork through his lips as another image melted in his mouth.

"Is everything okay? You seem a little distracted tonight."

"Everything would be fine if you would allow me to take you out for a drink after your shift here is done."

Ashley looked at the older man at the table and smiled. He came here every night this week. Honestly, he was a welcome source of articulate communication and professionalism. She had no idea what he did for a living. There was a certain intrigued about this man with the piercing blue eyes.

"I think maybe that could be arranged." "Good, I'll be waiting."

He picked up the phone while he waited and called a number. He let it route anonymously from the burner. It's time.

"Hello?"

"You are a hard man to reach, Mr. Santiago. I'll get right to the point since it sounds like I'm disturbing your rest. You've been receiving a series of strange envelopes and packages and you have not been able to connect them. I am the connection. You have an engagement tomorrow evening. I will contact you again and set up a time for us to meet."

"Wait a minute, who is this? What envelopes are you talking about?"

"You're very good. You give away nothing. Let me show you how serious I am. You have three envelopes. You've received one daily for the past four days. The first two contained information about two people who are no longer with us. The third requires us to meet for you to understand the fourth.

Did I pass interrogation?"

"Alright, where would you like to meet?"

"Be available to take instructions when they're given. Click." "Hello? Hello?"

Stretching lazily in his arms, Madison asked sleepily, "who was that"?

"A stranger with some answers I need."

Ashley sat across from him as he evaluated everything about her with his eyes. He looked at and through her simultaneously. It was remarkably similar to the way Madison could do it. It made you feel like a specimen under a microscope.

"I am pleased you seem to like our food. We take a lot of pride in creating repeat customers. It shows they're satisfied with our service. Our owner stresses service as a core value. My schedule typically only allows time for leftover entrees and watered-down sodas. Thank you for asking me to join you this evening." Ashley knew she was rambling nervously.

"Believe me, the pleasure is all mine. I've reached the age where if something or someone appeals to you, you should pursue it. You have captivated me from the first cup of coffee in your restaurant four nights ago. You are truly an aperitif for one's palate."

"Thank you. You're making me blush. Most men aren't so straightforward." "Most men don't know what they want or are too intimidated to say so. I've learned to examine closely and only pursue what interests me. That interest led us here. I would love to see you in a more intimate light."

"You move quickly, don't you?"

"Time doesn't belong to us. Those who waste it too often find it has run out. The result is a grave full of unsatisfied desire. Dance with me."

The way he held her made her understand something was missing in her life. A lover. Someone who gave a damn if she made it home safely at night. Someone to stand by her side and gave a damn when her side of the bed was cold.

For the past two years, she watched Madison and Pedro play the separate is okay game when, in reality, they were destined from day one. Ashley quietly envied the love they shared. Tonight, maybe, just maybe, the stars aligned for her.

She should have given him her phone number and thanked him for a lovely evening. She should have left him at the front door when he followed her home.

She should have asked him his name. Ashley should have gone slower, but time was not dictating pace. Loneliness was.

The way he forced his tongue inside her mouth set her on fire. She should have begged him to stop when he slammed her into the refrigerator door. Instead, she let the beast inside her connect with the animal inside him. It wasn't about love. It was about physical lust with the intent to satisfy oneself and hope the companion came along for the ride.

Someone who made love often would have called it abuse. He was aggressive and painful, and she was left longing for more. Who was he? It seemed so trivial when he was buried inside her this deeply.

His stamina was as exuberant as a teenager's. The evening left her before she had a chance to wish it well. It was the first time in many long-tousled nights that Ashley wasn't envious of other people as she drifted to sleep.

She awoke bruised and exhausted. The other side of her bed was empty. He was gone. Ashley jumped out of bed and ran to the window. His car was gone. She searched all the places people left notes in the movies after nights like the one she experienced. There was nothing.

All the proof she had it even happened was a bruised body sensitive to her own touch. At one point, she was bleeding from his forcefulness. It turned him on even more. If she hadn't been so aroused, she would have cried.

Hell, she couldn't even be angry because that would require someone to associate it with. She needed a name. All she had was a burned image of a pair of steel blue eyes she would never forget.

Dressing for work was a chore. She hurt all over, and the pulsating spray of the shower did nothing to satisfy her throbbing. It was the kind of pain that created a smile all day long if it had been attached to something meaningful.

Otherwise, you wished for an i.v. filled with morphine and a razor blade.

She learned from Madison and Pedro the art of personal sacrifice and survival. They endured loss, death, separation, and divorce. The least she could do was look a one-night stand in the face. As she drove to the restaurant, she turned on her compact disc player to drown out the ache in her head.

There it was. Her note.

"Ashley, what kind of man doesn't say good morning? The kind of man I am. In another man's life, last night would have been a journey I would be honored to make. For a fleeting moment, you made me human.

However, time is of the essence and there is a destiny I must fulfill. The passenger manifest is full. You are one of the few women whose generosity deserves the right to continue. At the beginning of this prophecy, I thought otherwise.

Loneliness should not be the cause of your demise. Call this one of the few generous moments I've ever had by normal human standards. Save this. One day soon, it will make sense.

She understands. You can't. The physical pain of last night will subside. Listen. Believe what they say. It will all be true. When it happens, you will wish I hadn't been so generous. A picture will be worth a thousand words."

She played the disc over and over as she drove into the parking lot of the restaurant. What in the hell was he talking about? Who was this man that left her longing to be ravished again? He enjoyed their evening, she thought.

Who was this she he referred to? How did she ever let him go? Who were they? Was this a tease or was he really gone? Well, at least the throbbing was bearable now. She smiled as she limped across the parking lot. If this is what a one-night stand was, she understood why it stood out in history!

Madison stood at the window and thought of the changes her life had undergone during this six-day journey. Finally, she and Pedro were on the right track. Last night was almost the final fatality where he was concerned. It ended in a serenade of him to Jonathan Butler's "I'm On My Knees" followed by "Do You Love Me." She thought she saw a tear fall from Pedro's eyes.

Tonight was their infamous date, and she was sure it was going to end with a ring. She told him her first ring was still quite exquisite, and they could splurge on a second honeymoon instead. He wouldn't hear of it.

"A new start requires new luggage," he said as he left for the office this morning.

So, why couldn't she shake this feeling of fear that kept surfacing?

Was she that terrified of being happy? She moved into the bathroom and tried to stare into the face that stared back at her. The mirror continued its part in reflecting what it saw. For all of ten minutes, she avoided contact with "them."

They'd been together for thirty-seven years, and she still couldn't win an argument. She saw the stranger move to the forefront as her mind made contact with her eyes. Like clockwork, the bile in her stomach began to churn as etched closer to sanity.

The vomiting was more violent today. She dreamt of her mother last night as she lay in Pedro's arms. There was additional footage in the dream. It included Helen and Victoria adorned in their burial attire. There were cameo appearances by Dominic and Ashley. They were looking over her shoulder and whispering inaudibly. It almost seemed like a warning.

She turned to Pedro in her tear-drenched state, and he assumed she was still regurgitating the events of the evening. She let him. No one, including Pedro, would understand why she was having conversations with loved ones from the grave that never took place in life.

The thing that really puzzled her was everyone was dead except Dominic and Ashley. She knew Ash was fine because she spoke to her last night. She was opening this morning. As for Dominic, she was feeling guilty because they were supposed to have lunch together a few days ago. She knew how to rectify that.

"Hey, can we have lunch today? I need to see you." She wanted to tell him in person about her decision to remarry Pedro.

"Can you get away for about an hour?" "For you, of course."

The drive over to Dominic's office was a little bit uncomfortable. It was only five days ago when he asked her about a fresh start between them. So much happened to keep that from ever being a reality. Now, she needed to explain it to him without comparison. She loved Pedro. Years earlier, she had lust for Dominic. Deep down, he knew. He still wanted to try and build something anyway. She pulled into a parking spot at his office and Dominic. He hopped in and kissed her cheek.

Madison smiled and drove to a quiet little Chinese restaurant where they ordered their food to go. They proceeded to a small park nearby. The fallen leaves made a beautiful kaleidoscope of colors for the eye to behold. Others enjoying their last few days of frolicking before winter. The ducks were enjoying the ponds before venturing south. It was the perfect day for endings and beginnings.

"You look great today," Dominic said.

"Thank you. I've been thinking a lot these past few days," she began. "I was hoping you would call me." He took a bite of Crab Rangoon.

"Dominic, I wanted to talk to you because I value your friendship. You came into my life at a point when I needed someone to hold onto both professionally and personally. You and I are like two crack addicts together. We thrive on need and are codependent. Not a healthy combination.

We work if we don't confront the real issues in our lives. The pain in our past was bearable because we were always willing to pour another round. Together with alcohol by our side we were invincible, until morning came. But Dominic, you and I both know, morning always comes."

"Wait a minute, Madison. In the beginning, that may have been true, but I love you. I've realized these past few weeks, you made me the happiest I have ever been. I screwed up."

"Dominic, I was upset last night, and I drove around trying to put some perspective on my life. While I was out driving aimlessly, I drove by your house, and I saw Pamela's car."

"Madison, I can explain."

"It's not necessary," she said softly. "It didn't upset me that your ex-wife was at your house. Precisely the point. If my love for you were different, it would have. Instead, I found comfort knowing she was where she should be. It helped me understand where I should be too, at home with Pedro. Neither set of us should be apart.

We are meant to be the best of friends. I love you dearly. I will always treasure the time we spent together. But we are a couple of lunatics, not a couple.

Dominic looked into her eyes. He recalled the first time those cognac beauties ever smiled at him. He saw the way they looked when she was caught up in a passion she couldn't control. He remembered the anger he'd seen at his height of stupidity.

Now, they offered him peace and tranquility. They were the eyes of a woman who knew what she wanted. He was not it. Madison St. John was a class act, and she did it her way.

"Pedro is too damn lucky to be human. I hope he understands how much you love him. In the meantime, I shall wait until you are a lonely widow and beg for my undivided attention. Pass the duck sauce, friend."

On cue, the ducks on the pond made a break for it. They formed a perfect line flying in the opposite direction. Dominic shouted, "sorry, fellas, it wasn't personal!" Madison threw her head back and roared with laughter. It was a wondrous sound. Dominic's heart memorized it for eternity.

She offered to give Dominic a ride back to his office. It was a lovely day, so he declined. He told her he would walk the few blocks.

"Hey, Santiago, change the song in your head. Since it's about me, I should choose it."

"Fair enough, Dominic Charles. What shall I listen to when I think of you?"

"That artist TEEKS I told you about has the perfect song for us. It's called "Remember Me". When you listen, know I mean every word."

"Seriously, Dominic?"

"Yes, Madison, I'm serious. The lyrics fit perfectly, and I know you are a lyrics fanatic."

"Alright, I promise I will find it and listen whenever I think of you. I have no idea what I am agreeing to, but I've never broken a promise to you. I will not start now."

"Hey Santiago, I love you."

"I love you too, Dominic. Always."

She gave him their first decidedly "friendly" kiss and smiled as she lifted a burden off her heart. She drove off with a peaceful feeling about the status of their relationship. They would continue to be the best of friends, without benefits! She was still thinking of their conversation as she navigated traffic towards her house.

She didn't hear the commotion from the nearby joggers. She didn't see the Jaguar parked across from where they sat moments ago. She didn't hear the frantic call for help as someone in the distance dialed 9-1-1.

To anyone passing from the rear, Dominic sat motionless enjoying a view of the ducks splashing in the pond. However, a frontal view revealed half his face was shattered. A silent gun fired the bullet with precision. A man slew Dominic because he perceived him as a threat. They never met. "Loose end," he thought as he drove the Jaguar away.

Day Six

Finally, the masquerade ball was tonight, and Madison was so excited she could hardly stand it. Pedro forgave her antics, she saw a therapist and filled a prescription for anxiety and depression, and she was relaxing today. She was so tired. This was supposed to be a week of relaxation, and it had been a whirlwind of madness.

She and Pedro were in a good place, finally. They talked about whose house would go on the market. He opted for his because Gray's school was in her district. They agreed to renovate Helen's house as an Airbnb to provide additional income streams to calm Madison's fear of additional security.

In exchange, she agreed to promote Ashley to GM so she could have more flexibility to be a wife and mother. They were going to meet at the Justice of the Peace on Monday and get remarried. They did the grandiose thing the first time. This time, she only wanted it to be legal. Pedro wanted a little bit of fanfare, but she insisted.

Madison decided to drive to Roz's house and used her spare key to enter instead of ringing the doorbell. Roz was drinking a glass of lemonade when she came into the kitchen.

"You know, I keep thinking I'm going to come in here one day and catch you in the middle of some torrid piece of ass and quietly escort myself out unnoticed."

"Is Pedro finally ready to experience a real woman?" "You tramp."

"Well, I keep waiting for my turn. From the look on your face, I have a better shot at catching rheumatoid arthritis. I take it you two have quit pretending to only be good parents?"

"You know, the downside to having old friends is they take all the elements of surprise out of any news you have. I came in here prepared to spring on you my newfound happiness, and you let the air right out of it."

'What can I say? I've seen you get laid for a long time. I know that certain look you get when you lay next to something warm and fuzzy all night. Let's go, I'm hungry. You can fill me in on the details over some Italian cuisine. Assuming there is some motion left in your facial muscles!"

Roz sat quietly for as long as she could. This was Madison's third round of cocktails. Even for her, this was a bit much.

"Is there a rule your glass is not allowed to be half empty today?" Madison rolled her eyes and changed the subject.

"This is the best wedding soup I've ever had! I'll save you some next time. It'll be as close to the real thing as you ever get!'

The laughter echoed out the door and down the street as Roz made this slurping noise with her mouth in Madison's ear. Roz ate while she watched Madison think she was going to have another drink.

"I'm sorry, she meant to say no more, not another." The effects are already taking hold," Roz told the waiter as he came with another drink for Madison.

Madison realized the drilling was about to begin. "How about we go shopping after this?"

"How about you tell me why your desire for Italian was replaced by your love of vodka?"

"I realize I don't drink, but I'm not feeling deprived either. You don't have to feel obligated to have my share of the bottle. If you wanted me to drive, why didn't you say so? I would be a little weary if you were driving after what you've consumed in the past twenty-three minutes. What's going on?"

"I'm starting the festivities of my masquerade ball early."

"Uh-huh, and I'm standing in as a Martha Stewart body double."
"Ouch! You really do need to get some soon!"

"And you really need to recognize by now, I will not be blown off. Speak!"

"I had another one of those dreams last night. This time, it included an appearance by Helen and Tori and a special guest cameo of Dominic and Ashley. I went to see him yesterday.

We lunched and cleared the air about a lot of things, especially the "us" that never should've been more than a trip to an ice cream social. I feel good he blessed me to move forward with Pedro. And before you say it, no, it wasn't necessary. It never hurts to have access to a friendly bridge in case of trouble."

"Some people characterize it as an unfamiliar word to you, Madison, but it's called happy. You're finally back together with the only man I'd trade our friendship for. Your kid is well-adjusted. You have more money than any bitch from a dot town on the map deserves. And you have me. What more could you need?"

" Another drink."

"That would be hell no. So, what's behind door number 2."

Although she tried to be coy about it, Roz watched Madi closely. Madison had been subjected to "dreams" since they were children. Typically, they played out very accurately to real-life events. She didn't want to startle her by lending credence to her uneasiness, but everyone in her dreams was dead except Dominic and Ashley. Roz hoped the "friendly stamp" was as well received as Madi seemed to think.

"Did this dream have a different ending than the normal one?"

"Yeah, actually, I remember calling you on the phone and whispering." "Me? You called me? Did I answer?"

215

"I don't know, I woke up in a strange panic and Pedro was there and it was over."

"Did something happen to me that you're not telling me Madi?" 'Rozalyn, I tell you everything else, why would I hold back something if I thought you were harmed. No, more like whatever happened, happened to me. I don't remember what it was."

"Have you ever told Pedro about your dreams?" 'No."

"Why not?"

"Because this one has been with me for fifteen years. Because a human is only allowed to leave this world once and in case you've forgotten most of my guest stars have. Now, can we talk about something else?"

Rozalyn watched Madison pick over the stuffed cannelloni she was using as a deterrent to keep from making eye contact with her. Madison was conveniently leaving out a small detail about her dreams. The older she became, the higher the percentage of accuracy became. Within the past five years, her rate was 100%.

For now, she would not push. She could see it was disturbing to her. The good thing was the original dream hadn't happened in the fifteen years she'd been exposed to it. The dreadful thing was the dream itself started to alter the players.

Madison never discussed her dreams with Pedro, only Roz. They agreed the dreams were a product of an enormously powerful gift Madison was bestowed and refused to accept. She had her own staff of guardian angels watching out for her. They were fully accurate in their cautions of sorrow and pain. Roz was once the recipient of that gift which began her concern about them.

Once they were in a theater and Roz wanted to retrieve her shawl from the car at intermission. Madison insisted she wait. Roz told her it would only take a minute. Madison insisted. Instead, she summoned a coatroom attendant and bought an unclaimed jacket for her.

During intermission, there was a bang as they passed by the bay windows leading outside.

They rushed outside to see what was going on. A bullet had pierced through Roz's windshield. A man aiming for his wife and her lover struck Roz's car instead. If Roz had been outside retrieving her jacket, she would have been killed. Roz made a note to never let Madison's "visions" go unchallenged. She also told Madison the hour was never too late or the timing too wrong if one of those dreams referred to her.

Roz also recalled when Madison worked at the accounting firm. Her visions always guided her on what actions to take and which to avoid. Her "spirit" as she described it, directed her to ask certain questions or not perform certain tasks. The meaning was not always obvious, but clarity evolved with time.

The exact replication of the dreams may not occur, but associations were clear enough to make connections between her "spiritual sensation" and her dreams.

Sometimes the meanings materialized within hours. Due to the longevity of this one, Roz hoped this sequence meant Madison was nervous about having the life she deserved without any further interruptions.

"Well, are you ready? I hear there is an awesome sale on linens at that store off Potomac."

"Fine, Madi but so help me if you don't buy anything because you are using this as a deterrent to talking, I swear I will push you into oncoming traffic!"

"Oh, alright already, I think I could use a new face towel!"

'You have become unable to feel me like you should Madison! You are simply confused about what real love between a man and a woman is like. You've been brainwashed into believing you need him. He's a pathetic sloth who spends his day gloating over winning an impossible war he has no idea about. He thinks he's better than the people who spend years behind bars unjustly.

Santiago is no better than the police who swore to serve and protect. They violate people's rights, ignore irrefutable evidence, and tamper with accurate testimonies to suit their own purposes. Look at the number of victims of police brutality! Most of them are no better than the people they label criminals. You married one of those barbaric bastards.

His mind turned to Madison's daughter and a smile crossed his lips. He could only imagine the joy he would feel as he got to know her in Pedro's absence. They would be much more of a family than Santiago could ever provide. I'm sure he poured on the Cuban charm and the lavish lifestyle. Where is he today? Out chasing rainbows!

He made this personal the moment lay with you. He contaminated something between us that will take you a lifetime to forget. But that is why you have my love unconditionally! I will purge him from your soul. You will understand no one will ever come between us again, not the judicial system, not Brock, not Dominic, and sure as hell not some ill-gotten obsession with a wasted spermatozoa like Santiago!

You are mine! There has never been another who deserves you the way I do. I sacrificed my life for this reunion and there will be nothing to stand in our way. I thought allowing Crenshaw to remain intact would be a valuable reminder of your past. Perhaps her situation needs to be rectified!

Stop it! You're getting sidetracked with insignificant things. Tonight is the end of a lot of patient planning.

Damn the little things! After this Madison will open up to me again like she did that night on the shore. I should have ended it all then. Instead, I let the sheer presence of her overwhelm me. She is a lovely creature. I am proud of my part in making her the woman she is.

Madison had two hours to prepare for her role as Penelope. Grayson was coming home tomorrow. This was her last night to be the wanton hussy she became when Pedro was around. Tomorrow the world would transform her once again into the role of mother and support system for the six-year-old sapphire she had borne.

She was anxious, almost fearfully so. She hadn't been nervous on her first date with Pedro. But why? She had been married to the man who was escorting her this evening. There was no part of his body unidentifiable in the dark.

Roz and she decided to have a massage and get her nails done. The receptionist said there was a cancellation, so they got in immediately. Pampering, every woman should succumb to the indulgence every now and then. It rejuvenates and erases all the cares of the world to be smothered in exfoliates, drenched in a milk bath, and rubbed with sea salts. Pure bliss. Madison felt fit for a presidential inauguration. As she applied the last amount of lipstick to her perfectly polished mouth to complete the look of the evening, the phone rang.

"Hello?"

"Hey sweetie."

"Hey yourself. You should see me; I took ravishing to a whole new level, if I say so myself."

"I'm sure you are beautiful. I wish I could see you, but something's come up that I can't get out of."

"What are you saying? Something like what? Are you going to be late?"

"No, baby, I can't go to the ball tonight. I must fly to New York tonight. I wish I could explain it to you, but I can't right now. I am so sorry baby. I promise you if it weren't critically important, I would not pass up the opportunity to be with you tonight."

"I believe you when you say it's urgent but, I am disappointed. I was looking forward to purring in rare form this evening."

"You still can. I saw Ashley earlier this evening and she looked incredibly stressed, so I gave her my ticket. Jesse agreed to stay at the restaurant tonight so, she should be ready to go when you are."

"Well, if you're sure you want us to go without you."

" I promised you an evening you wouldn't forget, and I intend for it to be exactly that. Unfortunately, I will have to hear about it through memories."

"I love you so much. When do you think you'll be back?"

"I love you too. I should be home tomorrow morning and I promise you I will make up every inch of this disappointment to you. Do me a favor."

"Anything."

"Listen to the song you walked down the aisle to me at our wedding before you leave for the ball. Know I mean every word right now as much as I did when we got married."

"Me too."

"Baby, I will come straight home to you from the airport." "That has a wonderful sound. I'll even let you in!"

"Well, have a safe flight and I'll get off and find out if Ashley and I need a cab or if we're driving."

The life of an Assistant District Attorney was difficult. It meant a lot of plans had to be postponed or changed if a case had significant updates. Typically, they don't travel because they are not investigators or police. This must have something to do with that strange phone call he received yesterday when they were in bed.

Their roles literally helped make the difference between someone's life and death. She understood. It was still disappointing sometimes, like tonight. Yet, knowing he was making a difference made her love him even more.

As she promised, she pulled out "If You Could See You Through My Eyes," by Kenny Lattimore and let the moment envelope her. This song would always remind her of one of the best days of her life. She got the prince that day. Later, they had a little princess to call their own.

After this, Madison will open up to me again like she did that night on the shore. I should have ended it then. Instead, I let the sheer presence of her overwhelm me. She is a lovely creature. I am proud of my part in making her the woman she was.

"Hey, Ms. I hear we have one hell of a night planned."

"I know I'm a poor substitute but, I need to have a night to remember." " Is everything okay? You sound kind of down."

'It's a long story. I will fill you in after I have about a pint of alcohol and a lengthy line dance out of my system. I should be over in about twenty minutes."

The phone went dead. Madison was suddenly concerned for Ashley. There was a certain selfishness Madison hadn't realized she'd been drowning in.

Ashley stood by her side for years without question. She didn't realize Ashley was burying herself in work since the relationship with Jesse soured.

They were still amicable in the workplace, but Ashley really loved him. When he pulled away and married Rebecca, Ashley shut down to life and feeling. Oh, she said she was okay, so Madison promised not to push. Inside she knew Ashley was lonely and hurt. Pedro offered to let her work in the Assistant District Attorney's office and pull her out of the restaurant. Ash refused. She said she wasn't a 9-5 kind of girl.

Madison could tell something happened. She sounded almost depressed. She also believed it was her duty to try and pull Ashley out of it. Maybe Pedro's sudden emergency was for the best. Tonight, they would be two women out having an enjoyable time for a worthy cause. No excuses!

The music could be heard for miles. Amazingly, when the judicial department was the source of the ruckus, no citations for disturbing the peace were being issued. He watched them one by one as they came in, some as couples and others-alone. "Who would want to crash a party given by all the important people of town?"

On cue, he saw her. She was draped in a lovely black coat accompanied by the substitute from the other night. He waited a long time for this moment. Ever so slowly, he disguised his limp and walked over to the gentlemen searching for something in his car. In less than sixty seconds, there was a stain on his shirt which added character to his costume. With an invitation securely in hand, he was now prepared for the night.

The beauty of the masquerade is one can be the angel or the demon of their choosing without explanation. Madison smiled as she saw quite a few familiar faces. All were exceptionally cordial to her and Ashley. The D.A. came over and expressed his apologies at Pedro absence.

He explained an anonymous crucial tip came in on a case that was shaping up to be a multi-agency situation. Attorneys and law enforcement were convening to weigh facts and authorities. Madison smiled and told him she was a judicial wife; she understood the unexpected. Joshua Curtis smiled before replacing his mask and reaffirming his role as Zorro.

He walked away but his train of thought did not. As he glanced around the room, he saw more than he had cast an enviable eye in the direction of their comrade's astoundingly beautiful wife/ex/lover. The way she moved was graceful.

It was the type of movement that commanded attention even though it was obvious that was not her intent. That was it, she was unintentionally, droolingly sexy. Many men would expect that mix of aura to radiate from a woman of half her stature. Madison St. John wore it with the delicacy of the runway.

She had the most delicious voice and the deepest cognac eyes he'd ever encountered. Pleasant and always understanding, the men at the office often discussed who would make a move on her if she and Pedro ever emotionally called it quits.

As his friend, Joshua had been equally as distraught as Pedro when they divorced. Over the past two years, he could see a part of Pedro was lost. It was a critically obvious part like an arm or an eye. He tried to patch it and move on, but everyone knew he had only one objective: crawling back into those arms. Seeing her this evening, every man in the room wanted to bash his skull for the opportunity to replace him.

The other woman, Ashley, was quite stunning as well. She didn't radiate confidence like Madison though. It was more a desire to experience something. In a way, the spotlight of Madison was diminishing her. Second choice but definitely not a left over. She wore her a 1920's whore outfit as though the character was a hidden fantasy of hers.

Joshua thought to himself, he would have to probe a bit deeper when Pedro returned to find out the rest of this woman's story. She provided few details about herself when she gave Pedro the scoop on Madison all those years ago. At the time, he was married, so he didn't pursue her.

Now that was over, so tonight, he would absorb as much information about her as he could. With precision timing, he walked over to Ashley to see if she was as wanton as the costume made her appear.

"Excuse me, I was wondering if you would have pity on the taxpayer's vice and dance with me?"

"Well, I suppose I may need to acquaint myself with you in case I need your assistance in a more formal capacity!" Ashley joked as Madison pushed her out of the chair.

She watched and thought of how attractive Zorro was with a woman of the night. Ashley would make a good match for Joshua. He'd been divorced about five years now. His wife Clarissa spent too many nights with television reruns and potluck. An affair came her way and she hopped on it with both feet. Her ticket to adventure and companionship.

No one could really blame her. There were times when Pedro's job caused its own indiscretion within their relationship. She shuddered as the image of Tamara came back to haunt her once again.

"You look cold; may I get you a brandy?" The voice was familiar. Madison turned to find Jack the Ripper standing behind her shoulder.

"Well, I guess that would depend on your explanation for what happened to the last girl, Jack." Madison teased.

"Believe me when I say nothing important."

"I guess I'd better help you change those odds."

He escorted her over to the bar and requested two neat scotches. The bartender complied quickly. Aware he should say something but unable to, Jack stared at Madison's profile as he tried desperately not to make eye contact with her.

As she began to sway to the music, he led her to the dance floor and created a spot perpendicular to Ashley and Joshua. Jack held Penelope close as they became two beings lost to the identities of their characters. A few brows went up as he dipped her and spun her into his arms. Graciously, Madison laughed and let the music ease the longing she felt without Pedro by her side.

The music ended and Ashley let Joshua lead her back to the table where she had been seated with Madison. He went in search of some drinks for them. Ashley searched for Madi.

As her eyes scanned the crowd, she saw Madi approaching with the rest of the group. Her escort vanished into the background. Recognition could not be afforded tonight. He had been human once if she flawed this evening that would be rectified.

"Well, you and Joshua seem to be hitting it off very well."

'This coming from Madame Slut herself is a royal compliment." "What!" Madison replied mockingly.

"I must say if I were the jealous type, I would claw your eyes out! Every man in this place including Joshua can tell you exactly how many centimeters there are between your thigh and your panty line. I do appreciate your respect for the rest of us mere mortals by allowing us to impede on your limelight.

Seriously, you look absolutely stunning in that outfit. I've never been attracted to pussy but if I were, Penelope, you would definitely be on the menu!"

"Did I already tell you that you couldn't drink anymore this evening?" Madison was absolutely shocked by the boldness rearing itself in her friend.

"If I make a real louse of myself maybe Joshua will file a motion to have me pardoned."

"All B.S. aside, are you alright? You seemed a bit down when we got here?" "Let's say I am not the one-night stand kind and leave it at that."

"What!" Madison's mouth hung open to reveal the crowding in her bottom teeth.

"Last night I accepted an invitation. Silly me, I didn't realize it was an invitation for last night only. Anyway, it made me realize I have got to get out more and see what the rest of the world does from 9-5. Do you think Pedro's offer will still be valid on Monday?"

"Well, you're not the only one who's ever had a night in need of a do-over. I think Pedro will be thrilled. He needs a new assistant anyway."

"Why does that sound like a loaded statement? What have you done?" "Let's just say I let the hood side of me pay a visit last night and it got my little Black ass in more trouble than I could cover. Almost. Film at 11:00!"

Roaring with laughter, the two didn't recognize the magnitude of gazes they attracted as two lovely women minding their own business. As a pair of older judges' wives wished for their bodies because their husbands couldn't tear their eyes away, two stark blue eyes grew restless with the closeness yet the distance of desire.

A second round of drinks was sent to the table as a congressman sidetracked Joshua. The margarita and daiquiri were sent with matching napkins to correspond with the intended addressee. Both ladies smiled and toasted the bartender. Searching the room to see whom they owed the obligatory thank-you, Ashley's eyes found him first. She set the drink down mid-gulp and stared at him. It was him all right.

There was a certain unmistakable aura about a man who treated you like a leftover slut and left you in the stillness of the dawn. He didn't wave or motion towards her, he only stared. She couldn't see his steel blue eyes, but she could feel them. Her thighs became moist, and her lips parched through the gloss and residue of the alcohol.

Ashley didn't know how to signal, "fuck me again" across a

crowded room without appearing desperately cheap. She put the glass to her lips and licked the rim while he watched her. Still, he made no move in her direction.

Recognizing Ashley left her behind about two sentences ago, Madison turned to her friend and realized she was more than two sentences behind. Obviously, Mr. Last Night was present and accounted for by the look on Ashley's face.

"Do I need to find another ride home?" "What?"

"It is very apparent Little Bo Peep your sheep isn't lost anymore. Why didn't you tell me Jack the Ripper was the one? I feel so used. To think I was being sucker-punched with that dip on the dance floor."

"What?"

"He was my dance partner a few songs ago when you were with Joshua. I didn't know I was being used. I'll tell you what, since it is obvious you are the newest resident of Sodom & Gomorrah, I'll make an excuse to Joshua if you need to suddenly vanish for the evening. I get the feeling your night has already been solidified."

"I wouldn't leave you here," Ashley said as she unconsciously fumbled in the dark for the keys to her car. Madison smiled at the back of Ashley's head as she went off in search of a two-night-stand.

"Damn her! He muttered as he watched her approaching. Well, then again, she could be useful."

Pedro got off the flight and drove straight to the address he'd been given by his mystery caller. The file folder in the passenger's seat was full of unanswered questions. This person was supposed to unravel the details for him. Right now, all he had was a lot of clues to several disconnected objects with no reason for the state of Connecticut to be involved. An investigator should be handling this. He should be chasing Penelope around the dance floor in a skunk suit!

The stranger made it clear Pedro would find the information quite relevant. A "group of depositions of sorts," he'd called it. He had never heard of any of these people. He wasn't sure if this was Tamara playing a game with him or Karla getting even for the way he handled Madison.

What Pedro did know for sure was that the items and photos in the couriered envelopes were very disturbing or someone had a very twisted sense of humor. The point of contact was a police officer. He didn't feel any sense of ease because of that fact. Some police officers had dirty laundry with stains acid couldn't remove.

He rang the doorbell after he checked the address, 4407 Austrian Drive, yes, this was the place. Unsure what awaited him on the other side of this quest he brought along a weapon at the insistence of Joshua and Brad, the chief of police.

"May I help you?"

"I'm looking for Major Sims."

"I'm sure Major isn't looking for you!"

"Look, Miss, I have flown in from Connecticut and am not in the mood to play which dick is the biggest! Is Major here or not?" Pedro felt himself getting more irritated by the second. He should put a bullet in this woman's head as a civil service.

"Who's looking for Major?"

"My name Pedro St. John. I'm the Assistant District Attorney of Connecticut, is Major home or not?"

"Yeah, come on in."

The first thing that struck Pedro as strange was the full arsenal of weapons within fingers reach all over the house. It looked like a military war zone. There was no feminine decor on the walls or floral arrangements on the tables. It was laid out in almost maze formation.

"What kind of nutcase was this Major Sims? Dear God, hopefully he's not unfortunate enough to be a Vietnam Veteran. Those poor souls never did get the justice they deserved and many of them never recovered from the shock their souls saw."

"So, speak."

"I thought you said Major was home. Look lady, you are really trying my patience. All I want to do is talk to the guy. I've got a folder full of mumbo jumbo and I have no idea what it means or why I'm even involved in this. I at least need to try and find out!"

She walked to the comer and opened the top of the liquor cabinet. Two glasses came out along with a bottle of scotch.

"I said you can talk to Major, and you are. Major is short for Marjorie." A small sigh of exasperation escaped her lips as she sat down and motioned for Pedro to do the same.

"So, why in the hell didn't you say so?"

"I don't owe you any explanation for my behavior. You came to me, remember?" She had quickly annoyed him with the defensive attitude. His concentration was already divided, and this woman was playing games. His patience was getting thin!

"Okay, let's start again. I don't know how you're supposed to help me. I got your name, address, and a plane ticket out here along with this series of envelopes. If you wouldn't mind, would you look at them and tell me if any of this means anything to you? Do that and I'll be on my way, okay?"

"Fair enough."

He spread the contents out before her one envelope at a time. Pedro watched carefully as she had no response to the photos. He realized she was a police officer, but something was off.

He had been a lawyer for a long time. He spent way more hours than he cared to remember watching people be interrogated. This woman was calm, too calm. Hell, he was a man, and images in these photos ignited stronger emotion than this from him.

The first envelope was a woman with a gash the size of Texas in her vaginal wall clearly made by a pair of scissors planted firmly there. She had clearly bled out. The point of the scissors crested where her navel cord should be. Several prescription bottles and an empty fifth of vodka were strewn about. There was a note written on her right breast in tattoo. It read: "The fight was too much."

The medical examiner stated this woman did not die immediately. Due to the depth of the wound and the sensitive area of skin damaged, this was a slow, painful, death. All of the tissue on the scissors aligned with the victim's height trajectory. He also indicated there were other signs of older self-mutilation scars. She did this to herself.

The second photo was of a woman with her neck secured to a bathtub fixture with an extension cord. A blender was plugged in and resting on the bottom of the tub. Electrocution was the apparent cause of death. A bottle of scotch was present. It could have been mistaken for a tragic accident had it not been for the note, scribbled in lipstick on the side of the tub: "Forgot the purpose of the battle."

The crime scene investigators indicated the words were written in a smudge proof lipstick and the water splashed over them. Meaning she wrote the message before getting into the tub. What kind of torment must one be suffering from to carry out that impending level of pain?

The third envelope contained Major's address and badge#. The fourth was blank except the note that read: "Everything becomes clearer with time."

"I told you I can't help you!" 'Can't or won't?" "Either way is still my choice, isn't it?" "I can't help you," was all Major said as she refilled her glass. Something about her defiance was shifting.

"All of this led me to you. You are prepared to fight something or someone to the death, from the looks of this place, so tell me what the hell this means. Why did I get dragged into this mess? You know something because you haven't asked one fucking question!

"What kind of person are you? This isn't for me! I'm still breathing! If these two women were only depressed then, I can close any connection to this. If they were murdered, some sick bastard needs to pay! Look at the goddamn photos again!"

"I don't need to look at the photos. I saw them both firsthand. I buried them."

She got up and poured herself another drink. A frustrated hand was run through what probably would have been beautiful hair if washed and conditioned properly. For the first time, Pedro looked at the woman standing before him drowning from something disguised by scotch. Major stood about 5'9" tall and very fit and even in this partially inebriated state she wasn't a bad looking woman.

Her eyes were green, and her hair was dark auburn. He could tell from her brows it was her natural color. She looked to be somewhere between 35-40 years old. Time might've been her friend had it not been for hard living. He had an overwhelming desire to stroke her hair like a veterinarian would soothe a battered animal. However, the stronger urge was to be humane and "put her down" to end her suffering if she didn't start talking!

"You buried them?" "Yes."

"They were your friends? They committed suicide?" "Yes."

"Then why does someone want me to investigate this?"

"Because he's a sick son-of-a-bitch that likes to weed out what he called the fittest and the fairest of them all!"

"He, who is he?"

"I don't know. None of us did."

"None of you? Begin at the beginning for me please because I'm missing a key piece of what is going on here. Who is us?"

"Any of us that was ever young and vulnerable to madness. Look, I've spent twenty-seven years leaving this behind. Suddenly, within a six-month span of time, I am thrust back into a hell I tried so desperately to forget. I know both people.

The scissor happy one used to be my best friend when I was eight years old. We grew up in a small town where everybody looked out for everybody else's children. It was a straightforward way of life. You never worried about who your children were with because everybody had their eyes out. Until they didn't. It was the perfect atmosphere for resident evil to breed.

Photo number one: Vanessa Thompkins. She and I were shy kids. We were considered misfits even back then with our big pigtails and hand-me-down clothes. The difference between the other poverty-stricken children and us was that they at least had a home life to go home to.

Van and I were more at home on the streets than inside the four walls with no address on the door. You can do a lot of harm to a person if you get deep enough inside their head, Santiago. Some people recover, some never do. Van never did. Neither did Shawna."

Photo number two: Shawna Washington. Did your investigation tell you that Shawna started out without an 'a'? She was a shy boy that also never fit in. He was two grades behind us."

"The autopsy did say that she was transsexual, yes. Not very many people knew that."

"I told you I buried them. As the song says, "I guess some things we bury are just bound to rise again, right." I took money from my pension to see that in death they were afforded a beauty they never got to experience in life. He should die a slow and painful death. Whatever kills him should not relinquish its hold until he experiences the ultimate amount of pain a body can handle and still breathe.

"You keep referring to a "he." Who is he?"

"I don't know his name. I spoke to Van about ten years ago and neither did she. They started a collection to cover the cost of digging her grave. She used to be the most brilliant girl in our class. The idea that she spent her last few years as an addict gets me right here!" She pounded a fist against her heart. She continued.

"That's what predators like him do. They have a radar for us. The ones who are products of dysfunction, mental illness, loners. The quiet, over-developed ones with attitude, potential, and possibility. They disguise themselves as unsuspecting family friends, neighbors, teachers, priests, counselors, or anybody the rest of the world programs us to trust.

They strike and leave a figment of who we could have been behind. We spend the rest of our lives with unanswered questions. Why me? What do I do now? Who knows I'm broken?

Who do I fight to get my soul back? One day the madness approaches like a freight train and they don't make enough legal prescriptions to stop it. Finally, you're left with an addiction to anything else: sex, drugs, alcohol, irrational behavior, self-mutilation, imposter syndrome, etc.

You spend the rest of your life running, unable to commit or trust like you should, like normal people. You wish it could be that simple for you. A normal existence without nightmares or the fear of letting anyone inside. Because if they get too close, they realize you are a hollow, lifeless being fighting every day to be functional.

Poor Shawna was a call girl that nobody wanted to admit knowing in the end. Amazing how the world can eat you up and shit you out without so much as a burp isn't it? An old friend of my stepdad's sent me the announcement. I flew right down and took care of all the arrangements that were left. I had Van exhumed and buried properly in a nice casket with a formal program.

All I could say to her was I tried to kill him. I tried but I only wounded the bastard! May he set up gangrene and become a human maggot on the outside to match the rotten soul on the inside!"

Recognizing he needed to keep her calm and sober for as long as possible, Pedro tried to draw her back out of the world she was quickly catapulting into. He needed some more information from her.

"You said you tried to kill him?"

"Yes, about six months ago, I was coming home from work, and I got the strange sensation that someone was following me. It sent chills down my spine. At first, I thought I was going crazy. Until I started to get these flowers that I couldn't connect to anyone.

Anyway, one night I got out of my car and starting walking across my yard, when someone grabbed me from behind. We struggled, I broke free, got to the service weapon strapped to my ankle, and fired a few rounds. We did a grid search. No body was found but there were some blood droplets. Our neighborhood is familiar with gun shots, so the DNA match was inclusive. I hit him somewhere, but I don't know where."

"And you think it was the man from your childhood?"

"Yes. He whispered it had been twenty-eight years since he'd seen my red hair up close and personal."

Suddenly, the obvious was gagging him. Pedro looked at Major very strangely for a moment. Her resemblance to Madison was eerie both physically and the way she sat staring through him. She could have been Madison's sister. "Do you have copies of the others' obituaries?"

"Yes, in that box, why?" He swallowed deeply because fear was overtaking him at avalanche speed. Pedro examined the "before" pictures of the victims and looked at Major. They all had the same natural hair color, approximate height, and build. He was looking at what could have been a family tree.

"Where did you say you were from, Major?" "The 49th precinct."

"No, where is your original hometown?" "Humphrey, Alabama, why?"

"Oh shit, I've been such a fucking idiot!" "What's wrong?"

"My wife is from Humphrey, Alabama!" "Your wife?"

"Yes, my wife is Madison Santiago, her maiden name is St. John."

Major looked at him and said, "The favorite." Dude if you are married to "the favorite" you need to catch the first thing smoking! I don't know what the son-of-a-bitch has planned, but if you are here, that means he is there! Let me see if I can get you a red eye back home.

The flight back was torturous for Pedro as he struggled to remember the last time he saw Madison's face. It was cloudy and that made him feel more desperate. She was a sensual woman. Everything about her from the casual elegance to that tomboyish smile made you want to take care of her. She could be aggressive, but she had taken care of herself a long time. People who've seen a lot don't surrender control easily.

He recalled the night they made love years after being apart. No matter how close he held her that night it wasn't close enough. She loved him. Surely, all those years of mass weren't for naught! Dear God do not take her from me now.

His mind drifted to Major. She had that same ability to look through you. It had always disturbed him about Madi because it was like she became entranced by something and suddenly you didn't exist. Now, he understood it was a defense tactic but also a symptom. A way to block the noise of other people's lives when events got too unbearable to process.

What did Major say about receiving some flowers? Madison received those gaudy carnations with roses as well. Whoever this bastard was, he had calculated the risk and meticulously executed his plan. "He knew he would have to kill me to get to her!"

He tried to construct a list of possible suspects. Could it be the new intern? No, he wasn't old enough to know these people when they were younger. Could it be Joshua? He'd been eager to get him to pursue and close this. Hell, Santiago, middle-aged white male meant it could be 25% of the damn country!

Madison knew something only she didn't know it. Had she witnessed something that drew him to her? Major made it sound like this man was stalking them for a reason. The reason. He ran out of her house so quickly when she told him her hometown, he didn't ask her the reason! Now, his phone was hostage in airplane mode.

Dammit! His imagination was crafting all sorts of scenarios, and he was afraid of them all. If none of them could identify him… What was it Major said, "Once you get inside someone's head…" Whatever "it" was, all of them were terrified of it.

Use your training, Santiago! Follow the evidence. What do you know?

Each of them referenced fighting. God knows Major was ready for WWIII! All of them have/had an unhealthy relationship with alcohol or drugs. The same severe mood swings that sometimes overtook Madison were a commonality. All were young at the time of the incident. All of them seem to have trouble maintaining relationships in their adult lives. None of them can identify him.

What had Major said, "one had been married four times." Major was emotionally invested in her alcohol collection. People self-medicate to suppress pain. He knew that personally. They lost contact and built different lifestyles. What drove the two of them to suicide?

Again, his mind went back to Major's comment, "they have more of a home on the streets than inside those walls with no address..."

Madison told him once, "Sometimes the only thing standing between a child and a tragic mistake is the love of a parent. Knowing someone loves you beyond compromise is sometimes the only thing in the world you can give a child. Many of us came home only because of that. "

He never pressed her to explain what that meant. Now, he felt like an idiot. The answer could save her life. She hadn't elaborated. Instead, she turned to another topic and declared the subject closed.

Madison had an insurmountable will. She was not easily intimidated. She always joked once you've had a date with a hoe and "made a day," the world is not that scary. Being the only woman or minority in a space was not a weakness to her. It was an obligation to show up and diversify the room by letting others know they had postponed their exposure to brilliance. If she walked away, she made it noticeably clear it was her decision.

She always left someone aching for more. Men loved her because she could bullshit with the best of them. Women loved her because she was the friend always willing to sacrifice herself for their happiness. He thought nothing of it when she said someone had been sending her flowers. He assumed it was appreciation for an act of martyrdom she didn't remember.

Now, he realized it was the calling card for a disturbed man she never mentioned. But who was he? Whoever he was it apparent she was the primary object of this game. Major called Madison "the favorite." What did it mean? Damn it, why wasn't hundreds of miles per hour fast enough!

He still isn't answering. Madison tried to call Pedro but got his voicemail. She left him a sultry message and hoped voicemail meant he was in flight and on his way home. She pulled off her costume and turned on the shower. When he surprised her in the middle of the night, she wanted to be wearing his favorite fragrance and waiting on his side of the bed.

Her mind traveled back to the beginning. This time would be the forever they always wanted. She thought of the night he came over with Ashley's recipe for success. The heat in her body found an outlet as she touched herself and found the vortex of her womanhood to be almost as moist now as it was then. He was a very "endowed" man with full control over his ability to execute his prowess.

Whenever Pedro looked into her eyes and touched the sides of her face before a kiss, there was no need for him to penetrate her. She reeked of an orgasm. He always said how much it aroused him to inhale her scent. A shiver ran down her spine at the thought of his tongue. It always found her in the most inviting positions and took full advantage of her generosity.

Her fingers glided themselves into the make-believe position of a lover. She stood touching her aroused breasts and remembered how he couldn't get enough of them when she was pregnant with Grayson. He thought they were indescribably erotic. The fuller they became, the mere touch of them on his skin was orgasmic for him. A smile crossed her lips.

She thought of the love she shared with the man who would once again legally be her husband. All she could do was part her legs and allow her imaginary Pedro to seduce her beyond words. She sighed so loudly she forgot he wasn't present.

This is how he would touch her, she thought, as it gave new meaning to the term "handshake." Madison fell against the wall of the shower as she climaxed. "Hurry home, sweetie," she whispered as she cleansed herself with the body wash and towel hanging nearby.

Ashley lay silently weeping as her life flashed before her. She had no idea what he injected into her, but she assumed it was like a date-rape drug. He said she would need to deliver a message to Pedro so whatever it was wouldn't kill her immediately.

How had she been so stupid? How had she failed to see he was an animal? Because you weren't looking for a wolf to be disguised in expensive wool! The way he fucked her left no room for any other conclusion. Was she so desperate for attention any male would do?

Losing Jesse devastated her. She tried to bury herself inside the walls of Satyre's and pretend it didn't hurt. He said she had too many restrictions and hang-ups sexually to satisfy him any longer. She never realized anal sex was now the norm in sexual encounters. Her ass was one-directional, and if that was the deciding factor in loving her, she guessed he really didn't.

When he desired to release in her hair, she let him; blindfolding her wasn't even an issue. She even agreed to let him watch while she fucked one of his friends. But she drew the line on having bananas, penises, or any other foreign objects lodged up her ass simply for his enjoyment. Her answer might have turned him off, but his friend still called her!

Obviously, strait-laced, sixty-nine was still good enough for some men in the world! Jesse moved on to Miss FreakNeak without any further ado. Well, she hoped every panty she owned had a rubber seat for leak protection and thick enough to capture an uncontrolled attack of the shits!

She was lying here with her body responding to the slow-burning sensation the chemical inside her caused. She hoped for a mild tingle of some sort to let her know she would not be immobile for life. Blinking her responses to questions could take quite a toll on one's sanity. Whatever he gave her drastically lowered her body temperature.

He was an animal! Yet, she discovered something primal about herself being with him. This man, without a name, slammed her into the wall and tore off her underwear with no regard for gentleness.

Ironically, she had the strongest orgasm she could ever recall. He bit at her breasts until she felt them ooze with blood. The whole ordeal was so erotic she collapsed in his arms.

The way he pulled her hair when she straddled him made her ache inside. He punished her body for a sin she couldn't remember committing but would love to do it again if it meant he wouldn't stop. As he drove into her, she cried out like a newly restored virgin. The more she laughed and cried, the more excited he became.

There was a welt on her ass from the bite he applied to it. Yes, he was an animal, so that made her what? He split her ass with his penis. She screamed and succumbed to the sensation. It didn't require explanations of why it should happen, or the guilt trip Jesse tried to induce her with. It had been the climactic end to a night of record-breaking orgasms and abandonment.

The whole time he was in pursuit of Madison. She had always been his objective. Was he an old lover? What the hell kind of puss did Madison have? All the men in her life never wanted to stay gone, so it had to be fire! What would make her leave him if he ravished her the same way? It was obvious his love for her was insatiable to go to these lengths to be with her.

Snap out of it, Ashley! You could be dying. The last thing on your mind should not be how aroused you were while an animal ravished your body! Greet St. Peter smelling like fish and explain why you should get into the Pearly Gates! And oh, by the way, I liked it.

Madison came out of the shower and froze. There were carnations and roses on her bed. The peignoir from her closet for her remarriage night with Pedro lay beside them. She raced to the phone; it was dead. She grabbed her cell phone from the bathroom vanity and locked the door. She dialed the first number who would not waste time with questions.

"Roz!" she whispered. "Yeah?"

"There is someone in my house. My phone lines are dead! This is from my cell! He's here ...!"

"Madi! Madi!" The phone went dead. Roz scrambled to an upright position.

Fully awake and heart pumping, Roz felt the blood in her veins run cold. She dialed 9-1-1 as she frantically grabbed her keys off the nightstand table.

"Hello, 9-1-1 operator."

"Send a car to 13951 Cherokee Lane. There's an intruder, and the phone lines have been cut. She called from her cell phone! Hurry!"

"Ma'am, calm down."

"Bitch, you calm down! I told you she is in danger! If something happens to her while you are exercising your right to be a stupid bitch I promise you, you will regret it! Play the recording back after you send the police to her now!

Roz threw the phone down and ran out of the house. The driveway never seemed this long before! Dammit Madi! Why do you have to live so far across town? Her mind was racing. She didn't even notice she was running red lights and stop signs. People were veering off the road and yelling obscenities at her. She heard nothing. All she could think of was Madison and if she got to her too late.

Roz remembered her jheri curl when they worked on a summer school program together. Madison teased her about wearing her newly extended hair "up or down." The laughter had been contagious. The guys with them enjoyed the female companionship. Although the summer was hot, the flirtations of Madison kept everyone entertained, including the passersby.

Every conceivable emotion known to human existence had been shared between the two of them. She recalled when her own mother was diagnosed with breast cancer. Madison still behaved as though the end wasn't near. She came to the house, sat around, and got yelled at as normal.

Madi loved her mother's cabbage and cornbread, so she still put in her request for after-Sunday supper as usual. Her mother obliged as strength permitted. She helped create the spoiled brat that was Madison. Madi was one of her children, too, and it kept some balance in the world as it was falling apart.

When the end finally came, Madison fell apart with everyone else. She also helped Roz realize she could still pursue her dreams and quietly kept the fact she was expecting her first child. Roz smiled. Madi never asked when she reconnected with the "old lover."

She didn't think it was any of her business. Madison set about making sure Roz stayed current on prenatal nutrition, vitamins, and doctor's appointments at the clinic. Meanwhile, Madison covered taking notes in class and turning in assignments on her designated sick days.

Roz was twenty-one when Charlotte was born. In between college romances, Madison took the role of overseer and paced with her when the labor pains came. She marched right up and down the dormitory halls with her as she made her trips to the bathroom.

When the first contractions hit, they loaded up the old Ford Grenada and headed for the hospital. The lack of brakes did not detour Madison from getting them there on the hospital curb in one piece. She told Roz to hold on. Madison hit the curb and drove up on the grass in front of the emergency room door!

Roz thought she was nuts between contractions! Madison flung the car door open and got her checked in. She sat all night and afternoon until Charlotte was born. Madison peeked at Roz, checked to make sure the baby had all vital parts, and went back to the dormitory and slept for 16 hours!

Roz was the first-person Madison called when her own mother

passed away. It was the second most painful experience of her life. They held each other to the truth about life. They were each other's matrons of honor.

Honestly, she never thought about her world without Madison. Sure, they talked about one dying and leaving the other, but in fairness, it had been in jest. However, with reality staring Roz in the face, it was hard to even comprehend. How could she possibly make it through the rest of her life without Madison's blunt honesty and outrageous sense of humor? Surely, the God she had sacrificed all those Sunday-go-to-meetings for would not be this cruel!

"Ms. St. John? Ms. St. John, are you all right? I got a 9-1-1 call from Judge Crenshaw you had an intruder."

Madison rushed to the stairs and saw a uniformed police officer standing on the stairwell. "Yes, I'm okay. I saw the front door ajar, and I heard you, and I thought... Oh, never mind. Someone was in my house. I have these flowers and these candles lit everywhere.

Your phone lines are cut as well. Are you sure someone isn't surprising you?"

"If they are, they have a really twisted sense of humor. If you want someone's affection, don't break into their home uninvited!"

"Come with me while I check out the rest of the house." "Don't worry, I am right behind you."

The officer walked from room to room upstairs and downstairs and checked the back door. It was locked and the windows were intact.

'Well, there's no one here but you and me now. The squad will be arriving shortly. I'll go radio in you are unharmed. Aren't you the Assistant District Attorney's ex-wife?" "Yes, yes, I am."

"Well, I'm sure he'll be happy to hear you're okay."

"He's out of town right now, but hopefully, he'll be home tonight."

"He lives here, too?"

"Yes, we've reconciled."

"That's good to know. I wouldn't want to accidentally shoot anyone by mistake. Death is one of those things you can't undo, you know?"

A chill went down Madison's spine at the thought. She turned to go upstairs because she realized she was very exposed in her current attire. The fact that the officer was older with a slight limp didn't justify her lack of clothing. Others would be arriving soon.

Her foot grazed the second stair, when she felt stinging in her shoulder. All her limbs suddenly became limp. Instead of falling straight down, she landed in the arms of the officer. "If we hurry, they'll be enough time to clear the air before those self-righteous sons-of-bitches show up!"

"Why," was the only word Madison could get out as her vocal cords became paralyzed.

"Soon, sweetheart, I'll explain everything, and we'll be together again. Right now, lie here and let me take care of everything. Roz will be here soon. I will ease her suspicions. She will be the most persistent." Her mind was racing as she lay where she was placed.

"He called her Roz. Only people who were in my intimate circle know I call her that. How did he know she was on her way? Wait, he said my phone lines were cut! He was in the house when I called Roz.

The front door being ajar was a decoy to send me upstairs! He told me about the candies being lit. The lights were on in my bedroom, so there was no glow. What is he doing with my blood?

What did he inject me with?? Why can't I move? How did he know this was done to the house? Why do I suddenly feel like a white woman in high heels running in a horror flick?

Madison heard the officer explain the door was open and her keys were still in the lock. He said a piece of her clothing was torn on the bush outside. It looked to have fresh blood on it. He found a shoe with scuff marks near the garage. The door was open, and the car was missing.

A few droplets of something lay near a genuinely nice wedding ring. He said he called her name but got no response. He did a perimeter sweep inside the house, but it looked undisturbed.

"He's lying! Her mind was screaming! I'm here! Help me, dear God, help me!"

She heard a car screech in the driveway. She heard Roz scream. The detective took her inside and had her look over everything.

"These goddamn pink ass flowers! Find out who in the hell is sending her these damn flowers. Once you find him bring the son-of-a-bitch to me!"

"Judge Crenshaw, I know you're upset, but please, I need you to try to calm down and work with me here."

"Detective, do you have anyone in your life who would die for you without a second thought?"

"Well, I would like to think my wife would."

"When you have a more definitive answer, get back to me, and I'll calm down. Until then, this woman you're looking for has changed diapers and exchanged more bad relationships with me than Tyson has slaughtered chickens. Do your part and bring me the bastard responsible. I'll do my part to save the taxpayers some money on his execution!"

Although nothing on her body worked, Madison smiled in her heart as she realized she and Roz had been good friends. She tried to be a decent friend to those in her life. Roz had tolerated her mood swings, complaints, indifference, and overall bitchiness longer than anyone. She still answered the phone when Madison called, day or night.

Roz held on to her during the storms in her life. She never asked why; she had just done it. When Madison's behavior landed her in predicaments that should have garnered an "I-told-you-so," Roz let her vent. Her philosophy on Madison's behavior was simple. When Mad was ready to talk about it, she would.

In her heart, Madison always knew that silently, Roz waited for the phone to ring. Roz knew one night she would need to identify Madison in the morgue. Even then, she would not judge the outlandish behavior that landed her there. She would make sure the world knew Madison was her friend and that was all they needed to know. She hoped the devastation was not so severe the casket couldn't be open.

Roz would mourn for the lost soul inside Madison, who never quite figured out how to be happy. She had been her rock on more occasions than she could recall. When alcohol got the better of her, Roz told the necessary lies to keep her respectable.

Alcohol deserved a special place in Madison's life too. It was a mind-eraser, a lover on a rainy night. Most of all, it had been permission, rejection, and a bandage on an amputated space in her soul. It answered the door when no one else was home, even Roz. It always amazed Madison no matter where you are in life, a liquor store is only a few blocks away. Her misery used to keep her company with Crown Royal and gin.

When Helen was dying, Pedro missed the nights she passed out on the floor. Brock missed the times she drowned the images of him touching JoAnne with Jose' Gold. When she buried her biological mother, she was drunk for about a week. Her professors thought she was grieving. She was, but it was also a perfect excuse for no one to question.

Alcohol was by her side when the distinction of valedictorian passed her by in high school. It sat by her when her first lover decided Christmas break was too long apart and found someone else.

She was a functional alcoholic. That's why she understood Dominic so well. She had pieced together a few more controlled drinking days than he had when they met. However, one difficult day can make everyone who struggles with addiction a backslider.

The length of sobriety does not matter. The substance of choice does not matter. Madison always smiled when she heard people refer to themselves as former addicts. They were still in the social judgement denial phase. One who has ever struggled knows there is no such thing as "former."

She thought if she could save Dominic, maybe she could look herself in the eyes and see the respectable person everyone else thought she was. She'd been wrong even with the love of a good man. She had the lifestyle she dreamt of through cotton stalks and summer heat but, there was still an empty inside.

The root was still under investigation. There is always a root cause. The trick is to be brave enough to uncover it then work it through. No one is born self-destructive.

Silently she thanked Roz for standing by her through the rough spots. Maybe one day, when Roz was visiting her grave, God would allow Madison to stop by and say so. Madison knew by the lack of feeling in her body this was not going to end well.

Whoever this man was, he had already fooled everyone on Connecticut's finest into believing he was one of them. That meant he had a plan and would not be deterred. She said a prayer for the soul she knew was supposed to be in the uniform he wore.

The killing obviously did not generate an emotional response from this man. There was something familiar in the way he addressed her. The limp was forcing her backwards, but fear was distorting her focus.

"Dear God, if he must take my life, so be it, but spare my child, my husband, and my friends. I am not Jesus, but please let my blood be enough. They still have the possibility of full lives. I accept mine has been detoured by an evil I stumbled across somewhere in this journey. While innocence can still be found, allow them the lives they should have. They will all make sure my child knows I loved her."

Her cell phone rang in the distance. She had it in her hand when he attacked her. "Hello?" Roz answered it.

"Roz? Where is Madi?"

"Oh, Pedro, she's gone! The police found blood on her costume outside. Her keys were in the door. Someone who sounded like Ashley was with her at the ball. No one knows where she is either.

Everybody saw Madison leave with Joshua, but he's not answering. Her wedding ring was found in the garage with blood on it. Her car is missing."

Roz waited for the fear she knew was coming from Pedro. He was completely silent. Roz knew he was still processing what she said. "Meet me at the restaurant. I told my mother to take Gray to my office and wait for me. I'm leaving the airport now. I will find Joshua and meet you there."

" What are you not telling me?"

"Meet me at Satyre's Roz. I'll explain there." The phone went dead. "Pedro! Dammit, I'm so sick of testosterone today!"

One of the detectives taking fingerprints looked at Roz as she threw the cell phone across the kitchen floor. "I know you have some work to do, and it does not involve being in my face! Find her!"

Roz ran to her car and drove like a New York cab driver to Satyre's. Pedro drove up and Joshua was right behind him.

"What in the hell is going on?"

"Why did you summon me over here?" "Where is Madison, Joshua?"

"At home."

"No, Mr. District Attorney, the evidence says Madi never made it inside the house."

"That's ridiculous! I dropped her off at home. I tried to walk her to the door, but she said it wasn't necessary. I asked her to let me know she was okay inside. She flickered her lights and waved at me.

Before she got out of the car, she asked me to give Ashley her keys back. I still have them because I couldn't find Ashley when I went back to the ball. Why in the hell are you saying Madi never made it home?"

"They found blood in the driveway and inside the garage on her wedding ring. Her car is missing. An all-points bulletin has been issued for it. There were these disgusting pink carnations on her kitchen counter."

"She mentioned something about some sick bastard who keeps sending them to her. Everyone knows Madi hates pink."

"Yeah, everyone but him."

"What him? Can somebody tell me what the fuck is going on? I have known her longer than both of you put together, and I'm getting really pissed off here. If there is something about those goddamn flowers, then somebody better fucking tell me right now!"

"Come inside, Roz. There's something I need to show you, but first, I need to check on my mother and Grayson."

"He really is scared," Roz thought, "he only calls their daughter Grayson when he is upset."

"Madre? Madre?" Pedro ran to the office door and found his mother pacing inside when he unlocked it.

249

"Pedro, what is going on? Is everything all right?" "How is Grayson?"

"She's been asleep for a while. I told her we were having an adventure. What's wrong?"

"Come with me for a moment, Madre." Pedro took his mother out into the hallway and told her Madison was missing. He omitted the part about the blood but told her about the stalking and her car was missing.

"Oh, Dear Mary, Mother of Jesus. Do you know by whom?" "No."

"Well, your child will not leave my sight." Pedro realized his mother had a sawed-off shotgun in her hand. "Madre?" He looked at her in disbelief.

"Do you think we were allowed to waltz out of Fidel's Cuba with our freedom, Miguel? Someone has one of my children, there are no rules. Find Grayson's mother while I talk to ours!"

Pedro rushed back to Satyre's and laid out the envelopes for Roz and Joshua. He explained everything he knew about the pictures. He detailed his conversation with Major. Roz sat back in her chair.

"I remember these girls growing up, but Madi wasn't friends with any of them. Only two of them were friends with each other. One was a loner. This doesn't make any sense, Pedro."

"Think Roz, something has to connect these people. Major referred to Madison as the "favorite." She said something about once someone gets inside your head. What could she have meant?"

"All of them had severe mood swings like Madi has. They were all from homes without fathers. There were rumors of promiscuity, but hell, we were teenagers in a small town. Sex with one guy could give you that reputation. Other than that, Madison didn't have anything in common with him or the other two women!"

"Do you think she's?" Joshua started, and Pedro gave him a glance that dared him to finish his question. Roz was not so kind.

"Look, if you are not on our side, then get up and walk away now! I'm not thoroughly convinced you're trustworthy anyway. Are your fingerprints on file at the station? The only reason I have entertained you this far is your eyes didn't slant down and to the left when you recanted your last contact with Madi. You could have been perfecting the lie for all I know!

She is not dead. I would feel it if she were. She wouldn't leave this world without my soul knowing it! She's in trouble, but she is still breathing!" Roz got up and went to check on Grayson. She couldn't stomach Joshua's reality any longer.

"You say she divorced her husband?" "Yes."

"Has anyone seen him since?" Pedro glanced at Joshua side-eye.

Across town, a different discussion was taking place. "Okay, Ashley, you need to figure out if you can move."

Slowly, she felt a tingle return to her legs. There was an incredible throbbing in her ears, but she could feel them. It had been nearly five hours since she was injected, but she was still alive. Her arms and muscles hurt like hell, but that was a good thing under the circumstances.

She wiggled her toes, and they obeyed slightly. Recalling the fetal position, she tried to roll over on her side. The daggers in her head were hitting their target with precision. She was dizzy and nearly vomited as she held onto the wall and tried to sit up. The motion took the wind out of her.

"Come on, Ashley Suzanne, no guts, no glory! "My fat ass has to lose some weight if I survive this ordeal!" Although she couldn't stand, she could slither. She did her best rattlesnake imitation to reach her purse. It felt like she had moved 18 tons of sand when she finally got to it.

The voodoo drums began in her head. She closed her eyes. She would have to dial by touch. Thank God for speed dial programming. She found the #2 and pressed it.

"Hello?"

"Pedro, this is Ash... Help me..." "Ashley, where are you?"

"Ball, hallway... stairs from the dance floor."

"Ashley! Ashley! Get the police to City Hall now! Ashley is in the stairwell off the ballroom dance floor! Pedro yelled as he slammed the cell phone shut. "Roz! We've located Ashley!"

"Does she know where Madi is?

"We don't know; we're going over there now."

"I'll stay here with your mother and Gray. Call when you know anything!"

"Okay!" Pedro and Joshua dashed out the door.

Pawn found. Now, you bastard, where is the Queen? Roz thought.

Roz kept thinking they missed something at that house, but what? She told Marisol she was taking a few officers and a crime scene investigator back over there. She had a spare set of keys so anything they found could immediately be collected as evidence. No chain of custody technicality was going to keep this bastard off death row!

"Be careful. The little one and I are not going down without a fight." Roz smiled. You want to see a bake sale mother become a vigilante on your ass, fuck with her kids!

The last officer finally left the house. No one knew to search for a second set of car keys. He used them to move her car. His plan had gone brilliantly. They considered themselves to be the finest profilers of the criminal mind. They probably were except, when they came up against a real criminal!

Amazing how the color of blue creates an invisible shield at all the right times. His badge had a serial number and the name of some pathetic individual who thought he could make a difference. The criminal element was like the poor; they would be among us always.

The caliber of intelligence possessed by the accused was an entirely different story. He suffered every hell imaginable to man, but none compared to seeing Madison with someone else. The struggle was worth it. He slipped back into the house through the back door.

He knew the layout by heart. Lighting was unnecessary. While she shopped and dined with Roz, he traced her house. The night she spent at Santiago's, he worked. It all came to fruition. The island in her kitchen was an expansive design. The best marble was used to store the finest bakeware.

Her pots and pans read like a culinary Who's Who. She probably spent thousands of dollars on these items to prepare food for herself and her little one. She was highly organized in a disorderly way. It was another trait he admired. The small holes in the corkboard were ideal for air. They also didn't draw attention to the non-culinary eye.

He placed her flowers on the other side of the room. No one would be cooking while investigating her disappearance. She was immobilized but hidden in plain sight. He carried her upstairs as she stared at him in dazed bewilderment.

They should have found her car near the river by now. It would be hours before they finished processing it, dusted it for fingerprints, and tried to determine if he was part of a car detail team or someone else. There would be a lockdown on all viable transportation for the next 5-6 hours while the city's finest searched for the abducted ADA's wife. Last seen at a judicial ball! The irony.

They would be alone and then disappear before sunrise. They would be on a luxurious cruise to South America as husband and wife by the time all the pieces were linked.

The freshly acquired passports he'd purchased would cement their new identities. All he needed to do now was make her blend in with the average woman of color. He was overcome by emotion as his eyes gazed upon her. Nothing in this world had ever moved him the way she did. He trembled as he laid her on top of the sheets. Her eyes asked questions. He began to answer her.

"Ahh, but you do know me. Look at me, Madison. Look at me closely. We've been together for a long time. You've known me since you were a child way back in Humphrey. I've had so many flowers delivered to you this past week I should try my hand at horticulture. Do you think you'd like that?

The color of them would all be pink. I love you in pink, Madison. Have you ever wondered why you detest the color so much? It goes deeper than a palette, doesn't it? Could it be something more psychological? Think about it."

Madison closed her eyes. He grabbed her hair and forced her to look at him. "Think! Look into my eyes the way you do Santiago when he's inside you!"

Her mind drew a complete blank. Partially out of fear and partially from the throbbing in her head. She could not place this man.

She knew each of her lovers. He hadn't been one. Was he the father of one of her friends? Her mind was racing through the pain. She felt dizzy. Her eyes must have conveyed her confusion. He moved closer. His voice finally registered in her head.

"Party," was all she could whisper.

"Yes, I held you in my arms as Jack the Ripper this evening. You were stunning. I wanted to ravish you right there, but I think intimacy should be a private act between a man and a woman.

I am disappointed you don't remember our conversation on the beach a few nights ago. The night when Santiago proved once again how unworthy he is to be your lover." Tears slipped from her eyes as she watched him. Her mind's eye retraced that night. She acknowledged him.

That explained why he was familiar to her at the ball. Now, some of the blanks were beginning to come together. He was in the Jaguar across the street visiting her neighbor when she received the first set of pink roses after lunch with Roz. Still, the question of why formulated in her eyes. As if he could tell she was struggling to connect all the dots. He leaned down close to her ear and whispered.

"I live down the street today. I don't know where I'll be tomorrow, but I'll always remember you. If you tell anyone, I'll be back for you. You kept your promise, but I couldn't keep mine. I had to be with you again. "

Sheer terror crossed Madison's face. She wanted to turn her head, but it wouldn't move. All she could do was stare at him as he caressed her hair with his hands. Those eyes. If only she could choke on her own vomit to end this torture. Her mind recoiled so quickly she closed her eyes to the pain.

It was a dark and stormy night. She was in Humphrey, Alabama. She was seven years old. That was twenty-eight years ago. Hence, the alternating twenty-eight carnations and seven roses bouquet. She and her babysitter were home.

Her mother worked nights as a nurse's aide forty-five minutes away. It was a small town. Everybody looked out for everybody else's children, except the night they didn't.

Madison was asleep in her room when the lightning flashed. She was awakened by someone touching her. She thought she was dreaming until she tried to turn over. A large hand clasped over her mouth and restrained her movements. Her eyes widened as she fought to no avail. A stranger touched her.

He ripped her panties and the gown off her childish body. Now she recalled the gown as pink with alternating carnation and rose patterns. She moved her head as he entered her. He put a knife to her throat and threatened to slit her throat if she moved. Quietly, she pleaded with him.

"I'm only seven years old. You're hurting me."

He stared at her with those eyes. Suddenly, it was over as quickly as it began. He left her lying there with blood-stained sheets, ripped underwear, and unrecoverable shame. He rose quickly and pulled up his pants and made an ominous threat.

"I live down the street today. I don't know where I'll be tomorrow, but I'll always remember you. If you tell anyone, I'll be back for you."

She lay there and drifted into her first encounter with depression. Later, she would learn it was sometimes accompanied by severe and violent mood swings. It was often the author of many suicidal thoughts. It could be associated with a fear of commitment and the inability to manage simple things in life. Failure or disappointment triggered an unhinged need to prove worth.

Trivial things could create a downward spiral that lasted for weeks. Some people suffer from obsessive-compulsive behaviors. Others hid their pain through promiscuity. Madison had chosen the latter mixed with alcohol.

Depressive personalities feel things deeper than other people. Self-destructive tendencies can be exacerbated when depression is compounded by post-traumatic stress or repressed memories. The fears of a self-destructive personality type are different from other people. Things that scare others shitless don't flinch a destructive if they have been provoked.

She and others like her called it "living on the edge". Science called it a disorder. Whatever the politically correct term was, for the past twenty-eight years it had created her personal hell. Sometimes after an emotionally challenging event she spiraled out of control.

Alcohol calmed her but also fueled her irrational and indulgent behavior. She used sex as a weapon instead of cowering from it as many sexual assault victims do. She withheld it for self-preservation and showered it on lovers for the exact same reasons.

Rejection was something she didn't manage well. Therefore, the more she thought she was losing, the more obsessive she became with something or someone. It wasn't even out of desire to have it. It was more to prove she was good enough to deserve it.

Intentionally, she sought out older men and unavailable lovers. It was about the chase and conquer, not the prize. Once they gave in, she discarded them like old tampons. She had a tough time connecting with anything in the realm of love.

She lived this cycle of boredom her whole life. The older she became, the more jobs she changed on a whim. On the flip side, the more reclusive she became as well.

There were days when she could not even force herself to go outside. It didn't bother her in the least. She spent a great deal of time in the darkness. The latest employee assistance plan (EAP) labeled it social anxiety mixed with severe introversion. Madison was honest with herself about it. Being around strangers and unfamiliar situations where she wasn't in control made her cringe.

People thought she had a brilliant mind. Lifelong learning gave her an outlet for her anxiety. It kept her from her greatest desire most days. She didn't want anything in life as badly as she wanted to break down. If she knew she would recover she would have surrendered to the madness years ago.

People in her life loved her fiercely. She always protected them from the knowledge she was one appointment from complete darkness. She kept breaking it because of the required commitment. For years, she had done battle with God, too. They argued violently.

She spent many nights in Socratic questioning sessions with Him. It was not fair because He chose not to answer and there wasn't anything she could do about it! She stayed awake for days demanding answers that never came. He would not honor her simplest plea to die and end her torture. What kind of God allows the mental anguish of a poisoned mind?

The Scripture, "God never puts more on you than you can bear.," always came to her mind in her youth. Appropriately so when the knife blade, bottle of pills, or drive off a bridge found themselves at hand. She always considered her life as God's personal punishment for angels out of control.

She was staring into the eyes of the beast. He had to have the mark. He left her a living suicide twenty-eight years ago. She had questions and she could not even speak. How fucking awesome is this shit!

"What does one have for breakfast when they decide to ruin a child's life?"

He answered the one that haunted her most, "Was he dead or alive? Up next… Did he know he destroyed someone's perception of passion? Did he care? Did he know she could not differentiate between love and obsession? Did he even know her name back then?

Had he watched her from afar on her way to and from school? Did he have a checklist of neighborhood kids and it had simply been her turn? Did it excite him to know he was her first? No matter who loved her since, he was still a novelty.

Was this his sick way of preserving himself to always be in the recesses of someone's thoughts? Was he another sick bastard who should have been sacrificed to abortion? Was he violated as a child?

Did he know there was no honor in what he had done then or now? Did he not understand self-esteem was a challenging thing to come by? Did he know her mind haunted her at all the wrong times in her life? Did he know she lived in this constant capsule of fear and shame?

Did he know he nearly destroyed the best relationship in her life?

Pedro thought it was her father's inability to commit that caused her erratic behavior. That was only partly true. This animal affected her far worse. The eating binges, the weight gain, the diet obsessions, the cycle was endless. It was not about appearance after a while. It was an attempt to control something in her life that belonged to her.

Was he aware every day for years she had to choose between insanity and depression? She had finally crossed the thin line back into sanity and now he was back! Did he really believe what he had done to her was love? Did he really think she would love him the way she loved Pedro? Maybe she was the delusional one because she was attempting to analyze the mind of a psychopath.

On some level of Christianity, she knew she should pray for him. Forgiveness was too much of a stretch. She was okay with that mark being permanently stained on her Book of Life.

She hated him with every fiber in her toenails! She had never really experienced the innocent things in life as most young girls did. All of those things had a stain of contempt for the way life really was and not how adults portrayed it. She learned early, observe, and reveal as little as possible. That is how you survive.

He was the cause of her trauma when she was eleven years old and got her period. Madison went to school in silence that day with half a roll of tissue in her panties. She thought this was her "issue of blood" for the next twelve years as atonement for the horrific secret he made her keep.

It was only after another girl started her "issue" the same day she realized it was called a menstrual cycle. The girl's mom brought pads and shared them as she explained this was normal physiology for girls their age.

She hated him for the years he stole from her! She hated him for ruining her chance at a normal childhood and adult life! She hated him for the fear he used to corrupt the simple pleasures of life. The first kiss, first date, and first sexual experience were all reminders that intimacy between a man and a woman can go horribly wrong if someone didn't take control. It wasn't until Pedro that she learned sex did not have to be used as a weapon.

There were nights she crawled into bed with Grayson because her mind would not rest and chills gnawed at her spine. As Grayson neared seven, she often sat at the foot of her bed. She held a knife in one hand and a drink in the other. Her thought was, "if he comes for you, I will slit his throat and send him straight back to hell!"

Roz told her about a child who was molested by a cousin. She was five years old. Madison had been physically ill for days. It disturbed her to the point of insomnia. At least the child knew who battered her life.

There was a certain type of relief associated with the horror of knowing. Every man of a certain age is not suspect. You can sort out physical characteristics to eliminate certain people. Those who know their abusers don't watch every action of the babysitter's brother, priest, cousin, teacher, storeowner, dentist, etc. If there is anything to help you cling to sanity it is the clarity in knowing.

Anonymity did not afford you a penthouse view of hell. Anonymous assailants made their victims view hell from bowel-level. Madison had gone through life hoping never to find herself here, reliving this smell, this touch, this gleam in his eyes.

Maybe in some sick recess of her mind she'd been looking for him all these years. In some twisted crevice maybe, she wanted this encounter as an adult to slaughter this beast in the bed he made for them both. It would have been so appropriate. If she could fucking move!

She wasn't afraid anymore. He would kill her. She found comfort in that thought. It would end her years of suffering and Pedro and

Grayson would have the opportunity to be loved by someone "normal."

She thought of the prostitutes she read about over the years. The ones who became someone no one knew. How many of them were battered by demons like him and suffocated under the pressure? How many priests and nuns chose celibacy as a form of escapism and learned to love God in the silences?

Did heaven hold 24-karat wings for those who lived through mental torture? How many turned to drugs or alcohol because it was easier to self-medicate than look into the soul of a stranger each time, they encountered a mirror?

"Tears, Madison? She didn't realize they were falling. Don't cry for us. We are together again. You are the last of my girls. After tonight, I will finally be with the one who kept her promise. Do you know how much I love you for your silence?"

One by one, he ran off the names of the other three victims from her hometown. One by one, their deaths made sense now. He told her how Shawn was destined to be Shawna all along but was too weak to fulfill the potential.

He told her Vanessa had married four times in search of the love they shared. In the end, she surrendered and took her old life to a new level by ending it. It gave her the notoriety she craved in life but never achieved.

Then there was Marjorie. She had not been the least bit happy to see him. He explained Marjorie was the reason he decided to inject her. He did not want his prized possession to try and kill him before she remembered who he was.

"But, he continued, the more I observed you and your lifestyle I knew you would never let that happen. You are a loving friend to a lot of undeserving people. Take Ashley, for instance. Had I known she was so needy; I would have killed her too.

Your daughter is exquisite. She looks so much like you did at her age." The look on his face made Madison's blood turn to molten lava! Madison was so repulsed she nearly vomited. He slowly ran his hand over her breasts, and she froze. "Steady, steady now," she thought. I can feel that! He took off his clothing and lay next to her. His hands started down to her thighs and she nearly passed out.

"You are so beautiful. I have come a long way to be with you this way. A lot of people have been sacrificed for us, darling." He kissed her breasts, and she begged God to remain immobile for a bit longer.

She felt his tongue slide down to her navel, and he kissed her hip. Fortunately, it was the one that lost all feeling when Grayson was born, or her plan would have been ruined. When he ran his tongue inside her thighs, she closed her eyes. "Not yet, St. John, not yet."

She allowed him to saturate himself with the taste of her. Why couldn't she at least have a yeast infection? He looked like a shimmering snake as her moisture slid over his cheeks and chin. His eyes took on a demonic glow as he positioned himself to penetrate her.

"Now!" Her body recoiled in contempt. She bolted like a wild stallion as one foot connected with his penis and scrotum while the other caught his chin and nose. Blood spurted everywhere!

"You bitch!"

"Timing is everything! she said and tried to make her way down the stairs.

Her head was spinning as she struggled to the bottom. He tackled her and fell forward. She fought him with superhuman strength. Another knee connected with him, and she was able to reach his gun. He grabbed her gown in an attempt to subdue her.

"Back off me, or so help me God, I will blow your goddamn brains out right now!"

"You won't kill me, Madison. It would be like suicide. Admit it, you've longed for me and this moment half your life. Sure, you're angry with me, but you need me as much as I need you. We are soul mates. No one else understands us. I was your first, and you were the only one I have ever loved."

Madison stood half-dazed and weak. She thought she saw him take a step toward her, but she wasn't sure. The gun was so heavy she could barely hold it steady. Her vision was blurred, and her head was spinning. All she could do clearly was hear him.

As he kept talking, her mind was racing. She knew he needed to die for what he'd done to all of them. She needed to be free. Madison closed her eyes. Her Aunt Wilsey could discern clearly in her blindness through sound. Where did he go?

"Madison, let's stop wasting time. I did all of this for us. We can raise Grayson Marisol to be the woman you are. Let me help you love her the way we love each other."

The next thing Madison heard was Roz.

"Madi, give me the gun. Come on, honey, give me the gun."

Madison stared at her blankly. She focused on Roz's face. Whatever was happening to her, Roz would make it okay. She had trusted her face most of her life. It would be all right now. Madison continued pulling the trigger even though the clip was empty.

Finally, she focused and stopped shaking long enough to hand Roz the gun. Neal White lay in a puddle of blood on the floor. Roz eased Madison into a chair and kept tapping her face because the shock was setting in quickly.

"Madi, stay with me, Madi. Madi, can you tell me what happened?" She didn't even notice the room full of policemen.

"Can somebody get me something to cover her, please!" Roz was yelling. Pedro dashed into the house.

"Oh my God, what happened?"

He took off his jacket and threw it over Madison's shoulders to cover her. Madison sat with a death grip on Roz's hand and recounted the whole ordeal for them. She was shaking as she recounted the molestation years ago that tied all the victims together. One by one, unknowingly, she accounted for each of the photographs.

She told them about the flowers and the lives of the others sacrificed for them to be together. She explained he placed her inside the hollowed-out island in the kitchen during the whole investigation. The decorative holes provided air circulation. She heard them looking for her but couldn't move or speak. Madison explained he planted the blood to make it look like she'd been abducted. He drove her car to the river.

"He was planning to kidnap us. He said Grayson reminded him of me when I was her age. I couldn't let him hurt Grayson. Don't you see, Roz? I couldn't let him hurt Grayson?"

"My God, sweetie, you've been carrying this around all these years?" "An officer taking the statement said, " A man has been murdered here, so a full investigation into these allegations still needs to happen."

"A man hasn't been murdered. A predator has been exterminated! Furthermore, I'll make sure I have the crack of your ass on display if this statement goes anywhere but to the District Attorney's office," Roz screamed at him. Then she glanced at Joshua, "You got this?' He nodded in agreement.

A doctor was permitted to examine Madison at Pedro's house because she became hysterical at the thought of going to the hospital. He carried her upstairs and let her check on Grayson. The doctor gave her a sedative, and she fell asleep immediately.

Pedro came back downstairs. He held out his own shot glass as Roz was refilling hers with scotch. "You never knew either?" they said in unison as they downed the liquid.

Joshua sat at his desk with the investigative report in front of him. He walked to the window and stared out as he recalled the whole sordid mess he was handed. To no one's surprise, the bastard's name wasn't Neal White. He adopted an alias to accompany his façade of being human. He came into this world as Jonathan Kemble.

He'd been incarcerated for the past ten years after a botched attempt to abduct a nine-year-old girl. He walked out of prison with one purpose in mind: reunite with Madison and annihilate anyone who got in his way. She was his most cherished victim, "the favorite."

The first sacrificial lamb on his quest for destruction this time was Diane Spiegel, a social security administration worker. She served his purpose by finding all his victims from the state of Alabama. One by one, he used their social security numbers to hunt them like game. When only Madison remained, he slit Spiegel's throat and neatly tucked her in the trunk of a vehicle in the parking lot where she worked.

Jonathan Kemble tracked Madison to Connecticut and arrived earlier this week. He stalked and memorized her patterns as he studied her interactions with friends. To prevent suspicion, he killed the neighbor two houses down for unrestricted access parking in her driveway.

It also allowed him to know when Madison's house was vacant or when Pedro stopped by. According to the manifesto in his rental vehicle, he planned to kill Pedro before he kidnapped Madison and Grayson. Joshua instructed the detective to withhold that information from Pedro. It can drive a man insane if he believes he is inept to protect his family. "Kemble you are one sick bastard!"

He overheard their conversation when Dominic Charles visited her. He waited for the perfect opportunity. Kemble put a bullet in Dominic's head without an ounce of remorse.

The final element of his plan was to distract Pedro and attend the masquerade ball. He sent Pedro pictures and put him together with Major's borderline delusions. Ashley satisfied his momentary lust until he could reach Madison. Then he lay in wait for her in the ballroom stairwell.

Joshua shuddered at the thought of Ashley in the arms of that animal. She was recovering slowly from an erratic heart rhythm and deep tissue bruises. That was the detectable trauma from her interaction with Kemble. Her emotional state was undetermined.

The officer at the ball lost his life because he forgot his invitation and returned to the car to retrieve it. Kemble snuck behind him as he leaned into the car and slit his throat. He hadn't stood a chance. Sergeant Bradford was a desk sergeant with 17 years of service.

All these events culminated in Kemble's death at the home of the woman he mentally and physically terrorized for 28 years. Joshua knew as District Attorney, he had to make a decision. Either way, he was going to pay a substantial fee to the piper.

If he tried Madison for murder, any self-respecting person in the state would think him criminally insane and morally bankrupt. If he let her go free, people would say it was because of her connection to the Assistant District Attorney.

Who was she, Madison St. John-Santiago? A woman who suffered mercilessly at the hands of a psychopathic pedophile for years. A woman who did it silently and alone, yet she built a world for herself despite the two worst times in anyone's life to have a demon come calling, childhood and happiness.

There were times when his job required him to deal with people who were not going to change with the coming of dawn. Those were the people he hated to see walk away on a technicality. Other times, being human outweighed any possibility of reasonable doubt.

Joshua glanced at the file on his desk. There was no crime. A community service was performed on behalf of every parent in the world this evening. People like Kemble proved they don't stop unless they are forced to.

One can only hope, his journey on the ferry to hell was soul-stirringly hot, with maggots chomping every inch of the way! Joshua closed his eyes and silently thanked the heavens for the one time in his career he was sure he could right a wrong.

He shut the blinds, walked to his desk, and filed her case under closed. He would take the criticism. People weren't created equal. Some, in fact, were poster children for abortion; Jonathan Kemble was one of those people.

Day Seven

Madison was dazed on the day of Dominic's funeral. Her thoughts drifted to Pamela. The first time they'd met, she immediately understood why Dominic couldn't completely leave her.

She was a kind and gentle woman with wide, innocent eyes. The kind captured in paintings of a doe. She sat quietly in the family section and beckoned Madison to join her. She was still allowing co-dependency even amidst her own grief.

"He would want you to be here," she whispered as she saw Madison's hesitation.

"I can't. This is all my fault if he'd never known me..."

"Then any true moments of happiness would have eluded him his entire lifetime. You are not responsible for other people's madness, Madison. I learned that from you through Dominic.

Pamela asked her to speak but Madison refused. Pamela left a space in the program for her anyway. Something inside her knew if Madison would come, she would do it. For that, she enlisted Pedro's help.

Their choir sang "He Looked Beyond My Faults" and "Have a Little Talk with Jesus." The obituary was read silently to "We Will Meet Again." Vanessa Bell Armstrong, Dr. Watts, and Oleta Adams would have been proud. Now, all eyes turned to Madison. She rose unsteadily to pay tribute to her friend. She spoke beautifully from memories of Dominic.

"He was from Beaufort, South Carolina," she began in an unsteady voice. Her mind had brilliant flashes of him as she shared their story. They used to joke because it was one of the only places in the world besides Humphrey with "slop jars."

She included his love for Pamela through the years they'd been together. Privately she kept his secrets. Only those in his inner circle knew of the infidelities. No one ever doubted he loved Pamela; it wasn't enough to save him from himself.

She spoke of his passion for life and how it sometimes got him into trouble. Yet, he was forever the comedian and got himself out. His love for the Dallas Cowboys never wavered.

"He was flawed, and he was broken, but he loved God, his African Methodist Episcopal Church, and his family. He fought enemies before and after his stint in the Army about which he didn't talk. Most days, they won, but he kept fighting. Dominic knew he was damaged, and fiercely protected those he loved. His big heart paused long enough to open and swallow me whole.

Dominic recognized I was broken, flawed, and damaged, too. He was my friend, and I loved him. I didn't even know he was gone. Otherwise, he would have received a formal military ceremony, including "dress right dress."

He deserved more than an "honorable mention" website with three entries on the sympathy page. He didn't deserve to be "found" in this battle. No one should die alone. He didn't deserve to have his war end this way." Madison was overcome with emotion. Pamela came and wrapped her arms around her and guided her from the podium. There was not a dry eye in the church.

After the service, as Madison was turning to leave, Pamela came to her and quietly said,

" I knew he left me for you. I know you tried to persuade him to stay. I was prepared to hate you, but, on the contrary, I see exactly why he loved you so much. He carried it with him until the end. I couldn't compete. There's nothing you can do when the love of your life finds it with someone else.

I also see you loved him very deeply. Thank you for allowing me to continue my world of making believe a little longer. He was a blessed man. Two vastly different women loved him, and we understood why he needed it.

Be well, Madison. Dominic would not want to be the source of any more pain for you. I pray you can find peace. Enough of this nightmare has been yours for far too long." She gave Madison a hug and walked to the hearse waiting for her. Madison refused to attend the interment. No one tried to convince her otherwise.

Pedro stared after her in disbelief. Pamela must have thought he knew the extent of Dominic's relationship with Madison. Dominic Charles had gone from victim to his wife's former lover and his potential replacement in 36 seconds! Madison wasn't only grieving for a friend; she was also grieving for an old lover. Obviously, it was requited!

The tales told by the dead are much more detailed than the explanations offered by the living. Pedro had to quell his jealousy. A man was dead. Who he had been to Madison didn't matter. He could no longer be anything to anyone. Pedro understood the hours Madison had spent listening to TEEKS sing "Remember Me."

After the service, they all returned to Pedro's house. Madison quietly slipped outside and sat on the deck alone. She sat there staring into some unknown abyss. Shock was the only company she kept close by her side. She hadn't spoken a word on the ride from the church.

"You've seen her cry for Charles, Major, Vanessa, Shawna, Detective Thomas, her neighbor, the social worker, and you've even seen her cry for Ash, but have you seen her cry for herself?"

Pedro pondered the question for a moment. "Actually, no."

Joshua continued, "That's what's wrong with her. You can't get in because she can't get out! The room is at capacity. She is traumatized. Hell, who wouldn't be? Until she exhales some of the grief, we can't get to her.

Think about it, P. We've seen this reaction in rape victims, murder cases, and family members who have lost loved ones. Unfortunately, Madison was cast in all three roles simultaneously in this maniac's insane production."

"So, what in the hell am I supposed to do? Sit back and lose my wife to some form of certifiable madness?"

"There isn't a lot you can do except love her and realize she has to find her own way back. You can't do it for her. This is Madison's pain, P. We all want her to overcome it. You are underestimating the amount of time she has lived with this thing inside her.

She constructed a whole life around a tragedy to have it magnified once she found a way to tolerate it. Lesser things have pushed people over the edge. If there is a way to get through this, Madison will find it."

"I can't lose her, Joshua; Marisol can't lose her mother. We've been through too much to be destroyed by someone I can't fight. I don't even have the privilege of killing the bastard!"

Joshua tried to reassure his friend. "She knows, but, more importantly, God knows."

Outside, Madison's mind flashed backwards to his face. He seemed almost human before she knew who he was. He really believed he had honored her by branding her "used" before her eighth birthday.

She thought of how he kept talking about the sacrifices he'd made to be with her. It was as though killing innocent people was acceptable under his circumstances. The newspaper neatly printed a layout in jigsaw puzzle formation of his timelines. The dates of all the lives he dishonored/killed to get to her were choreographed like a psychotic dance. Madison recalled thinking as she read it those were victims on the trail. He started somewhere.

By the time he reached Humphrey, Alabama, he was a serial deviant in his late twenties. Slipping into alleys, picking locks, and raising bedroom windows unnoticed became second nature to him. In his mind, he was sampling a piece of privilege he had been wrongfully denied. Criminal and self-serving psychopath were not words he would have used to describe himself. Those were insulting.

Jonathan Kemble thought of himself as a knight in shining armor.

He fought many a foe to rightfully reunite with the one person the world denied him. His favorite. He didn't consider himself a pedophile. That descriptor would be highly offensive to him. Quite the contrary, he considered himself a refined gentleman with a few obstacles in his past.

Those obstacles happened to be the lives of innocent people. He was a man on a destination driven by love. The fact that his love was for the stolen virginity of a seven-year-old child was irrelevant to him and abhorrent to her. All perpetrators can find the justifiable "why" no matter how reprehensible the deed is. They already granted themselves the needed permissions.

He told Madison killing him would be like killing herself. Tragically, he had been right in a very twisted way. Now he was dead, her hatred had no place to rest. Healing sounded like a cliché.' It took 19 minutes to start this nightmare, twenty-eight years to make it bearable, six hours to end it, and the rest of her life to figure out how to live with the madness of it all.

Fortunately, he wasn't out there anymore; she knew that for certain. His brains were scraped off her living room walls. She recalled the moment she pulled the trigger and flinched. He really was a part of her story now. He was embedded even deeper.

Madison kept thinking about what would have been different if she had gone with him. Nothing. Based on the timeline in the paper, every one of his latest victims was already dead by the time he'd reached her house.

I need closure, God; can you help me find closure? They kept saying I wasn't responsible for what happened. Not yielding the weapon yet being the objective of the fight, doesn't make me sleep any better. Madison wasn't sure the war was over. She wasn't sure if her mind could wield itself to move forward one more time.

Suddenly, as if to answer the unspoken question, a hand softly cupped her shoulder. It was accompanied by the one face that came closest to understanding. Madison searched Ashley's hazel eyes to see if there was a possibility sanity still existed.

"He was an animal Mad. He was an abominable creature who died much more mercifully than he deserved. Every bullet freed the soul of a child he destroyed. I don't know the extent of the damage you have after being haunted and then hunted by him. I need you to know you set all of us free tonight. You, Madison St. John-Santiago, are a heroine. Don't ever forget that.

In 48 hours, I glimpsed his devastation. The fact that you survived and flourished all these years is a true testament to the resilience within your spirit, not the evil of his. I speak for everyone who matters in the world of decent folk when I say a lesser person could not have survived this. All of us respect you now more than we did two weeks ago. It was not tarnished by learning about the atrocities of this psychopath.

Your daughter thinks you hung the moon, and Pedro is willing to jump over it for you. None of your friends living or transitioned, she paused for Dominic, regret knowing or loving you. You have not fallen from grace before our eyes; you have exemplified it. We tremble in awe of your courage."

The tears came to Madison then. She cried for the one person who needed it most: herself. Ashley held her. However long it took, she would sit by her friend's side and reassure her she was not damaged beyond repair or love.

Joshua, Pedro, and Roz stood and watched through the patio door as, one by one, a soul was released through Madison's tears. The actual number of casualties Kemble consumed was unknown, but one was on the road to recovery. For those such as Vanessa and Shawna, who lost their lives in battle long before they died, Pedro, Roz, and Joshua believed they were protecting Marjorie, Madison, and the unknown others with 24-karat wings.

Day Eight

Madison took a deep breath. It was her wedding day, a day of new beginnings. She would officially become Mrs. Pedro Santiago once again. The wedding was in one hour; the guests were seated on the grounds surrounding the gazebo. She let Pedro have his audience. Madison was trying to keep calm.

Roz was downstairs explaining to Pedro he could not go up and see her. "The only way she is escaping is with bat wings. Fortunately, for you, Batman is using them at the moment, so you're betrothed is safe. However, if you want to ditch this rat trap, we can be hitched before she walks down the stairs. Just say the word!" Pedro cracked up. "Thanks Roz, but I think we have all had enough side piece drama!"

Meanwhile, Ashley was barricading the door just in case. Gray was tickled by the whole thing. "Mr. Joshua, my parents are getting married. I get to be a flower girl!"

"Yes, sweetheart, they are renewing a love that has stood many tests." Joshua was still glowing after a wonderful night with Ashley. They spent the time discussing where he might assist in her personal restructuring.

The phone rang downstairs. Madison could hear Pedro say, "Hello." Roz started going off, "If that is a goddamn reporter, you tell them…!"

"No, I don't think so. She wants to speak to Madison. Babe, pick up the phone, he yelled upstairs. "

Ashley held her breath. "Dear God in heaven, please let this pass for her. For all of us."

"Hello."

"I saw his picture in the paper. I would have turned right past it had it not been for the eyes. They took me backwards to a place and a horror locked away by a key I buried. Thank you for ending this for all of us." The line went dead.

Madison fought back tears as she held the receiver. The quiet buzz filled the room. For the first time in her life, Madison understood God doesn't call the qualified; he qualifies the called. She glanced in the mirror to dab her eyes and paused. Her spirit let her know "He may not come when you want him, but God is always on time."

Printed in the USA
CPSIA information can be obtained
at www.ICGtesting.com
LVHW081618090124
768552LV00023B/1525